D1553287

GETTING

Schooled

New York Times Bestselling Author

EMMA CHASE

Getting Schooled / Emma Chase – 1st ed.
Library of Congress Cataloging-in-Publication Data
ISBN-13: 978-1984370617

For our teachers. We remember you.

CHAPTER
One

Garrett

E very town has its stories. The urban legends, history and heroes, that set it apart from the surrounding areas. Lakeside, New Jersey, population 8,437, has some real winners.

That boarded-up brick house at the end of Miller Street? Three hundred years old and haunted as fuck. If you stand in front of it at midnight on Friday the 13th, you'll see the ghosts of two creepy 18th- century boys looking down at you from the attic window. True story.

Then there's the Great Goose Plague of 1922. Geese are not the friendliest of feathered beings—but they've got balls; you got to give them that. In Jersey, wherever you find a body of water, you'll find geese. And wherever there's geese, there's an abundance of goose shit. It's basically indestructible—if there's ever a nuclear war, all that'll be left are the cockroaches and the goose shit. Anyway, in 1922, either by

1

accident or the most ill-conceived prank ever, those durable turds made their way into Lakeside's water supply and wiped out almost half the town.

The old-old-timers still hold a grudge, so it's not unusual to see a little gray-haired lady pause midstep on the sidewalk, to give the finger to a flock flying by overhead.

In 1997, Lakeside received the distinguished honor of being named the town with the most bars per capita in the whole US of A. We were all very proud.

And we're not too shabby in the celebrity department. This town has given birth to five decorated war heroes, two major league baseball players, an NBA coach, one world-renowned artist, a Rock & Roll Hall of Fame inductee and a gold-medal Olympic curler.

We keep that last one kind of quiet, though, because . . . curling.

The guy I'm jogging towards on Main Street right now is a different kind of celebrity—a local one.

"Ollie, look alive!" I call out.

He doesn't make eye contact, but he smiles and lifts his hand from the arm of his folding chair so I can slap it with a high-five, like I do every Sunday morning I run past.

Oliver Munson. Every day he plants himself on his front lawn from morning until late afternoon, waving to the cars and people on the sidewalk. Like a Walmart greeter—for the whole town.

Legend has it, when Ollie was a kid, he fell off his bike, hit his head on the curb, and ended up in a coma. When he woke up, he had lost the ability to speak and the doctors said he'd never be "quite right" again.

Now, it's possible that this story is bullshit—just a cautionary tale the moms cooked up to get kids to wear helmets. But I don't think so.

Though the doctors recommended Ollie be committed—because society was a real asshole back in the day—Mrs. Munson wasn't having any of it. She brought her son home, taught him the skills and routine he follows to this very day—one that gave him independence and dignity and, from the looks of it, fulfillment.

Mrs. Munson's gone now, but Ollie's neighbors check up on him and a social worker comes around once a month to make sure he's good to go. When he needs something, there's never a shortage of volunteers, because he's a fixture around here—extended family—as much a part of this place as the lake that gave us its name.

Behind me, three boys on bikes whizz past Ollie in single file.

"Hey, Ollie!"

"S'up, Olls!"

"Ollimundus!"

See? It's like that Bon Jovi song that says your hometown is the only place they call you one of their own.

And Ollie Munson's one of ours.

My sneakers slap the sidewalk as I continue to run—picking up my pace, pushing myself until sweat soaks my T-shirt and dampens the strands of my dark hair. I'm a big believer in sweat—it's good for the body and the soul. Forget Zima, or Yogo or Pi-kick-my-ass, if you want to look and feel good? Work up a hard, real sweat once a day—doesn't matter if it's from running, sweeping, or screwing. Though screwing is my preference.

I am a creature of habit—most guys are.

I'm also superstitious—all athletes are. It's why there's so many shaggy beards in professional sports and why if you ask a player on a winning streak when he last washed his jock—hope he lies to you.

A streak trumps personal hygiene every time.

The last fifteen years of my life have basically been one long winning streak. Don't worry, I wash my boxers every day, but the other parts of my life—the Jeep Wrangler I drive, the T-shirts I wear that will have to be pried from my cold, dead corpse before I throw them away, my workout routine—those do not fucking change.

I run this same way every day—past the string of brick capes and ranches, with small grassy yards and well-used Fords and Chevys.

Lakeside started as a brick town—back when communities sprang up around the mills, factories, and industries that offered employment. California had gold in its hills; Jersey had red clay. The demographics really haven't changed. Most of the people around here work with their hands—proud blue collars, union members, and small business owners.

It was an awesome place to grow up—it still is. Safe enough to be stupid, big enough not to get dangerously bored, small enough that every street feels like yours.

I finish my five-mile run, like always, at the corner of Baker Street, and walk the last block to cool down, stretch my hamstrings, and wipe the sweat from my forehead with the bottom of my T-shirt.

And then, I walk through the door of The Bagel Shop.

This place is never empty—besides the bagels being awesome, it's where old guys shoot the shit all day and young guys come to hide from their wives.

I grab a bottle of water from the cooler, next to a table filled with locals.

"Daniels!"

"Hey, Coach D!"

"Morning, Coach."

Not to go all Ron Burgundy on you, but . . . I'm a pretty big deal around here. I think I'll run for mayor after I retire, erect a statue of myself in front of Town Hall to replace the one of old Mayor Schnozzel. He was an ugly son of a bitch.

Anyway, long story short—I'm a history teacher at the high school, but more importantly—I'm the head coach of the best football team in the state. I know they're the best because I made them that way. I was the youngest head coach ever hired and I have a better record than anyone who came before me.

Those that can, do; those that can't, teach . . . those who know how to play football like a fucking god but have a bum knee—coach.

"How's it going, fellas?"

"You tell us," Mr. Zinke replies. He owns Zinke Jewelers—which gives him the inside track on almost every relationship in town. Who's getting engaged, who's coming up on a big anniversary, who's in need of an "I screwed up" two-carat apology tennis bracelet. The man's a vault—what gets sold at Zinke's stays at Zinke's. Figuratively. "How's the team looking this year?"

I swallow a gulp of water from the bottle. "With Lipinski starting quarterback, we'll take states—no doubt."

Brandon Lipinski is my masterpiece. I've coached him since he was a small pop warner player . . . that's peewee or youth league football to you non-New Jerseyans out there. And like God made Adam in his own image—I made Lipinski in mine.

"Justin's been working his butt off all summer," Phil Perez tells me. "He drills every morning—throws fifty passes every day."

I keep a mental catalog of upcoming talent. Justin Perez is a seventh-grader with a decent arm and good feet. "Consistency is key," I reply. "Gotta build that muscle memory."

Mrs. Perkins calls my name from behind the counter, holding up a brown paper bag. "Your order's ready, Garrett."

The Perkins family has owned The Bagel Shop for generations—Mrs. Perkins and her two brothers run the place now. Her oldest daughter, Samantha, was a gorgeous, wet dream of a senior when I was a freshman. She took my buddy Dean to the prom—they got wasted in the limo and missed most of the dance screwing in the bathroom—forever solidifying Dean's player status.

"Have a good day, guys." I tap the table and head over to pay my bill.

Mrs. Perkins hands me my sack of carbs and my change. "Is your mom going to Club this afternoon?"

Ah, the Knights of Columbus Ladies Auxiliary Club—where the women plan bake sales, get buzzed on sherbet-topped alcoholic punch, and bitch about their husbands.

"She wouldn't miss it for the world." I give her a wink and a smile. "Have a good one, Mrs. P."

"Bye, Garrett."

With my bagels tucked under my arm, I walk down Fulton Road and cut through Baygrove Park, which takes me to Chestnut, around the bend from my parents' house. Theirs is the dark-blue colonial with the white shutters . . . and practically neon-green lawn.

Retirement hit my old man hard.

In the winter months, he spends hours in the garage, working on classic car models. But the minute the frost breaks, it's all about the grass—trimming it, watering it, fertilizing it . . . talking to it.

He's spent more quality time with this lawn than he ever did with me and my brothers—and there were four of us.

I walk through the front door that's never been locked and step into chaos—because the gang's all here.

The Sunday morning talk shows are on TV. Volume level: blaring—because my dad has a hearing aid he doesn't wear. Jasmine, my mother's formerly feral, still-evil black cat hisses as I close the door behind me, foiling her perpetual attempts to escape. My dad's in his recliner, wearing his typical August uniform—plaid boxers, knee-high white socks with sandals, and a T-shirt that says: *If lost, return to Irene.* My mother's in front of the stove, with the vent fan clattering above her head, wearing a shirt that says: *I'm Irene.*

Enough said.

I pass the bagels to my mom with a kiss on her cheek—'cause out of the four of us, I'm her favorite. Sure, she'll give you the whole "I love my sons equally" spiel if you ask her . . . but we all know the truth.

My youngest nephew, Spencer, my oldest brother Connor's son, wrinkles his nose at me from the kitchen table. "You smell, Uncle Garrett."

Puppies learn how to be dogs by roughhousing with bigger dogs. Boys work the same way.

"Yeah—like a winner." I haul him out of the chair, lift him up, and rub my damp, sweaty head on his face. "Here, get a better smell."

He squeals, then laughs as he pushes me away.

On either side of Spencer's chair are his two older brothers—thirteen-year-old Aaron, whose light-brown, John Travolta, *Saturday Night Fever*-era hair needs a trim, and the middle child, in every sense of the word, Daniel.

Yes, they named him Daniel Daniels—I don't know what the fuck my brother was thinking—they might as well have tattooed a target on his forehead. His middle name is Brayden, so we all call him that.

At the other end of the table are my nieces—my brother Ryan's daughters—the pretty, perfect little girls my mother always prayed for. Thirteen-year-old Josephina and seven-year-old, curly-haired Francesca—also known as Joey and Frankie.

I pour myself a cup of coffee while my mom slices and butters bagels and passes them out to the kids.

Then my petite, dark-haired sister-in-law comes walking down the hall from the bathroom, clapping her hands at the children. "Come on, kids, eat quick. We're going school shopping and we gotta get going."

She's Ryan's wife. Angelina Bettina Constance Maria, maiden name Caravusio.

She's just a little bit Italian.

Angela's a Jersey transplant—her family moved here

from Brooklyn her junior year in high school. Her and my brother got together that same year and haven't been apart since.

"I don't wanna go," Brayden whines. "I wanna stay at Nana and Pop's and play Xbox."

Angela shakes her head. "Nana has Club today. Your dad's going to pick you up at my house this afternoon after his meeting."

That would be Connor's meeting with his divorce lawyer.

My brother's an attending ER doctor at Lakeside Memorial. He's been living at my parents' house for the last few months—since his wife, Stacey, told him she didn't want to be married to him anymore. *Ouch.* Fifteen fucking years—up in smoke. While they're separated, she's got the house—a five-bedroom McMansion on the newer, fancier side of town—and he's got the kids every other weekend.

My little brother, Timmy, walks in through the sliding glass door from the backyard.

"Hey, Pop." He smirks, "You've got some crab grass growing out by the tree. You really should get on it."

That my father can hear.

He springs out of his recliner and heads to the garage to get his crab grass spray.

There's a two-year age difference between my oldest brother, Connor, and my next older brother, Ryan. And there's another two-year difference between me and Ryan. The third time was definitely the charm for my parents, and they frankly should've quit while they were ahead.

But, seven years later, my mom wanted to give it one last try for a girl. And that's how we got Timmy.

Timmy's kind of a dick.

Don't get me wrong—he's my brother—I love him. But he's immature, selfish, basically . . . a dick.

"You're kind of a dick, man." I tell him because we both know there's not a blade of crab grass on my father's lawn.

He laughs. "That's what he gets for not letting Mom get me that Easy-Bake Oven I wanted when I was ten."

Like a lot of guys of his generation, my father is a staunch believer in separate toy aisles for boys and girls and never the two shall meet. He thinks progressive is a brand of soup.

Unlike my niece Frankie, who looks at me determinedly and announces, "I want to play football, Uncle Garrett."

This is not news to me. She's been saying she wants to play football—like her uncles, and her cousins—since she started talking. She's the one who watches the games on Sunday with my brother while wearing her pink Giants jersey.

"Oh yeah? Have you been working on your kicks?"

She nods enthusiastically and steps back from the table to demonstrate. And she's not bad—the family football gene didn't skip her.

I clap my hands. "You can play pop warner when you're nine."

Frankie beams, until Angela rains on our future-Heisman parade.

"Knock it off, Garrett. You're not playing football, Francesca. I'm not spending three thousand dollars on braces so you can get your teeth knocked out of your head."

Well, that's offensive.

"You think I'd let my niece get her teeth knocked out?"

Angela points at me. "When you have a daughter, we'll talk."

Timmy checks the clock on his phone. "Hey, Mom, I

have to get going. Can you get my laundry?"

Yes, my mother still washes his laundry every week. Like I said—dick.

I'm about to tell him to get his own god damn laundry, but Angela beats me to it.

"What the hell is that? Get your own goddamn laundry!"

"She likes doing my laundry!" Timmy argues. "It makes her feel needed."

Angela sneers. "Nobody likes doing frigging laundry, Tim. And you don't ask a sixty-three-year-old woman to haul your laundry up the basement steps. What kind of fireman are you?"

Timmy's a firefighter in Hammitsburg, two towns over.

"Ma! Mom, tell Angela you like doing my laundry!"

Angela takes a step towards him. "I'm going to smack you upside the head." Timmy takes a step back—'cause she'll do it. "I'm gonna smack you in front of your nieces and nephews if you don't move your ass down those steps and get your laundry."

My brother throws his hands up in the air.

Then he moves his ass down the basement steps to get his laundry.

And this is my family. All the time. If they seem crazy . . . that's because they are.

My mom helps Angela herd the kids from the table towards their shoes. As Frankie passes me, I crouch down next to her and whisper, "Hey, sweetheart. You keep working on that kick, okay? When you're a little older, Uncle Garrett'll hook you up."

She gives me a full crooked-fence-toothed smile that warms my chest. Then kisses my cheek before heading out the front door.

The coolest thing I've ever bought is my house on the north side of the lake. Two stories, all brick, fully refurbished kitchen. There's a nice-sized, fenced-in backyard with a fire pit next to the path that leads down the steps to my private dock. I've got a bass boat and like to take her out a couple times a week. My neighbors Alfred and Selma live on one side, retired army captain Paul Cahill on the other, but with the spruces and pines that border the property, I don't see them unless I want to. It's private and quiet.

I toss my keys on the front hall table and head into the living room to find my best friend curled up, asleep on the couch. He's soft, snow white—like a baby seal—and weighs about twenty-five pounds. He's a great listener, he gets fired up at the TV when a ref makes a bad call, and his favorite pastime is licking his own balls.

I found him, small and dirty, in the ShopRite parking lot my senior year of high school. Or maybe . . . he found me.

"Snoopy," I whisper, pressing my nose into his downy fur.

His dark eyes spring open, lifting his head sharply, like my old man when he catches himself falling asleep in the recliner.

I stroke his back and scratch his ears. "What's up, bud?"

Snoopy stretches, then steps up on the arm of the couch to wash my face with his tongue. His tail wags in a steady, adoring rhythm. Can't beat this kind of devotion.

In people years, he's seventeen, so not as spry as he used

to be. He's also partially blind and diabetic. I give him insulin shots twice a day.

Snoopy's my boy. And there's nothing in the world I wouldn't do for him.

After a shower, I put the Steelers game on, and as I pick up my phone to order Chinese, the front door opens and Tara Benedict walks into the living room.

"Worst day ever." She groans. "If I have to listen to one more woman tell me the size of her new Gucci boots *must* be off, I'll rip my hair out. The boots are fine, bitch—your chubby Fred Flintstone feet are nowhere close to a size six!"

Tara's an online customer service rep for Nordstrom's. She was a year below me in high school—we started hooking up a couple months ago when she moved back to town after her divorce.

I raise my eyebrows. "Sounds rough."

Snoopy hops on the couch, stretching his neck, preening for Tara's attention. He's such a needy bastard.

"Sorry I didn't text before I came over. Are you busy?"

Tara was cute back in the day, but now, at thirty-three, she's gorgeous—an avid tennis player with long dark hair and sweet curves.

"Nope. I was just going to order Chinese. Hungry?"

She unzips her black skirt and lets it slide to the floor—leaving her thigh-high stockings and shiny black heels on. "Later. First I need to fuck away some of this frustration."

Tara's a great girl.

I drop the Chinese menu like it's on fire.

"You've come to the right place."

She strips her way up to the bedroom, leaving a trail of clothing behind like an awesome porn version of Hansel and

Gretel's breadcrumbs. I start to follow, but pause in the hall-way—because Snoopy's the best . . . but he's also a voyeur. His eyes are round and attentive as I point at him. "Stay here, dude. And don't listen—I told you—it's fucking weird."

Two hours later, a much less frustrated Tara and I sit at the kitchen counter, eating great Chinese food out of takeout containers.

Tara dabs her lips with her napkin. "The County Fair is coming up."

The County Fair—beer, great barbeque, decent live music, and rides worth risking your life for.

"Joshua's really excited—every time we pass a sign, he asks me how many more days until he can go." She picks up a piece of steamed chicken and holds it down to Snoopy's drooling mouth. "So . . . I was wondering, what you thought about you, me, and Joshua going together?" She looks up at me meaningfully. "The three of us."

I narrow my eyes, confused. "That's . . ."

"I know that's not what we said when we started seeing each other . . . we agreed to nothing serious. But . . . I like you, Garrett. I think we could be good together." She shrugs. "I'm a relationship kind of girl—and even though my marriage crashed and burned, I'm ready to start over. To try again."

I like Tara—but even if I didn't, I wouldn't bullshit her. A man gets to a point in his life when he realizes that honesty—even if it's not what someone wants to hear—is just simpler.

"I like you too. But I also like my life the way it is. A

lot." I gesture towards the next room. "I bought a Ping-Pong table last week, for the dining room. I like that I didn't have to discuss it with anyone—that I didn't have to consider anybody else's feelings. I like that the only emotional worry I have is wondering how the hell I'm going to get around North Essex High School's defense this season."

"You should have kids, Garrett," Tara insists. "You'd be an amazing father. It's a sin you don't have kids."

"I do have kids. Thirty of them, six periods a day—and another forty every day after school during football season."

Interest is the key with teenagers—with getting them to listen—they have to sense that you give a damn. That you care. You can't fake it—they'll know.

I don't know if I'd be as good of a teacher as I am if I had kids of my own—if I'd have the energy, the patience. It's not the only reason I'm not married with kids, but it's one of them.

Like I said—I don't mess with a winning streak.

Tara pushes back from the table and stands. "Well. Then, it looks like it's Match.com for me. And I don't suppose a new guy is going to be real keen about me keeping a piece of hot coach on the side."

Gently, I push a strand of hair behind her ear.

"No, I don't think that'd go over too well."

"This was fun, Garrett." She reaches up and kisses my cheek. "Take care of yourself."

"Yeah, you too, Tara. I'll see you around."

With one more smile and a nod of her head, she picks up her purse, pats Snoopy good-bye, and heads out the door.

Snoopy watches her go, then turns to me—waiting.

I tilt my head towards the glass doors that frame the setting sun as it streaks the sky in pinks and grays and oranges.

"You wanna go bark at the geese on the lake?"

Snoopy's ears perk high, and he rushes over to the back door as fast as his old little legs can take him.

CHAPTER
Two

Callie

Looking back now, I should've known it was too good to be true. The best things in life usually are—long-lasting lipstick, Disneyland, dual action vibrators.

"Okay, let's check you out," Cheryl says, bending her knees, so she's eye level with me. At five-seven, I'm not exactly short, but Cheryl is like a warrior woman of Sparta at over six feet tall with eye-catching dark red hair and a broad, often-laughing, always-louding mouth.

Cheryl works in the back office, here at the Fountain Theater Company. We crashed into each other—literally—on campus when we were both students at the University of San Diego, sending the papers in her hands scattering like leaves on a windy day. It took twenty minutes for us to catch them all—and by the time we did, it was the beginning of a beautiful friendship.

I open my eyes so wide my eyeballs would fall out if they weren't attached to my head.

"Corner makeup gunk?"

"You're good," Cheryl confirms.

I pull back my lips and grit out, "Teeth?"

"Clean and shiny like a baby's hiney."

I tilt my head back. "Nose?"

Real friends make sure there aren't any bats hanging in the cave.

"All clear."

"Okay." I shake out my hands and whistle out a deep breath. "I'm ready." I close my eyes and whisper the words that, through the years, always helped settle my nerves. Words that aren't mine.

"Visualize the win. See it happen, then make it happen. You got this."

"What's that?" Bruce asks.

I open my eyes at the blond, lanky, impeccably attired man in a gray tweed jacket, camel pants, and red ascot standing behind Cheryl's right shoulder.

"Just something my high school boyfriend used to say." I shrug. "He played football."

Bruce is an actor with the Fountain Theater Company, like I was years ago, before I moved behind the scenes for a steadier paycheck and worked my way up to general manager.

"I don't know why you're nervous, Callie. Dorsey is a jackass, but even he has to see you should be executive director. You've earned this."

Theater people are a rare breed. For the truest of us, it's not about money or fame or getting our picture on the cover of *People* magazine—it's about the performance. The show. It's about Ophelia and Eponine, Hamlet and Romeo, or even chorus girl #12. It's the magical connection with the audience, the smell of backstage—dust and makeup and costume fabric—the warm heat of the lights, the swoosh of the velvet curtain, the roll of the sets, and the clip-clap echo of shoes across a stage. It's the piercing thrill of opening night, and the tear-wringing grief that comes with the closing performance. Behind the scenes or in front, cast or crew, stage left or right—there's nothing I don't love about it.

But for our newly retired executive director, Madam Lauralei? Not so much.

She was more concerned with her television production work on the side and her recurring voice-over role for a successful string of inflammatory bowel disease medication commercials than growing the company. Than putting in the time and energy to expand our audience and choose innovative projects that could turn us into a cultural fixture in Old Town, San Diego.

But I could change all that. As executive director, I'd be equal to the artistic director, below only the founder, Miller Dorsey, who enjoys the prestige of owning a theater company but tends to take a hands-off approach in the actual running of it. I'd have a say in budgets and schedules, marketing and advertising and how our resources are allotted. I would fight for the Fountain, because it's a part of me, the only place I've ever worked since college. I would throw down like the Jersey girl I am—get in faces, bribe, barter, and blackmail if I had to. I've got the experience, the skills, and the determination to make this company the powerhouse I know it can be.

I want this position—I want it bad. And that's why I'm so nervous. Because the harder you reach for something, the more it hurts when you end up slapping the pavement with your face.

Mrs. Adelstein, Miller Dorsey's secretary, comes out into the hall. "Miss Carpenter? He's ready for you now."

Cheryl gives me the thumbs-up and Bruce smiles. I take another deep breath, then follow Adelstein through the office door, hearing that steady, strong voice in my head.

"You got this, Callie."

⎯⎯⎯⎯⎯⎯⎯⎯

"Wooooohooo!" My lips pucker as I down a fourth lemon-drop shot. "I can't believe I got it!"

"Of course you got it, girlfriend!" Cheryl yells, even though we're standing right next to each other.

We started out at a hip, too-cool-for-school wine bar—because that's where thirtysomethings are supposed to go to celebrate. But we end up at a dirty dive bar in the seedy end of town because that's where the real fun is.

The large, burly bartender with tattooed arms as big as my head gives Cheryl a smile from beneath his bushy blond beard as he pours us another round. Cheryl catches his smile and bats her false eyelashes.

But they get stuck together, so the overall effect is less flirty, more seizure-like.

Bruce is in the back corner, chatting up a friendly, middle-aged blonde in a tank-top and leather pants. He's charming, suave with the ladies . . . but he also has the "nice guy" curse. It's awful and stereotypical—but true. Bruce is too polite—there's no edge to him, no excitement. I should know. He and I tried dating when we first met, years ago, but it was quickly apparent that the only spark for either of us was a friendship ember.

With one eye open, Cher turns to me, lifting her shot glass. "I just thought of something! This means you can finally move out of that rinky-dink building that's teeming with piss-poor graduate students and move into that place you've been creaming over for years—the one with the seals!"

I still live in the same apartment I lived in my senior year of college. But I've been saving up, year by year, little by little, for a down payment on a beautiful two-bedroom, ocean-front condo in La Jolla.

There's one unit in particular, with a balcony and perfect view of the rocks where seals come to sun every afternoon. It's peaceful and magical—my dream home.

Excitement buzzes up from my toes, spreading through my body, and I feel just like Kate Hudson in *Almost Famous*.

"It's all happening!" I pick up my glass, sloshing a bit of cloudy liquid because I'm literally bouncing.

And scary-bartender-man raises a glass for himself, toasting with us. "To the seals. Love those fuzzy little fuckers."

As the night winds on, me, Cheryl and Bruce get the kind of drunk they make montages out of in the movies. Life is reduced to snapshots of moments—moments like Bruce swinging his ascot over his head like a helicopter blade, like Cheryl dancing on a chair . . . right before she falls off of it, like the three of us forming a personal conga-line and choo-chooing around the bar as "C'Mon Ride the Train" plays from the speakers.

Eventually, we make it back to my tiny one-bedroom apartment. I kick off my shoes in the corner and Cheryl does a trust-fall onto the couch.

Bruce spreads out his sports coat on the beige carpeted floor, then lies on top of it, sighing.

"Oh! Oh," Cheryl yells, reaching into her blouse to pull a balled-up napkin out of her bra, "Look what I got! Mountain Man's number!"

"Mountain Man?" Bruce asks.

"The bartender." She breathes out, then mumbles, "Gonna climb him like a mountain." Cher's an avid climber in her spare time. "He can sink his crampon into me anytime . . ."

Her voice drifts off and I think she's fallen asleep. Until Bruce rips the beige throw pillow out from under her head.

"Hey! What the hell, dude? I need that pillow."

"You have the couch, Cheryl. If you get the couch, I get the pillow," Bruce grumbles.

"I can't lie flat after drinking. My acid reflux will burn a hole in my chest."

And this is how you know you're old.

"You have selective acid reflux," Bruce argues. "You only bring it up when you want something."

"Screw you, Brucey."

Cheryl and Bruce are like a cat and a dog that have been raised in the same house.

"Settle down, children. I have extra pillows and blankets in the closet."

When things are good, it's easy to forget Murphy's Law—*anything that can go wrong, will go wrong.* But that's when you need to remember it most. Because Murphy's Law is like a quiet snake in the grass at a picnic. When your back is turned, when you're not expecting it . . . that's when it reaches up and sinks its fangs into your left ass cheek.

As I step towards the hall, my phone rings. I try to fish it out of my messy purse, but the little bastard's hiding, so I end up having to dump my whole bag out, pelting Bruce with rogue Tic Tacs as they bounce off the coffee table.

I peer at the screen and see the smiling face of my big sister staring back at me, with my adorable nieces surrounding her, sticking their tongues out. I took the picture last Thanksgiving at Lake Tahoe—where my parents, my sister, and I rented a cabin for the holiday.

It doesn't occur to me that she's calling me at two in the morning. I just answer.

"Hey, Colleen! What's—"

Her words come out in a rush. And I think . . . I think she's crying. Which is weird, because—there's no crying in Colleen. My big sister is rock solid. Badass. She gave birth to three children au natural . . . nothing rattles her.

Only, right now, something definitely has.

"Col, slow down, I can't understand you . . ."

Between my drunkeness and her hiccups—I can barely make out her words.

"Mom . . . Dad . . . car a-acc-accident."

Ohmygod. Oh. My. God.

I turn to Bruce and Cher, instantly stone-cold sober—any thought of my promotion dissipating from my mind like mist in the morning light. There's only one thought, one focus.

"I have to go home."

CHAPTER
Three

Callie

It turns out, Colleen wasn't crying.

She was laughing.

And twelve hours later, while I'm standing in the harsh, white, sunlit hallway, outside my parents' room on the sixth floor of Lakeside Memorial Hospital . . . she's still chuckling.

"Their legs?" I ask the doctor, hoping I heard her wrong. "They broke their legs?"

I didn't hear wrong.

"That's correct." Dr. Zheng tiredly pushes back her dark hair and adjusts her glasses. "One leg each."

My sister snorts into her hands behind me, sounding like a horny goose.

"I want them to stay in the hospital another day or two for observation, however, given their ages, your parents are in surprisingly good health."

Yeah. It's their vices that keep them young.

My parents sent Colleen and me to Catholic school, but that's not why we were "good girls" growing up. That was because nothing your parents do can ever be cool. It's why some behaviors skip a generation. If your parents have tattoos, tattoos are not cool. If they have long hair, crew cuts are way cooler. If they dress in tied-off, midriff-exposing tops and skin-tight jeans, nuns become your fashion icons.

My parents' heydays were the '70s Disco balls and bell-bottom pants, Woodstock and psychedelic drugs—they ate that stuff up with a spoon . . . literally. And in their minds, it's still the '70s—it will always be the '70s. Lung cancer? It's a con-spiracy from the money-hungry medical establishment—go ahead, light up another menthol. Liver disease? It only strikes the weak—pour me another whiskey sour. Monogamy? It's unnatural—where's the next key party? Yeah, before me and my sister came to be, our parents were swingers.

At least, please, for the love of God, let it be "were."

I push that line of thought right out of my head and focus on what Dr. Zheng is saying.

"With their advanced ages, the bones will take much longer to heal. They'll require extensive physical therapy—for months. I've given your sister all the paperwork."

I nod, numbly. "All right. Thank you, Doctor."

I turn around and gape at Colleen, who's leaning her blond head against the wall.

"How did this even happen?" I ask.

My sister holds up her hands. "How it happened? That's a whole other story."

I flinch. "Do I want to hear it?"

"Nope." She grins evilly. "But I had to, so you're going to also."

Colleen fixes her gaze behind me. "Ryan, you're back. Perfect timing."

I turn around—and look at that—Ryan Daniels is a Lakeside cop. I did not know this. He's also the older brother of my high school boyfriend—I practically lived at his house for those four years. The last time I remember seeing him was when he came home from college early and caught me and his brother dry-humping on his parents' living room couch. *Great.*

He smiles at me warmly. "Hey, Callie. Good to see you."

"Hi, Ryan."

He must be thirty-six or thirty-seven now, but he looks almost the same as I remember—just with some new, light wrinkles around the eyes and a few strands of gray in his dark hair. But he's still broad, tall, and handsome, like all the Daniels boys.

"So . . . I reviewed the report again and, I'm sorry, but I'm going to have to give your dad a ticket for the accident. There's really no way around it. Reckless driving."

Colleen nods, suppressing a giggle. "It's fine."

"It's not fine!" My father yells from inside the hospital room. "I've never gotten a ticket in my life and I'm not paying the man now!"

Then he starts to sing "Fuck tha Police," by NWA.

"Dad!" I yell. "Stop it! I'm so sorry, Ryan."

"They've got them hopped up on a lot of painkillers," Colleen explains.

He chuckles. "No problem."

"Fuck, fuck, fuck the police . . ."

I clench my teeth. "How does he even know that song?"

"The new Buick he bought came with a free satellite radio subscription," my sister says. "He's been listening to Urban Yesterday, all the classics are on there—NWA, Run-DMC . . . Vanilla Ice."

My father stops singing and goes back to yelling. "I remember you, Ryan Daniels—puking in our rosebushes after drinking that crap liquor you brought to Colleen's sweet sixteen!" Then he does a spot-on impression of *Scarface*. "You're not giving me no stinking ticket."

A pink flush crawls up Ryan's neck. "Wow. Your dad has a really good memory." He calls into the room, "Sorry about those rosebushes, Mrs. Carpenter."

"That's all right, honey," my mother's gravelly voice calls back. "You can regurgitate in my bushes any day—as long as you rally afterwards."

I cover my eyes. Praying for a tear in the space-time continuum to swallow me whole.

"So, a reckless driving ticket?" I ask Ryan. "Dad's usually a great driver; what happened?"

"His mind wasn't on the road, that's for damn sure," Colleen answers.

Ryan's flush burns brighter. "Your parents were being . . . affectionate . . . at the time of the accident."

"Affectionate?" I repeat, happily clueless.

Until Colleen ruins it.

"Mom was blowing Dad," she busts out, then folds over with horrified laughter.

I think I scream. Because those words should never, ever be put together in the same sentence.

"We had a good night at the slots in AC," my mother yells back. "We were celebrating." Then her tone turns disgustingly proud. "I've still got it. Though I think taking out the dentures might've helped."

I'm stunned, speechless—afraid to say anything that could make it worse. With my mom and dad it can always be worse.

"Your parents are so much funnier than mine," Ryan says, and now he's cracking up with my sister.

"Oh yeah?" I raise my eyebrows. "Wanna trade?"

Coming home to Lakeside always feels kind of odd—the way everything seems smaller and yet, no different at all. It's been longer this time since I've been back . . . years. I look out the window as my sister drives us from the hospital to my parents' house, passing the streets I know so well and the sweet ghosts that live on every corner. Colleen fills me in on the latest happenings around town—who's having babies, who's getting divorced. There was a fire at Brewster's Pharmacy a few months ago, but they rebuilt, painted it an ugly orange color.

It wasn't really a conscious decision for me to come home less often . . . life just sort of worked out that way. Money was tight my first few years of school; my parents were footing the bill for two full-time college tuitions, and a plane ticket from California to New Jersey wasn't cheap. I waitressed my way through those first Thanksgivings and spring breaks at a diner near campus . . . only coming home for Christmas.

It wasn't bad—I liked San Diego—the newness of it, the sunshine. And my mom had, once upon a time, hitchhiked her way from one corner of the country to the other—so she was always encouraging me and Colleen to get out there, see the world, make their own nests, and get to know the birds on all the other branches . . . to fly.

I started doing theater productions in the summers, so coming back to Jersey in May when the semester ended was out. My third year in school was a game changer. Money was better with Colleen having graduated and I got an off-campus apartment. My parents came out to visit and met Snapper, my glaucoma-afflicted, medical-marijuana-card-carrying neighbor. He was like their soul mate—I swear they would've adopted him if he wasn't forty-seven.

He lives in Oregon now and my parents still send him Christmas cards.

The year I graduated, I came home to be the maid of honor in my sister's wedding. But then, I sort of became my family's time-share—their excuse to go on a vacation every year. Them visiting California eventually evolved into all of us picking a different place each year to spend each holiday. Sometimes it was Lake Tahoe, sometimes it was Myrtle Beach . . . but only once in a rare while was it Lakeside, New Jersey.

On Main Street my sister gives two quick beeps on her horn and Ollie Munson waves at our car. I smile and raise my hand against the glass, waving back.

My voice goes soft. "Ollie's still here, huh?"

Colleen makes a *duh* face at me. "Of course he is. I would've told you if something happened to Ollie."

A few minutes later, we pull into my parents' driveway— the same brown ranch I grew up in, with the neat front yard, white wicker chairs on the front stoop, and my mom's dreamcatcher wind chimes hanging beside the door.

"So." My sister turns the car off. "We need to talk about a schedule. How we're going to handle Mom and Dad's recovery."

It's the "we" that hits me, right between the eyes. A big red flag with a bull right behind it that signals my life is about to change.

"I hadn't thought about it."

It's been like a tornado since her phone call—a whirlwind of throwing stuff in a bag, getting the first flight to New Jersey that I could, and grabbing a taxi to the hospital.

Colleen's head tilts with disappointment. "Callie-dally. I realize you have this whole shiny, single life going on in California—but you couldn't really think I'd be able to do this all by myself."

Embarrassment thickens in my blood—because that's exactly what I thought. Maybe it's little sister syndrome, but Colleen's always so on top of everything, a regular Super Woman, I've never considered there's something she can't handle alone.

"Can we hire a nurse?"

"Ah, no. Medicare won't cover that. Gary does okay at the insurance company—well enough for me to stay home with the kids—but we can't afford a private nurse. Not for the amount of time they'd need help."

My brother-in-law, Gary, is a nice, average guy—in every way possible. Medium height, average build, medium brown hair—even the tone of his voice is average—not too deep, not too high, always spoken at a steady, even volume. And like Colleen said, they're not rolling in dough but he makes a good enough salary to take care of his family, to allow my sister to be the stay-at-home, PTA-warrior, dinner-on-the-table-at-five soccer-mom she always dreamed of being. Just for that, I love the guy way above average.

"I can take care of Mom and Dad during the day, after I get the kids on the bus," my sister says. "I can take them to their doctor and rehab appointments. But at night, you're going to have to be here in case they need anything, fixing them dinner, keeping them out of trouble. You know Dad—he'll be trying to hobble out the door with Mom in his arms and squeeze both their freaking casts into the Buick for a joyride, on day one."

I laugh. It's funny because it's true.

And then I rub my eyes, exhausted, like mustering that laugh took all the energy I had left in my bones.

I give my sister my big news, with considerably less excitement than I'd felt yesterday. "I got a promotion. I'm the new executive director."

She hugs me tight and strong, the only way Colleen knows how. "That's awesome! Congratulations—I'm so happy for you." Then the joy dims on her face. "Is taking time off going to screw that up?"

The tendons in my neck feel stiff and achy. "I don't . . . think so. I have to look into it, but I'm pretty sure they'll let me take an emergency family leave and hold the position for me. But the pay for that kind of time off is only a fraction of my normal salary. It won't cover my rent."

And if I start dipping into my savings, I can kiss my seals goodbye forever.

My sister skims her palms over the steering wheel, thinking.

"Julie Shriver, the theater teacher at the high school, is pregnant and just got put on bedrest."

"Julie Shriver is having a baby?" I ask.

Julie Shriver was always the odd girl around town. Her hobbies were beekeeping and pen-paling with the prison inmates in Rahway.

"Yeah! One of the inmates she wrote to was released last year and turned out to be a really nice guy. They got married a few months ago—he plays on Gary's softball team and is the new deacon over at Saint Bart's. Adam or Andy . . . something like that. But the point is, Miss McCarthy is in desperate need of a theater teacher for the year—she'd hire you in a heartbeat."

Miss McCarthy was the grouch-ass principal when I went to Lakeside—and I can't imagine the seventeen years since have made her nicer.

"Teaching? I don't know . . . that would be weird."

My sister waves her hand. "You have a master's degree in theater arts." Her voice takes on a teasingly fancy tone. "And you're the *executive director*, now, la-dee-da. A high school theater class should be a piece of cake for you."

Note to Past Callie from Future Callie: *Should be*, are the operative words there.

"Is, uh . . . is Garrett still teaching at the high school?"

"He sure is." Colleen nods. "Still coaching too."

"That could make it even weirder."

"Oh come on, Callie," my sister says. "That was forever ago—it's not like you guys ended on bad terms. Would it really be so bad to see him again?"

My stomach does a little tumble, like Alice falling down the rabbit hole, because seeing my high school boyfriend again wouldn't be bad at all. Just . . . curiouser and curiouser.

I blow out a breath, vibrating my lips. "Okay. This could work. It might be a clusterfuck . . . but it could work. I'll make some phone calls first thing in the morning."

My sister pats my arm. "Come on, let's go inside, you're probably beat. I stopped at the store for some supplies before; I'll bring them in."

I love the scent of my parents' house—it's unique, no place on earth will ever smell just like it. A whiff of April Fresh fabric softener from the laundry room, and I'm eleven years old again, climbing under the cool summer sheets in my bed. The hint of cigars and Old Spice in the living room, and I'm instantly seventeen—hugging my dad as he puts the keys to his prized Buick in my palm, my freshly laminated driver's license heavy in the back pocket of my jeans and my head buzzing with the excitement of freedom. A whiff of roasted turkey from the kitchen stove and a dozen years of family dinners dance in my head.

It's like a time machine.

My sister walks past me into the kitchen and sets the brown paper bag in her arms on the counter. Then she pulls a bottle of wine out and slides it onto the wine rack below the cabinet. And then another bottle.

And another.

"What are you doing? I thought you said you bought groceries?"

Colleen smirks. "I said I got *supplies*." She holds up a bottle of pinot noir. "And you and I both know, if our sanity is going to survive the time it takes for those old leg bones to heal up, we're gonna need every bottle."

My sister is wise.

And it's true what they say . . . life comes at you fast. Then it runs you right the hell over.

CHAPTER
Four

Garrett

"Y ou're a good kid, Garrett."

Michelle McCarthy. She was a crazy piece of work when I was a student at Lakeside, and now she's my boss. I sit across the desk from her, in her office, a half hour before I have to be on the football field for the start of the last week of August practices.

"You always were. I like you."

She's lying. I wasn't that good of a kid . . . and she doesn't like me. Miss McCarthy doesn't like anyone. She's like . . . Darth Vader . . . if Darth Vader were a high school principal—her hate gives her strength.

"Thanks, Miss McCarthy."

Even though I'm an adult, I can't bring myself to call her by her first name. It's like that with all the adults I grew up with around town—it'd be like calling my mom Irene.

Michelle . . . nope . . . too fucking weird.

The fact that she looks almost exactly the same as when I first met her, only makes it worse. She has one of those ageless faces—firm, round cheeks, hazel eyes, a bob of reddish-brown hair—the kind of woman who looks better with a little extra weight, who would look like a flabby, deflated balloon if she were too thin.

Miss McCarthy takes a blue plastic bottle of TUMS out of the top drawer of her desk, tips her head back, and pours some into her mouth.

"You're a leader in this school," she tells me as she crunches the chalky tablets. "The other teachers look up to you."

Not every teacher has their shit together, like I do. In fact, the majority are frighteningly hot messes. Messy personal lives, messy relationships with their children, messy head cases who can barely put up a stable front for seven hours a day with an occasional crack in the veneer. Those cracks are what you read about in the papers—when a teacher finally goes apeshit on a smartass student or throws a chair through a classroom window because one kid too many came to class without a pencil.

That's how our former vice principal, Todd Melons, went out last year.

And that's how I know what McCarthy is going to say next.

"Which is why I want to promote you to vice principal."

She leans forward, staring me in the eyes like a Wild West gunslinger on a dusty, tumbleweed-scattered Main Street at high noon, waiting for me to reach for my piece so she can shoot it out of my hand.

But I don't have a piece—or, in this case, excuses. Too

complicated—I'm all about being a straight shooter.

"I don't want to be vice principal, Miss McCarthy."

"You're ambitious, Daniels. Competitive. The VP position is one step closer to being top dog around here. You could institute real change."

Change is overrated. If it's not broke, don't fix it—and from where I'm sitting, there's nothing broken about Lakeside High School.

I like being in charge; I like calling the shots. But I'm not a fucking idiot.

Being vice principal sucks. Too many headaches, not enough upside. And the kids hate you because you're the disciplinarian—in charge of detentions, suspensions, and enforcing the dress code. By definition, the VP's job is to suck all the fun out of high school, and while high schoolers can absolutely be selfish, shitty little punks . . . sometimes they can also be really funny.

Like last year, a sophomore brought a rooster to school on the first day. He unleashed it in the halls—shitting and cock-a-doodle-doo-ing everywhere. The maintenance guys were terrified. I thought it was hilarious.

But Todd Melons didn't think it was hilarious—he couldn't—he had to come down hard on the kid, make an example out of him and babysit him through six weeks of Saturday detention. If he hadn't, he would've had fucking farm animals roaming the school halls every day of the year.

Non-administration teachers can still enjoy the funny. And some days, the funny is the only thing that gets us through the day.

McCarthy lifts her hands, gesturing towards the cramped, insane-asylum-beige-colored walls. "And one day, when I retire, this could all be yours."

She'll never retire. She's single, no kids, doesn't travel. She's going to die at that desk—clutching a bottle of TUMS— probably from a massive, stress-induced heart attack brought on by the stupidity of my co-workers and the senility of her long-time secretary—sweet little Mrs. Cockaburrow.

No thanks.

"I don't want to be principal, Miss McCarthy." I shake my head. "Not ever."

McCarthy scowls—giving me the pissed-off principal face I remember from my youth. It makes me feel seventeen-and-just-got-caught-getting-lucky-in-the-janitor's-closet, all over again.

"The students respect you. They respond to you."

"My players respect me," I correct her, "because they know I can make them run until they barf up both lungs. The students think I'm young and cool—but they won't if I move into the vice principal's office. Then they'll just think I'm a douche. I don't want to be a douche, Miss McCarthy."

Her eyes narrow and her pretty, pudgy face twists. "So, it's a no?"

I nod. "A hard no."

And *schwing* . . . out comes the flaming red light saber. "You're a cocky little shithead, Daniels. You always were. I never liked you. One of these days, you're going to need something from me and I'm going to laugh in your smug, pretty-boy face."

I'm not offended. *Sorrynotsorry.*

"That's a chance I'm willing to take."

She pushes her chair back from the desk. "Cockaburrow! Bring me those god damn résumés."

Mrs. Cockaburrow scurries into the office like Dr. Frankenstein's Igor.

Then McCarthy shoos at me with her hand. "Get the hell out of my office. Go get that team ready to win some football games."

"That, I can do for you, Miss McCarthy." I tap the door jamb as I walk through it. "That I can do."

"Nice job, Martinez! Donbrowski—I said left! You go left! Jesus, were you absent the day they taught left and right in fucking kindergarten?!"

Times have changed since I was a football player on this field. The things a coach can say—and can't say—have changed. For instance, my coach—Leo Saber—liked to tell us he was going to break our legs if we screwed up. And if we *really* screwed up, he'd rip our heads off and take a dump down our necks.

Today, that would be frowned upon.

These days, it's all about behavior-centric criticism. We can't *call* them dumbasses, but we can tell them to stop *acting* like dumbasses. It's a minute difference, but one me and my coaching staff are bound by. Some changes have been good, important—vital. Back in the day, coaches weren't as aware of health issues, like multiple concussions. It didn't matter if you were hurt—we were always hurt—it mattered if you were *injured*.

I'll never forget the day, the summer before my junior year, when Billy Golling had a seizure in the middle of a two-point conversion. Heat stroke.

That'll never happen to one of my kids. I won't let it.

But the fundamentals of this game haven't changed. It's brotherhood, mentorship, hero worship—it's dirt and grass, confidence and pain. It's hard . . . it takes real commitment and real sweat. The best things in life always do.

We spend practice breaking them down, like in the military, then building them up into the champions they can be. And the kids love it. They want us to scream at them, direct them—fucking coach them. Because they know in their hearts if we didn't care, if we didn't see their potential, we wouldn't bother yelling at them.

We treat them like warriors, and on the field . . . they play like kings.

That's how it worked with me—that's how it works now.

"No, no, no—god damn it, O'Riley! You drop that ball again, I'll have you doing suicides until you can't see straight!"

Dean Walker is my offensive coach. He's also my second-place best friend, after Snoopy. He was my go-to receiver in high school, and together we were an unbeatable combination. Unlike me, he didn't play football in college; he majored in math—and is now the AP math teacher at Lakeside.

Dean's a real Clark Kent kind of guy, depending on the time of year. He's a drummer in a band—having summers off allows him to tour all the local haunts up and down the Jersey shore. But from the end of August through June, he hangs up the drumsticks, puts on his glasses, and assumes the Mr. Walker, math-teacher-extraordinaire persona.

He grabs O'Riley's face mask. "You're pulling a Lenny! Stop squeezing the puppy to death!"

Some players are chokers—they freeze up when a big

moment arrives. Others, like our sophomore receiver Nick O'Riley, are what I call clenchers. They're too eager, too rough, they clasp the ball too hard, making it easy to fumble the minute another player taps them.

"I don't know what that means, Coach Walker," O'Riley grunts around his mouthpiece.

"Lenny—*Of Mice and Men*—read a frigging book once in a while," Dean shouts back. "You're holding the ball too tight. What happens if you squeeze an egg too hard?"

"It cracks, Coach."

"Exactly. Hold the ball like an egg." Dean demonstrates with the ball in his hands. "Firm and secure—but don't strangle the bastard."

I have a better idea. "Snoopy, come here!"

Snoopy loves football practice. He runs around the field and herds the players like a sheepdog. In a white furry blur he runs and leaps into my arms.

Then I put him in O'Riley's. "Snoopy's your football. You hold him too tight, or drop him, he'll bite your ass." I point down field. "Now run."

Across the field, my defensive coach barks at my starting line. "What the hell was that?"

Jerry Dorfman is a former all-state defensive back and a decorated marine. "I piss harder than you're hitting! Get the lead out! Stop acting like pussies!"

He's also Lakeside's only guidance counselor and our emotional management therapist.

So . . . yeah.

A few hours later, when the air is cooler and the sun is on its downward descent, and the team is hydrating and the field is quieter, I watch my quarterback, Lipinski, throw long passes to my wide receiver, DJ King. I check their feet, their form, every move they make—looking for weakness or error and finding none.

Watching them reminds me of why I love this game. Why I always have.

It's those seconds of perfect clarity—when time freezes and even your heartbeat stops. The only sound is your own breath echoing in your helmet and the only two people on the field are you and your receiver. Your vision becomes eagle-focused and everything snaps into place. And you know—you feel it in your bones—that now, *now* is the time. The raw energy, the strength, rushes up your spine, and you step back, pump your arm . . . and throw.

And the ball flies, swirls beautifully, not defying gravity but owning it—landing right where you've commanded it to go. Like you're a master, the god of the air and sky.

And everything about it is perfect.

Perfect throw, perfect choreographed dance . . . the perfect play.

I clap my hands and pat DJ's back as he comes in. "Nice!" I tap Lipinski's helmet. "Beautiful! That's how it's done."

And Lipinski . . . rolls his eyes.

It's quick and shielded by his helmet, but I catch it. And I pause, open my mouth to call the little shit out . . . and then I close it. Because Lipinski is a senior, he's feeling his oats—that cocksure, adrenaline-fueled superiority that comes with being the best and knowing it. That's not necessarily a bad thing. I was an arrogant little prick myself, and it worked out well for me.

A kid can't grow if he's walking around with his coach's foot on his neck 24/7. You have to give the leash some slack before you can snap it back—when needed.

My players huddle around me and take a knee.

"Good practice today, boys. We'll do the same tomorrow. Go home, eat, shower, sleep." They groan collectively, because it's the last week of the summer. "Don't go out with your girlfriends, don't frigging drink, don't stay up until two in the morning playing Xbox with your idiot friends across town." A few of them chuckle guiltily. "Eat, shower, sleep— I'll know if you don't—and I'll make it hurt tomorrow." I scan their faces. "Now let me hear it."

Lipinski calls it out, "Who are we?"

The team answers in one voice: "Lions!"

"Who are we?!"

"Lions!"

"Can't be beat!"

"Can't be beat! Can't be beat! Lions, lions, LIONS!"

And that's what they are—especially this year. They're everything we've made them—a well-oiled machine. Disciplined, strong, cohesive—fuck yeah.

Before I head home, I put Snoopy in the Jeep and walk down to my classroom, where I'll be teaching US history in a few more days. I have a good roster—especially third period—a nice mix of smart, well-behaved kids and smart, mouthy ones to keep things from being too boring. They're juniors, which is a good age—they know the routine, know their way around, but still care enough about their grades not to tell me and my assignments to go screw myself. That tends to happen senior year.

I put a stack of rubber-band-wrapped index cards in the top drawer of the desk. It's for the first-day assignment I always give, where I play "We Didn't Start the Fire," by Billy Joel and hang the lyrics around the classroom. Then, they each pick two index cards and have to give an oral report the next day on the two people or events they chose. It makes history more relevant for them—interesting—which is big for a generation of kids who are basically immediate-gratification junkies.

Child psychologists will tell you the human brain isn't fully developed until age twenty-five, but—not to go all touchy-feely on you—I think the soul stops growing at the end of high school, and who you are when you graduate is who you'll always be. I've seen it in action: if you're a dick at eighteen—you'll probably be a dick for life.

That's another reason I like this job . . . because there's still hope for these kids. No matter where they come from, who their parents are, who their dipshit friends are, we get them in this building for seven hours a day. So, if we do what we're supposed to, set the example, listen, teach the right things, and yeah—figuratively knock them upside the head once in a while—we can help shape their souls. Change them—make them better human beings than they would've been without us.

That's my theory, anyway.

I sit down in the desk chair and lean back, balancing on the hind legs like my mother always told me not to. I fold my hands behind my head, put my feet on the desk, and sigh with contentment. Because life is sweet.

It's going to be a great year.

They're not all great—some years suck donkey balls. My best players graduate and it's a rebuilding year, which means a lot of *L*'s on the board, or sometimes you just get a crappy crop of students. But this year's going to be awesome—I can feel it.

And then, something catches my eye outside the window in the parking lot. Some*one*.

And my balance goes to shit.

I swing my arms like a baby bird, hang in the air for half a second . . . and then topple back in a heap. Not my smoothest move.

But right now, it doesn't matter.

I pull myself up to my feet, step over the chair towards the window, all the while peering at the blonde in the navy-blue pencil skirt walking across the parking lot.

And the ass that, even from this distance, I would know anywhere.

Callaway Carpenter. Holy shit.

She looks amazing, even more beautiful than the last time I saw her . . . than the first time I saw her. You never forget your first. Isn't that what they say? Callie was my first and for a long time, I thought she'd be my only.

The first time I laid my eyes on her, it felt like getting sacked by a three-hundred-pound defensive lineman with an ax to grind. She looked like an angel. Golden hair framing petite, delicate features—a heart-shaped face, a dainty jaw, a cute nose and these big, round, blinking green eyes I wanted to drown in.

Wait . . . back up . . . that's not actually true. That's a lie.

I was fifteen when I met Callie, and fifteen-year-old boys
are notorious perverts, so the first thing I noticed about her
wasn't her face. It was her tits—they were full and round and
absolutely perfect.

The second thing I noticed was her mouth—shiny and
pink with a bee-stung bottom lip. In a blink, a hundred fantasies had gone through my head of what she could do with that
mouth . . . what I could show her how to do.

Then I saw her angel face. That's how it happened.

And just like that—I was gone.

We were "the" couple in high school—Brenda and Eddie
from that Billy Joel song. The star quarterback and the theater
queen.

She was the love of my life, before I had any fucking idea
what love was . . . and then, still, even after I did.

We broke up when she went away to college and I stayed
here in Jersey—couldn't survive the distance. It was a quiet
ending when I went out to visit her in California, no drama or
hysterics. Just some hard truths, tears, one last night together
in her dorm-room bed, and a morning of goodbye.

She never really came home again after that. At least, not
long enough for us to run into each other. I haven't seen her in
years—in a lifetime.

But she's here now.

At *my* school.

And you can bet Callie's sweet ass I'm going to find out
why.

CHAPTER
Five

Callie

I was fourteen the first time Garrett Daniels spoke to me. I remember every detail—I could close my eyes and it's like I'm right there again.

It was after school, a week into my freshman year, TLC was singing "Waterfalls" from the radio on the floor next to me. I was sitting on the bench outside the school theater when I saw his black dress shoes first, because football players wore suits on game days. His suit was dark blue, his shirt white, his tie a deep burgundy. I looked up, and those gorgeous brown eyes, with long "pretty" lashes that should've been given to a girl, gazed back at me. His mouth was full and soft looking and smiled so easily. His hair was thick and fell over his forehead in that dark, cool, careless way that made my fingers twitch to brush it back.

Then he uttered the smoothest opening line in the history of forever.

Do you have a quarter I could borrow? I was gonna get a soda from the vending machine but I'm short.

I did, in fact, have a quarter and I handed it to him. But he didn't go to get his soda—he stayed right where he was and asked me my name.

Callaway.

I'd mentally cursed myself immediately for using my full name because of its weirdness.

But Mr. Confident didn't think it was weird.

That's a really pretty name. I'm Garrett.

I'd already known that—I'd heard a lot about Garrett Daniels. He was a popular "middle school" boy because he'd gone to Lakeside public schools, as opposed to me, who was a "St. Bart's" girl because I'd spent grades one through eight at the only Catholic school in town. He was a freshman, already playing on the varsity team, because he was just that good. Garrett was the third of the Daniels boys. Rumor had it he'd had sex in eighth grade with his then-girlfriend, though I would come to find out later that that was just the middle-school gossip mill run amuck.

Are you going to the game tonight?

He asked, and seemed genuinely interested in my answer.

I glanced at my theater friend, Sydney, who was watching the whole exchange in wide-eyed, open-mouthed silence. Then I shrugged.

Maybe.

He nodded slowly, staring at my face, like he couldn't look away. Like he didn't want to stop watching me. And I was perfectly happy to watch him right back.

Until a group of varsity jackets called his name from the end of the hallway. And Garrett started walking backwards towards them, eyes still on me.

You should come to my house after the game—to the party.

There was always a party after a home game, usually at an upperclassman's house. That week, word around the school hallway was the party was at Ryan Daniels' house.

Technically, it's my brother's party, but I can invite people. You should come, Callaway.

Another flash of devastating smile.

It'll be fun.

I went to the game. And the party.

Although my sister didn't exactly run in the same circle as Ryan, she had some friends on the cheerleading squad and had already planned on going.

We were there a few minutes, in the basement, with Bruce Springsteen playing on the stereo, when Garrett walked up to me. He handed me a red plastic cup of beer that was mostly foam and kept another for himself. It was loud in his basement, teenagers shoulder to shoulder and wall to wall, so we ended up in his backyard, just the two of us. We sat on the rusty swing set and talked about silly things. Our classes, what teachers we had, the star constellations we could see and name, why a quarterback was called a quarterback.

And that's how we started. That's how we began.

That's how we became us.

"Callie!"

Although I haven't seen Garrett in years, I would know his voice anywhere—I hear it in my head all the time. So when my name bounces off the parking lot pavement in that rich, steady tone, I know right away who's calling it.

"Hey—Callie!"

Garrett's leaning out of a first-floor window on the east side of the high school. I wave, and my smile is instant and genuine.

He points at me. "Wait there."

I wait. His head disappears from the window and a few moments later, he emerges from the door, jogging over to me with those long strides I remember so well, but on a fuller, more mature frame. My eyes recognize him, and so does my heart. It speeds up as he comes closer, pounding out a happy greeting inside my chest.

He's smiling when he reaches me, that same, easy smile. Then he hugs me, envelops me in a warm, friendly embrace. His arms are bigger than I remember, but we fit together perfectly.

We always did.

My nose presses against the gray cotton of his Lakeside Lions T-shirt . . . and he smells the same.

Exactly the same.

I've dated many men through the years, artists and actors and businessmen, but not one of them ever smelled as fantastic as Garrett: a hint of cologne, and that clean, male, ocean scent.

And just like that, I'm sucked back to being seventeen again—standing in this parking lot after school. How many times did he hug me right here in this spot? How many times did he kiss me—sometimes quick and fleeting, sometimes slow, with longing, cradling my face in his large hands?

"Wow. Callie Carpenter. It's good to see you."

I tilt my head, gazing up into those same gorgeous eyes with the same pretty lashes.

It's a strange sensation standing in front of someone you've loved deeply—someone who, once upon a time, you couldn't imagine not seeing, not talking to every day. Someone who used to be the center of your whole world . . . that you just don't know anymore.

It's kind of like when I was eight and my Grandma Bella died. I stood next to her casket and thought, *it's her, Grandma, she's right there.* But the part of her that I knew, the part that made her who she was to me . . . that wasn't there anymore.

That was forever changed. Forever gone.

I know a version of Garrett intimately, as well as I know myself. But do those intimate details still apply? Does he still like room-temperature soda with no ice? Does he still talk to the television when he watches a football game—like the players can hear him? Does he still fold his pillow in half when he sleeps?

"Garrett Daniels. It's good to see you too. It's been a long time."

"Yeah." He nods, his gaze drifting over my face. Then he smirks devilishly. "You just couldn't stay away from me any longer, huh?"

I laugh out loud—we both do—because there he is.

That's him . . . that's the sweet, cocky boy I know.

"You look great."

And, God, does he ever. Garrett was always cute, handsome, the kind of good-looking that would make teenage girls and middle-aged moms alike drool while watching him play football or mow the lawn shirtless.

But here, now—Man-Garrett? Oh, mama. There's no comparison.

His jaw is stronger, more prominent and chiseled with a dusting of dark stubble. There are tiny, faint lines at the corners of his eyes and mouth that weren't there before—but they only add to his handsomeness, making him look even more capable and adventurous. His shoulders and chest are broad, solid, and the muscles under his short-sleeved T-shirt are rippled and sculpted. His waist is tight, not an inch of bulge to be seen. His hips are taut and his legs powerful. The way he carries himself, the way he stands—head high, back straight and proud—it radiates that effortless confidence, the unwavering self-assurance of a man who takes charge.

Grown-up Garrett is knee-weakeningly, panty-incineratingly, H-O-T, double-fuck, *hot*.

"You look great too, Cal, as beautiful as ever. What's going on? What are you doing here?"

I gesture in the direction of the principal's office and stumble over my words, because I still can't wrap my mind around it.

"I'm . . . getting a . . . job. Here. At Lakeside. I just met with Miss McCarthy . . . she really hasn't changed at all, has she?"

"Nope. Still bat-shit crazy."

"Yeah." The wind picks up, whipping at my hair. I tuck the blond strands behind my ear. "So . . . I'm subbing for Julie Shriver—teaching her theater class. I'm staying with my parents for the year while they recuperate."

His forehead furrows. "What happened to your parents?"

"Oh, God . . . You're not going to believe it."

"Try me."

I feel my cheeks go pink and warm. But . . . it's Garrett, so only the truth will do.

"My mother was giving my father a blow job on the way home from AC. He crashed into a ditch—breaking both their legs. One each."

Garrett tilts his head back and chuckles. His laugh is smooth and deep. Then he sobers to a smartass grin. "Yeah, my brother already told me—I just wanted to hear you say it out loud."

"Jerk." I push at his chest, and it feels like warm stone beneath my fingers. "It's so embarrassing."

"Nah, it's awesome." He waves his hand. "You should be proud. Your parents are seventy years old and still getting jiggy with it in the big, bad Buick. They've officially won at life."

"That's one way of looking at it." I shrug. "How are your parents? I saw Ryan at the hospital but we only talked for a minute. How's the rest of your family?"

"They're good. Everyone's pretty good. Connor's getting divorced, but he got three boys out of the deal, so it's still a win."

"Three boys? Wow. Carrying on the great all-boys Daniels tradition, huh?"

"No." He shakes his head. "Ryan has two girls, so we know who got the weak sperm in the family."

I roll my eyes, laughing. "Nice."

"I'm just kidding—my nieces kick ass and take names. Yours do too from what I hear. Colleen's oldest is a freshman this year, right?"

"Yeah. Emily. I've told her to get ready; high school is a whole new world."

And it all feels so un-awkward. Seamless. Talking to Garrett, laughing with him. Like riding your favorite bike down a smooth, familiar road.

"Are you still in California?" he asks.

"Yeah, I'm executive director of the Fountain Theater

Company in San Diego."

"No kidding?" Pride suffuses his tone. "That's amazing. Good for you, Cal."

"Thanks." I gesture towards the football field behind the school building. "And you're teaching here . . . and coaching? Head Coach Daniels?"

He nods. "That's me."

"You must love it. My sister says the team's been outstanding the last few years."

"Yeah, they are. But I'm their coach, so outstanding is to be expected."

"Of course." I smile.

Then there's that quiet lull . . . comfortable . . . but still a lull, that always comes towards the end of a conversation.

I gesture towards my rental car. "Well, I should probably . . ."

"Yeah." Garrett nods, staring down at my hands, like he's looking for something.

Then his voice gets stronger—taking on that clear, decisive tone he always had, even when we were young.

"We should hang out, sometime. Since . . . you're going to be in town for a while. And we're going to be working together. We should catch up. Grab dinner or get a drink at Chubby's . . . legally, for once. It'll be fun."

My eyes find his—the eyes I grew up loving. And my voice is quiet with sincerity.

"I would really like that."

"Cool." He holds out his hand. "Give me your phone. I'll text mine, so you have the number. Let me know when you're free."

"Okay."

I put my phone in his hand and he taps the buttons for a minute, then gives it back. I slip it into my purse. And then I stop and just look at him. Because there were so many times, so many days when I thought of him—when I'd wondered, and wanted the chance to look at him again, even just one more time.

My voice is gentle, breathy. "It's . . . it's so good to see you again, Garrett."

And he's looking back at me, watching me, just like the first time.

"Yeah. Yeah, Callie, it really is."

We hold each other's gazes for a moment, taking each other in, absorbing these new, older versions of ourselves.

Then he opens the car door for me—and I remember that too. He used to do this all the time, every time, because Irene Daniels' boys were rowdy and rough and a little bit wild, but she raised them right—to be men. Gentlemen.

The feeling of being precious and protected and cared about warms my muscles as I climb into the car, the same way it always used to. Garrett closes the door behind me and taps on the hood. He gives me one last breathtaking smile and steps back.

Then he stands there, arms crossed, watching me pull out of the parking lot and drive safely away.

Later, once I'm parked in my parents' driveway, I remember my phone. I take it out of my purse. And when I read what Garett texted to himself I laugh out loud, alone in the car:

Garrett, you're even hotter than I remember.
I want to rip your clothes off with my teeth.
~Callie

Nope—Garrett Daniels hasn't changed a bit.

And that's a wonderful thing.

Garrett

"**Y**ou called her name out the window and ran across the parking lot to talk to her? Jesus, did you hold a boom box over your head too?" Dean asks.

"Shut up, dickweed."

"Why don't you borrow the pussy costume Merkle wore to the women's march last year?"

Merkle is Donna Merkle—the megafeminist art teacher at Lakeside.

I flip him off.

We're sitting down at my dock later that day, fishing and drinking a few beers while I tell him about seeing Callie again, the story with her parents, and how she's going to be subbing at the school this year.

Dean shakes his head. "Just be careful with that, D."

"What do you mean?"

"I mean, I was here, dude. I remember how you were when you came back from California after you guys broke up. It was *rough*. And that's being really fucking generous."

I reach down to where Snoopy is lying on the dock and scratch his belly. He rolls over to give me full access, the shameless bastard.

"That was years ago; we were kids. We're adults now. We can be friends."

He shakes his head again. "See, it doesn't work like that,

man. Like, take me and Lizzy Appleguard. We were neigh-bors, friends—borrowing cups of sugar, I helped her hang her TV, shit like that. We screwed for a few weeks and it was good while it lasted. And then, we went *back* to being friends. I was an usher in her wedding. You and Tara, same thing— you knew each other in high school, passed each other in the halls, you bumped uglies for a few months, now you're friends again, passing each other in the grocery store, *"Hey, how you doing? What's up?"*

Dean reels in his line, giving his fishing pole a little tug. "But you and Callie . . . I remember how you two were back in the day. It was intense. A ton of heat, and there was love . . . but I don't remember a single day when you two were anything close to *friends*."

CHAPTER
Six

Callie

ays go by, and I'm not able to text Garrett to catch up. Because time really flies when you have ten thousand things to do: paperwork, fingerprints, background check—all so I can get emergency certification to teach in New Jersey. There are phone calls to make—to the HR department to set up my emergency family leave, and to Cheryl and Bruce who prove their BFF worthiness by packing up my whole wardrobe and other essentials and shipping it all to me.

My parents coming home from the hospital is a fiasco in and of itself. Between picking up the medical equipment—matching wheelchairs and crutches—and the stress of ordering and fitting a double-wide hospital bed in the middle of the living room—Colleen and I drink through half of her "supplies" in the first week.

Then, before I know it—before I'm anywhere close to prepared or organized—it's the day before the first day of school, and I have to report to the high school at 8 a.m. sharp for a staff in-service meeting.

I step through the side door of the auditorium a few minutes early. The rows of dark seats, the thin black carpeting beneath my feet, the dim lighting, and quiet, empty stage hidden behind the draping of the red velvet curtain . . . it all takes me back to twenty years ago.

Like it was just waiting here for me, frozen in time.

I made a lot of memories in this room—on that stage and in the secret lofts and caverns behind it—and there's not a bad one in the bunch.

The heavy metal door shuts against my back with a resounding clang, turning every head in every seat my way. Of course.

Most of the faces are new, but some I recognize—Kelly Simmons, who was the head cheerleader and top mean girl of our graduating class. Her eyes drag up and down over my body before she gives me a tight, unfriendly smile—then whispers to the two equally blond, long-acrylic-painted-fingernailed women on either side of her. Alison Bellinger adjusts her yellow-framed glasses and gives me a vigorous open-palmed wave. She was the student council president in the class above me and judging from her unruly, brown curly hair, effusive expression, and brightly colored Lakeside sweatshirt, she's just as boisterous as she was then. And look at that—Mr. Roidchester, my old bio teacher, is still alive. We figured he was like a hundred-years-old back then, but his crotchety, gray, wrinkled self is still kicking.

Obviously voodoo.

Towards the back, I spot Garrett's dark hair and handsome face. He lifts his chin in greeting, then tilts his head towards the empty seat next to him. I smile, relieved, and head straight for him, like he's my own hot, personal dingy in a sea of choppy water.

Something I can hold on to.

Before I reach him, Dean Walker stands up from the seat behind Garrett and meets me in the aisle. In relationships, friend groups usually mix, meld together. When we were young, Garrett knew a lot more people than I did—his brothers' friends, the football players and their girlfriends, were a crew, a pack. Over the years we dated, my old friends became acquaintances, people I'd talk to in school and celebrate with at the cast parties after the fall drama and spring musical but didn't hang out with otherwise. I was pulled into Garrett's group—and his friends became mine.

"Hey, sweetness," Dean purrs, giving me a hug that lifts me off my feet. "Adulthood looks good on you."

"Thanks, Dean. Good to see you."

He hasn't changed, at all—still tall, blond, wearing hot-nerd glasses with a swagger in his stance and a naughty smirk on his lips. Dean was a player with a capital "play." He had a different girlfriend every few weeks and he was faithful to none of them—though that never stopped the next girl from wanting a crack at taming him. But he was a good, loyal friend to Garrett—to both of us.

"You too, Callie-girl. Welcome home." He spreads his arms, gesturing to the building around us. "And welcome to the jungle, baby. Just when you think you're out . . . your parents' BJ pulls you back in, amiright?"

My eyes roll closed. "I'm never going to hear the end of that one, am I?"

"Never. It's officially Lakeside legend—I've deemed it so."

"Lovely."

Dean sits back in his seat and I slide into the one beside Garrett. Our elbows share the armrest, and our biceps press against each other—sending dancing, ridiculously excited sparks through my body.

"How's it going?" he asks softly.

I sigh. "It's going."

"How are your parents?"

"They're home, mending, but already starting to get on each other's nerves. They're stuck in bed next to each other basically every hour of every day. One of them may not make it out alive."

Garrett's lips curl into a grin. "My money's on your mom. I could see her pulling off a *Gone Girl*."

I laugh at that imagery. Then I ask, "Why were Kelly Simmons and the Plastics looking at me like they hate me?"

"Because they hate you. Don't you remember what it was like for the new kid in school?"

"But we're teachers. We're not kids anymore."

Garrett holds up his finger. "Connor has a theory about that. He told me once that teachers like me, who've only ever lived by the school calendar—winter break, spring break, summers off—never really leave high school. Add to that the fact that we're trapped in this building with a thousand teenagers, and we absorb their energy and personality traits—he thinks our brains are still partly stuck in adolescence. That we're all still teenagers, just walking around in grown-up bodies." Garrett shrugs. "Kind of like *Invasion of the Body Snatchers*." He scans the room, glancing at Kelly and a few of the other teachers. "It would explain a lot."

Wait. Hold on . . . what the hell did I sign up for?

Before I can challenge his theory, Miss McCarthy walks down the main aisle clapping her hands. "Let's get started, people. Everyone sit down."

There's a gust of shuffling and muted whispers and then everyone settles in and turns their attention to Miss McCarthy, standing in front of the stage, with Mrs. Cockaburrow bowing her head behind her like a scared shadow.

"Welcome back. I hope you all had a pleasant summer," she says, in a tone that indicates she really doesn't care if our summer was pleasant or not.

"I'd like to welcome Callie Carpenter back to Lakeside—she's taking over the theater classes for Julie Shriver."

Miss McCarthy motions for me to stand, and I do, straight and smiling, feeling the weight of fifty sets of judging eyes.

"Hi, Callie," some in the crowd murmur in unison, sounding like an unenthusiastic group at an AA meeting.

Cockaburrow hands McCarthy a folder, and she holds it out to me. "Callie, here's your class rosters for the year." She addresses the others in the room, "The rest of you should have gotten your rosters last week. Check your emails."

I walk up to get the folder, then head back to my seat, while Miss McCarthy talks about changes to the parking lot regulations.

Garrett leans over my shoulder and Dean huddles behind me.

"Who'd you get, who'd you get?"

And I have déjà vu—an image of our fifteen-year-old selves comparing sophomore-year schedules. Right in this room.

Garrett looks at the list and grimaces.

"Tough break."

Dean shakes his head. "Oh boy."

I look back and forth between them. "What? What's wrong with it?"

"That's D and B all the way," Dean says.

"D and B?"

"Dumb and Bad," Garrett explains. "See, some kids are dumb—not book smart, no matter what you do."

"Jesus, Garrett, you're a teacher."

"I'm honest. And I don't mean it in a shitty way. My dad didn't go to college—he was an electrician. The world needs electricians, and pipe layers, garbage men, and ditch diggers. Nothing wrong with that."

"Okay, so those are the D's. What about the B's?"

"Some kids are bad. They might be smart, they might have potential, but they're still bad. They like to be bad. Major pains in the asses, and not in a fun way."

"Hey! You three in the back!" McCarthy barks. "Do I need to separate you?"

And the déjà vu strikes again.

I shake my head.

"No," Garrett says.

"Sorry, Miss McCarthy," Dean says, leaning back in his seat. "We'll be good. Please, carry on."

McCarthy narrows her eyes into slits and points to them with her two fingers, then points those same fingers back at us.

And, Jesus, if I don't feel like she might give us detention.

The real fun starts when Miss McCarthy begins talking about the student dress code. And a frizzy, red-haired woman shoots her hand up to the ceiling.

"That's Merkle," Garrett whispers against my ear, giving me delicious goose bumps. "Art teacher."

"Miss Merkle?" McCarthy asks.

"Will we be adding MAGA articles to the banned clothing this year?"

Before McCarthy can answer, a square-headed, deep-voiced man in a USA baseball hat inquires, "Why would we ban MAGA clothes?"

"Jerry Dorfman," Garrett whispers again. And I can almost feel his lips against my ear. Automatically, my neck arches closer to him. "Guidance counselor and assistant football coach."

Merkle glares across the aisle at Dorfman. "Because they're offensive."

Dorfman scoffs. "There's nothing overtly offensive about a MAGA shirt."

"There's nothing overtly offensive about a white hood, either—it'd still be a bad idea to let a student walk around in one," Merkle volleys back.

"Anyone ever tell you you're delusional?"

"Stick it up your ass, Jerry."

"That's enough, you two!" McCarthy moves down the aisle between them. "There will be no talk of sticking anything up any asses! Not like last year."

Miss McCarthy takes a deep, cleansing breath. And I think she might be counting to ten.

"MAGA clothes will not be banned—it's a can of worms I don't want to open."

Merkle gives Jerry the finger behind McCarthy's back. Then he returns the favor.

And I feel like I'm in the twilight zone.

"Speaking of clothing," a younger-looking, light-brown-haired man in a gray three-piece suit volunteers, in a British accent, "could someone advise these lads to pull up their trousers? If I glimpse another pair of Calvin Klein pants, I'll be ill."

"Peter Duvale, pretentious asshole. Teaches English," Garrett says, and I feel the brush of his breath against my neck. Delicious heat unfurls low and deep in my pelvis.

"Jesus Christ, Duvale—I am too hungover to listen to your bullshit British accent today. Please shut the hell up."

"Mark Adams," Garrett says, whisper soft. "Gym teacher, fresh out of college. Only, don't call him a gym teacher—he'll be insulted. They're physical education teachers now."

I swallow, my skin tingles from the sound of Garrett's voice so close.

Another man raises his hand. This one middle aged with dark, thick hair sticking up at all possible angles.

"Speaking of dress code, can we make sure Christina Abernathy's breasts are covered this year? There was nipple-peekage last year. Not that I was looking—I wasn't. But if I had looked, I would've seen areola."

"Evan Fishler—science teacher," Garrett tells me quietly, and I squirm in my seat, rubbing my thighs together. "He spends his summers in Egypt researching the pyramids. Believes he was abducted by aliens when he was a kid." A smile seeps into Garrett's tone. "He'll tell you all about it, for hours and hours . . . and hours."

I turn my head and Garrett Daniels is right there. So close, our noses almost touch. And there's the familiar, thrilling sensation of falling, hard and fast. There's not a cell in my body that doesn't remember feeling this way, whenever he was near.

"Thanks."

He gazes at me, eyes drifting from my neck to my chin, settling on my mouth.

"You're welcome, Callie."

Then the moment is broken.

Because Merkle and Jerry go at it again.

"Breasts are not sexual objects, Evan," Merkle says.

Jerry snorts. "The fact that you believe that is exactly your problem."

"You're such a pig."

"I'd rather be a pig than miserable."

"No. Miserable would describe the women who've had the misfortune of going out with you."

"Don't knock it till you've tried it." Jerry winks.

Dean groans. "Jesus, would you two put us out of our misery and just bang already?! I hear the janitor's closet is nice—there's probably still lube in there from last year's senior lock-in."

Miss McCarthy yells, "There is no lube in the janitor's closet, Dean! That's a vicious rumor!"

"There's definitely lube in the janitor's closet," someone says. "Ray the maintenance guy hangs out in there way too long not to be whacking it."

Then the whole auditorium erupts in a debate over whether or not there is lube hidden in the janitor's closet. Then the conversation quickly turns to the mystery of the still unclaimed dildo that was apparently found in the teacher's lounge after sixth period last May.

Amidst the chaos, Miss McCarthy throws up her hands and talks to herself.

"Every year. Every fucking year with these shitheads."

Wow.

In fifth grade, my school gave us "the talk"—the birds and bees, where babies come from, biology talk. My mother had already given me the rundown, so I wasn't surprised— unlike some of my poor classmates, who looked like they were being scarred for life.

What was surprising was my epic realization . . . that my teachers had, at some point in their lives, had sex. Old Mrs. Mundy, the librarian, whose husband was the school gardener, had had sex. Young, handsome Mr. Clark, who taught social studies and who eighth-grade girls—and a few of the boys— majorly crushed on, had had sex. Cheery, energetic Mrs. O'Grady, who had seven children . . . she'd had a whole bunch of sex.

It blew my mind.

Because it was the first moment I comprehended that my teachers . . . were human.

They ate, they drank, they had sex, they went to the bathroom, fought, probably cursed—just like real people. Like my parents. Like anyone.

Teachers were people too.

And looking around the room now, I feel another realization coming on. Were my teachers also this crazy? I don't know if it's a question I want answered.

So instead, as the arguing and insults continue, I lean closer to Garrett. "Is it always like this?"

"No, it's a lot calmer this year." He glances at the Poland Spring bottle in his hand. "I wonder if McCarthy spiked the water bottles with chamomile."

Again . . . wow.

Garrett looks over to me, smirking. "Is this what your theater company's meetings are like?"

All I can do is chuckle.

"Ah . . . no."

CHAPTER
Seven

Garrett

The doors open for the first day of school at Lakeside High, and the students surge, filling the hallways. There's a rush of sound, shuffling feet, the metallic clang of opening and closing lockers, a clamor of chatter. It's how I imagine hell sounds when it receives an influx of souls through its gates—the sounds of the damned, who don't want to be there, groaning and crying for release.

I don't know who thought starting the school year off on a Friday was a good idea, but they're a fucking idiot. Probably the same genius who thinks suspension is an actual punishment. *Moron.*

The first day of school always has a Groundhog Day vibe to it—you've been here before, you know how this goes, you could swear you were just here yesterday.

Freshmen resemble tourists wandering through the big, dangerous city, trying desperately not to look like tourists.

Sophomores are unkempt, stressed out, and borderline depressed. Juniors congregate en masse in the halls—laughing with their friends, kissing their boyfriends and girlfriends, making plans about where they'll hang out that night. Seniors are like the old, wise lifers—everything bores them, they've seen it all. Some of them may take a scared, vulnerable freshman under their wing, pass the torch, show them the ways of the force . . . but most of them just want to fucking leave.

I held an early team workout in the weight room before first period, because games aren't just won on the field. Afterwards, I didn't see Callie in The Cave—aka the teachers' lounge because they don't give us windows—to wish her luck on her first day.

But if the look on her face at yesterday's meeting was any indication, she's going to need it.

My first two periods are average, uneventful, and then third arrives—my sweet spot. It's not unlike *The Breakfast Club*—a movie before its time. The kids file in and take their seats. We've got Skylar Mayberry—your basic overachiever, type-A, academic club brainiac.

Then there's Nancy Paradigm.

Nancy's a Queen B kind of popular, a pretty brunette at the upper end of the social status food chain, who's obsessed with the latest trends in makeup, hair, music, and clothes.

"Hey, Big D. Welcome back." She smiles as she passes my desk.

The Big D. As far as teacher nicknames go, it's not bad, but it's important to keep the lines between friendly-student-teacher and messed-up inappropriate clearly drawn.

If not, you're just asking for a shit-ton of problems.

"Let's keep it Coach D or Mr. Daniels for the year, okay, Nance?"

She bats her lashes. "That's what all the girls call you behind your back, you know."

"Yeah, let's keep it that way."

Nancy shrugs and slides into a desk.

DJ King, my starting wide receiver, moseys in next.

"S'up, Coach."

I just saw him two hours ago in the weight room, but we bump fists. Damon John reminds me of me—good family, long-term girlfriend, Rhonda, and a good head on his shoulders. He's gonna do okay.

After the final late bell, I shut the door and start class, talking to them about their summer, laying out how grading works, and explaining the Billy Joel assignment.

And ten minutes later, David Burke breezes in. Low-slung, saggy jeans, flannel shirt, oversized dark-gray trench coat—he's the rebel, the disaffected youth whose extracurricular activities include petty theft, dealing pot, and occasional vandalism.

I saw from her roster that Callie has him in fifth-period theater class.

"Sorry I'm late, Coach D." He presses a hand to his stomach. "I shouldn't have eaten that burrito for breakfast, you know?"

"You're so gross," Nancy hisses, her face twisting from her front row seat.

David winks at her, unabashed. Because girls still go for the bad-boy—that hasn't changed. But the weird thing about kids today? Their cliques are less defined, the parameters permeable. A goth can be a hard-core jock, a dork can be prom king, a druggie could be president of the French Club, a pretty cheerleader can be a criminal.

David's smart—really smart—he could be in honors classes if he wanted to be. Instead, he uses his intelligence to figure out the minimum amount of work he has to do to not get kicked out of school, and no more.

"Sit down," I tell him. "Don't be late again. It's disrespectful."

He salutes me and takes a seat in the back of the class. I continue my lecture. Until Brad Reefer—in the back corner seat, glances out the window and announces, "Runner! We've got a runner!"

And the whole class moves to the windows for a better look. Some of the students grab their phones, filling the room with the sound of snapping digital shutters and the *ping* of recording cameras. They point their devices at the skinny, light-haired boy—likely a freshman—dashing across the school lawn towards the Dunkin' Donuts across the street and doing a piss-poor job of it. Stealth is not this kid's friend.

He glances behind him.

Bad move. When running, always keep your eyes on the prize—where you want to go. Unless you want to go backwards, don't fucking look there.

The runner misses the police officer who steps out from behind a tree, raises his arm, and clotheslines the kid across his throat, knocking him on his ass.

"Damn."

"Ouch!"

When I was a student here, we had security guards, basically mall-cop-level enforcement. But today it's the real deal. Armed officers patrol the grounds and halls—if you get into it with them, you're looking at a charge for assaulting an officer—minimum. And there are all different kinds of cops. Level-headed, calm realists, like my brother Ryan. And aggressive, power-high live wires, like Officer John Tearney, who's currently hauling the runner up by the back of his shirt, cuffing him, and dragging him back into the building.

Remember my theory about the soul? How it doesn't change after high school? Tearney is Exhibit A. He was a grade above me in high school—he was a prick then, and he's a prick with a badge now.

"All right, guys," I tell my class. "Show's over. Back in your seats."

Midway through the period, my door opens and Jerry Dorfman, school guidance counselor and assistant coach, lumbers through.

"What's up, Jerry?"

He hands me a slip of paper.

"I need David Burke."

"I didn't do it." David holds up his hands in surrender and the class laughs.

From what I hear, David lives with his grandmother. His mom's out of the picture, his dad's still around, but the situation is not good.

"On your feet, Burke!" Jerry barks. "I didn't ask for your lip. Move it, monkey, move it!"

Jerry's big and rules with the tough love he learned from his marine days. He's a hardass—but he's not a dick. I wouldn't let him coach my team if he were.

With a final compulsory eye roll, David stands up and

walks out of the room with Jerry.

Twenty minutes later, the bell rings and the mad, *Hunger Games*-worthy fight for the door ensues. I give them the same send-off I do every Friday.

"Have a good weekend. Don't be idiots."

You'd be amazed at the amount of bullshit you can save yourself by following those three simple words.

My fourth period is free—a prep period—thank you, teachers' union. I plan to spend it in my office next to the locker room. But on the way, I'm stopped by the view of three football players—my quarterback, Lipinski, and two junior varsity players, Martin and Collins, surrounding another student— Frank Drummond. Frank's a special needs student in the self-contained classroom.

Lipinski has Frank's navy Yankees hat in his hand, holding it just out of his reach—letting him get close, then yanking it away like a yo-yo. Martin and Collins laugh as Lipinski taunts him.

"Hey!" I call out, walking over. "Knock it off, right now."

Martin's face pales when he sees me and Collins' eyes shift like he's looking for an escape hatch. I snap the hat out of Lipinski's grasp and put it in Frank's hands.

"Apologize."

"Sorry, Frank."

"Yeah, sorry."

"Just joking with you, Frankie." Lipinski sneers. "You don't have to freak out."

I look at him, hard—come practice I'm going to rip the

little shit's head off.

"There you are, Frank." Kelly Simmons walks up to us, threading her arm through her student's.

Kelly is beautiful, in a light-tan dress that only reaches her mid-thigh, and high, suede, brown fuck-me boots—she definitely stars in the hot-for-teacher fantasies of the majority of the male student population.

"Sorry about this, Kelly," I tell her as she scowls at the three players. "I'll take care of it."

"Thanks, Garrett." And walks with Frank down the hall.

"My office," I growl at the remaining jackasses. "Now."

Once the three of them are inside, I slam the door.

"What the hell did I just see?" I snap.

"We were joking." Collins squeaks out, eyes on the floor.

Lipinski juts out his chin. "It's not a big deal."

I step closer. Brandon's almost his full height, but I still have two inches on him and I use them to my advantage. "It's a big deal to me."

Martin lifts his shoulder meekly. "Guys bust on each other, Coach. We were messing around with Frank, that's all."

My voice is clipped, sharp, and damning.

"Guys bust each other's balls, yeah, but Frank wasn't in on the joke. Only assholes punch down—don't act like assholes."

"Punch down?" Lipinski challenges. "That almost sounds like you think Frank isn't as capable as the rest of us. Pretty messed up, don't you think?"

"Frank has challenges that you don't," I fire back. "I can't figure out why in God's name you would go out of your way to make his life even harder. Are you hearing me?"

"Yeah, Coach," Martin mumbles.

"Yeah, we hear you," Collins adds. "Sorry."

Lipinski says nothing. And his silence is loud.

First rule of dealing with a kid who's acting out? Take away his audience. He'll back down easier if there's not anyone else there to watch him do it.

I scratch out two hall passes and hand them to Collins and Martin.

"Go back to class. And if you pull this shit again, it'll be the last time you ever wear a helmet for this school. Got it?"

"Yeah, got it."

"Okay, Coach."

I point at Lipinski. "You—sit."

Collins and Martin shuffle out the door, closing it behind them. Lipinski sinks down into the chair and leans back, knees spread, without a care in the world.

I walk around my desk and sit down.

"You're a team captain—every move you make is a reflection on the team, and more importantly, a reflection on me." I point at the door. "That bullshit and your attitude right now does not fucking fly with me—you know that. What the hell is your problem, Brandon?"

He smirks. "I don't have a problem, Garrett . . ."

Garrett?

I mentally choke.

I watched *Inside Out* with my niece this summer, and if that film is any indication, my little red guy's head just exploded into flames inside my mind.

". . . I've just figured out a few things."

"Oh yeah? What have you figured out?"

"Dylan has mono, Levi's got pins in his arm . . ."

Dylan and Levi are my second- and third-string quarterbacks, who are both on the injured list for the year.

". . . I'm all you've got. You don't have a season without me. So . . . I'm done jumping when you snap your fingers. I'm done with your bullshit rules. I do what I want, when I want . . . and you can't say dick about it."

Huh.

Interesting.

Confidence is a tricky thing with athletes. They need to believe they're invincible, the best of the best—it makes them better players. But this isn't arrogance. This isn't some little shit testing boundaries, because deep down he wants to be snapped back in line. This is a challenge to my authority. Mutiny.

I speak steadily, evenly, because truth stands on its own.

"That's not how this is going to go, Brandon. You either straighten up and kill the attitude or, I promise, you will not step foot on that field."

I don't know when Lipinski changed. When he went from shining all-star to Frankenstein's monster.

He leans forward, staring me down.

"Screw that."

Harsh lessons are always learned the hard way.

"I'm going to tell you something I hope you'll remember—life will work out better for you if you do."

"What's that?"

"No one is irreplaceable. No one." My tone final, definite—the last hit of the hammer that drives the nail in.

"You're off the team."

For a second he doesn't respond. He swallows and blinks as the words sink in. Then he shakes his head, starting to laugh. "You . . . you can't do that."

"I just did."

I scribble on the pad and hold the slip out between my fingers. "Go back to class; we're done here."

He darts out of the chair. "You can't fucking do that!"

I regard him calmly. "Shut the door on your way out."

"Fuck you!" His voice goes sonic-boom loud and his face turns a radioactive red, eyes bulging, probably breaking a blood vessel.

He goes for the bookshelf along the wall, knocking it over, scattering the frames and books and trophies onto the floor with a metal crash that echoes in my ears.

I don't react. I don't even stand up. I don't give his tantrum any more energy or validation than I would a two-year-old, kicking and screaming on the floor because he doesn't want to take a nap.

With a final kick to the bookcase, Lipinski stomps out of the room.

Slowly, I walk around to the front of my desk and lean back on it, looking down at the mess on the floor. I wrap my hands around the back of my neck and tug.

God damn it.

Dean's blond head appears in my doorway. He eyes the toppled shelf and steps into the room, adjusting his glasses.

"Looks like you're having an interesting day."

I fold my arms across my chest—my mind swirling, reassessing my options.

"I just kicked Brandon Lipinski off the team."

He takes that in, blowing out a slow breath that sounds like an imitation of an atomic bomb going off. "Well, D, that's . . . *fuck.*"

Yep, my thoughts exactly.

After school, I tell the assistant coaches to get practice started without me and I head over to the freshman field.

"Tell me you've got something for me, Jeffrey. A wonder rookie, a new kid who just moved to town . . . a foreign exchange student with a golden arm."

Jeffrey O'Doole is the freshman coach and an old teammate of mine from back in the day. He scans the team roster on the clipboard in his hands, then glances up at the players running drills on the field.

It doesn't look good for me.

"You know all the kids as well as I do, Daniels. Dylan was my starter last year; when he moved up, I knew it'd be a rebuilding year."

I tilt my head back, cursing the sky and hating the words "rebuilding year" with a passion hot enough to melt steel.

But when I open my eyes, across the field, I see a small, scrawny kid step back and throw a sweet pass to his receiver. It was short, only a few yards, but it was nice, and his form wasn't half-bad.

"Who's that?" I point.

Jerry follows my finger with his eyes.

"Parker Thompson. Second string, a young freshman, good kid, but kind of the runt of the litter—hasn't hit his growth spurt and don't know if he'll have one. His brother was already a monster his freshman year."

Thompson, Thompson . . . Thompson.

"James Thompson's little brother?"

James Thompson was a player of mine six, seven years ago. He went on to be the quarterback for Notre Dame until he was sidelined by multiple concussions.

"One of them, yeah."

"I thought Mary wouldn't let the other boys play after James was injured?"

Jeffrey shrugs. "Guess she changed her mind for Parker. He's the youngest."

You can't underestimate the power of genetics—the natural athletic gift that's impossible to duplicate through training alone. And desperate times call for working with what you've fucking got.

I watch the kid throw another pass. And another. Then I watch him for the next fifteen minutes—his feet are decent, his attitude is good—he's scrappy, quick, and it's obvious he loves the game. I can work with him.

Jeffrey calls Parker over.

He's even shorter up close—a kind-looking boy—with gentle bone structure, intelligent eyes, and light-brown hair.

When I tell him I want him to be my starting varsity quarterback for our first game two weeks from today, his lips go gray, and his face, cloud white.

"I'm not . . . I'm not my brother, Coach Daniels."

"You don't have to be. You just have to do what I say. The greatest skill the best athletes in the world possess is their ability to listen. I'll work with you. If you listen to me, Parker . . . I'll take care of the rest. Okay?"

He thinks it over, then he nods jerkily. "O-okay."

I put my hand on his shoulder and try to sound enthusiastic.

"You're gonna do great. I believe in you."

He nods again, forcing a smile.

And then he bends over . . . and pukes all over my shoes.

After cleaning off my shoes, I walk out of the faculty bathroom in The Cave and spot Callie coming down the hallway. And she looks . . . a lot like Parker Thompson before he upchucked. Shell-shocked, drained, the curls at the end of her long blond hair limp and defeated on her shoulders.

"Cal?" I ask tentatively. "You okay?"

Her mouth opens and closes. "I . . . they . . ."

Her chest rises and falls quickly and a barky hiccup bursts from her lips. "They were so mean, Garrett. I didn't think kids could be that mean."

"Yeah. Sorry." I grimace. "High school kids are kind of assholes. Somebody should've told you."

She shakes her head, covering her sweet face with one hand. "They were—they were *total* assholes! They knew where I went to grammar school, what roles I played in the high school plays—they had pictures! That really awkward one from fourth grade when my mom permed my hair and I looked like an electrocuted poodle! They passed it around. And they had one from my friend Sheridan's divorce party— of me kissing a sex doll! They called me a degenerate!"

Huh—that's a picture I'd like to see.

I put my arm around her, patting her shoulder.

"Social media's evil. You need to slash and burn your accounts if you want to survive."

Dean's voice called out from midway down the empty D-wing hallway. "Yes! We have tears—pay up, Merkle."

"God damn it," Donna Merkle curses next to him, then slaps a bill in his hand. She shakes her head at Callie. "I believed in you, Carpenter. And you let the team down."

Merkle walks away, and Callie narrows her eyes at Dean. "You bet on me? You bet on how bad my first day would be?"

"Sure did."

"You . . . dick."

He holds up the folded bill between his fingers, grinning. "Easiest fifty I ever made."

"That's not cool, Dean," I say, like I'm lecturing one of the kids.

He rolls his eyes, then makes a whipping motion with his hand—sound effects included. "*Wapsshh.* I don't even know you anymore."

He wiggles his eyebrows at Callie. "If you quit the first week, Evan has to cough up a cool hundred."

And my chest tightens, way more than it should.

"She's not fucking quitting." I look down at her. "You're not quitting. You got this, Callie."

She shakes her head, and the fist squeezing my heart loosens its grip.

Dean may have a point about my whipped status. *Shit.*

"I'm not quitting. But I could really use a drink."

I nod. "We all could. Chubby's does a special every year . . . if you show your teacher's ID, you get half off."

There's a lot of bars in Lakeside, but Chubby's is the favorite among old-timers and locals looking for a beer after work. It's dim, windowless, quiet except for the old jukebox in the corner and the one, small television above the bar that's only ever been tuned to ESPN. My brother Ryan used to bartend here in the summers when he was home from college—and because we were cool about it, he'd slip me and my friends beers. Callie's old theater friend, Sydney, owns the place now. She's divorced with two kids and gorgeous—a far cry from the granny-glasses-wearing, frizzy-haired shy girl she used to be.

None of my current students would be caught dead here—they prefer to try their fake IDs at the newer, younger, more New York club-like Colosseum, down the highway.

Me, Callie, Dean, Merkle, Jerry, Evan, and Alison Bellinger head to Chubby's and commiserate over a few pitchers of beer at a table in the back corner.

"Two weeks . . . I don't smile for the first two weeks of school."

Alison Bellinger is one of the nicest, happiest people I know. If you told me she shits rainbows and pisses sunshine, I'd believe you. Apparently, she's also quite the actress.

"They all think I'm a grade-A bitch," she tells Callie, wiping foam off her upper lip with her sleeve. "Mean, nasty, stone cold and heartless."

You wouldn't know it to look at her, but little Alison can also chug like a fucking champ. I've seen her drink guys twice her size under the table without missing a beat. It's impressive.

"But it's what I have to do—scare them. I'm young, small, if I'm nice right off the bat, they think they can get away with murder. My first year teaching, nobody did classwork, no one brought pens to class—it was bathroom passes and trips to the nurse all period long. Chaos."

She shakes her head, remembering. "If they're afraid of me, they respect me, or at least pretend that they do. Then, as the year progresses, I can slowly relax—let them get to know the real me. But the respect sticks."

Callie draws her finger across the side of her frosty mug.

"I think I need to be taught how to teach." She snorts, maybe only half-jokingly. "You guys know any available tutors?"

No less than three awesome, tutor-and-the-naughty-student fantasies spring into my head at once, and every one stars me, Callie . . . and her old Catholic school uniform.

I lean forward, and go for it.

"Come to my house tomorrow night. I'll make you dinner and tell you everything I know about teaching. I'm awesome at it—ask anyone. By the time I'm done with you, you'll be awesome too."

Alison's eyes dart from me to Callie above her beer.

Callie's smile is shy and her voice is just a little bit breathless. Good sign. And then . . . she shoots me down.

"I would love to . . . but my parents . . . I can't leave them."

I hold out my hand. "Give me your phone."

Callie watches as I pull up her sister's number.

"Colleen, hey, it's Garrett Daniels. I'm good, thanks. Listen, I need to borrow your sister tomorrow night. Can you cover for her with your parents?"

Colleen starts to give me shit about how she already has daytime parent duty and how her kid has basketball practice Saturday nights.

"Okay, I get all that, but she needs a night off once in a while. You want her to snap?"

Callie's green eyes shine at me, making my heart rate run faster, harder . . . because she's so damn pretty. And I can't remember the last time I wanted to hang out with someone so much—just talking, laughing, listening, looking at them. Probably not since high school.

Not since her.

"Give her Saturday nights and I'll give your kids driving lessons, free of charge. Emily's only a few years away from her permit, right? It's a good deal for you, Col."

She thinks about it for a second . . . and then she agrees. Because even over the phone, no one can resist this face.

"Awesome. Great, thanks."

I hang up and slide the phone back over to Callie.

"You're free. I'll pick you up at your parents at six."

A bright, beautiful smile stretches across her face—a face I've dreamed of more times than I can remember.

Her eyes darken and her voice is sweet. "It's a date."

I have a date with Callie Carpenter. Fuckin-A right I do.

I wink. "Yeah, it is."

CHAPTER
Eight

Callie

I really like my boobs.

Every woman has that one body part she's especially proud of. Colleen always said she'd make a great foot model, because her toes are stunning. For me, it's my boobs—nice, full C-cups—firm, perky . . . happy-looking breasts.

I turn sideways in the hallway bathroom mirror and smooth down the plain white T-shirt over my dark jeans. I work out a few times a week, try to sleep enough, eat right, drink plenty of water. I use moisturizer and under-eye cream— after I hit the big 3-0, it was a must—but I've been lucky in the complexion department.

I lean in closer and pull the skin back at my temples. Then I do the same to my cheeks, erasing the laugh lines around my mouth . . . making me look like a demented, hungry fish.

I think I've held up pretty well through the years. But, I wonder . . . does Garrett think so too?

I bang my head against lime-green-tiled wall, trying to knock out the frustration.

"Stop it." I scowl at myself in the mirror. "It doesn't matter what Garrett thinks. That's not what tonight is about."

He agreed it was a date. He winked, Bad Callie whispers.

I roll my eyes and mirror Smart Callie does the same.

"Garrett's a flirt, charming—he doesn't know how to be anything else."

Garrett's single, I'm single . . . we could be deliciously, dirtily single together. The boy's got moves . . . you remember. I bet his man moves are spectacular.

Smart Callie shakes her head. "I can't complicate this. I'm here for ten months and then it's back to real life. The seals—remember the seals!"

Ten months is a long time. And did you see him with his students . . . with his players on the field? Admit it—you spontaneously ovulated on sight!

"My dream job is waiting for me on the other side of the country. Garrett's going to give me some pointers so I don't get fired or go crazy."

"Pointers" really isn't what I was hoping Garrett would be giving me tonight.

"We'll be coworkers," Smart Callie insists, like the practical girl she is. "Friends . . . good friends."

With benefits. We both know Garrett's benefits "package" is in a class all. Its. Own.

Damn, Bad Callie is persuasive.

I hear a knock at the front door, and my brother-in-law lets Garrett in—the steady rumble of their small talk drifting through the walls. His voice is clearer when he walks into the living room, where my parents are playing Dance-Dance Revolution, '70s edition, from their hospital bed.

"Hey, Mr. and Mrs. Carpenter."

"Garrett! It's so good to see you." My mother's smoky voice is high with excitement. She always loved him.

"How are you guys feeling?"

"Not so bad," my dad joins in. "Where's a three-legged race when you need one? We'd be champs."

"I'm happy you're spending time with Callie tonight," my mother says. "She's been very tense lately. You were always good—"

I'm out the bathroom door and down the hall, faster than Flash Gordon.

"Hey!"

Garrett turns and meets my gaze with an amused smirk. His body fills the entryway and he's wearing a light-blue button-down shirt and worn, relaxed jeans that hug his taught, fantastic ass perfectly. My mouth goes dry and my breath races from my lungs.

"Ready?"

His eyes drag over me, pausing briefly on my boobs. They were always Garrett's favorite too.

"Sure." He leans in, voice dropping, smelling like man and awesome outside sex on a fall day. "You look great, Cal."

"Thanks."

My mother waves her long, red fingernails at us. "Have fun, you two!"

Out on the lawn, Garrett puts his hand on my lower back, guiding me towards his Jeep. And the déjà vu strikes again.

It was a different time and a different Jeep . . . but Garrett and I made a lot of memories in one just like this. We were young and wild and couldn't get enough of each other. To be climbing into the passenger seat with him at the wheel is as familiar as it is exhilarating.

"How long do your parents have to stay in that bed?" he asks. "They remind me of the grandparents in *Willy Wonka*."

I laugh. "Not much longer. The doctors want them to start getting up and out to prevent pneumonia or bed sores. That'll be interesting."

We pull up to Garrett's house across town about ten minutes later, just after the sun has set and the sky is a soft, dove gray. It's beautiful here on the lake—quiet, except for the gentle chorus of crickets and buzzing dragonflies.

I stand in the gravel driveway and look up at the stately redbrick house. It fits Garrett, reminds me of him—simple, handsome, solid, and sturdy.

"Wow," I breathe out, teasing. "The north side of the lake, huh? When did you become Mr. Fancy-schmancy?"

Growing up around here, if you lived on the north side, everyone thought you were rich.

Garrett gazes up at the house too. "Signing the mortgage for this place was one of the scariest days of my life. Even with the extra from coaching and driving lessons on the side, I gave new meaning to the term house-poor. But . . . it worked out."

"Yeah, it did." Affection and warmth climb up my throat and pepper my words. "I'm happy for you, Garrett. You have everything you always wanted."

His eyes drift from his house to me, lingering.

"Not everything." Then he shrugs, grinning. "But it is a

great fucking house."

Inside, it's easy to tell a man lives here alone. It's clean, comfortable—with neutral-color walls and well-used furniture and a Ping-Pong table where a dining table should be. There are curtains that I'd bet my left boob Mrs. Daniels bought and hung for him. There are a few framed family pictures on the walls and in a glass case in the corner of the living room, the dozens of football trophies and awards Garrett earned through the years—first as a player, and then as a coach.

A barking ball of white fur comes leaping off the recliner at us, his nose sniffing and tail wagging at about a hundred miles per hour.

"Snoopy!" I gasp. "Oh my God . . . is this Snoopy?"

I reach down and pet his sweet little head, his familiar floppy ears. He whines excitedly and fidgets and twists like he can't get close enough.

There's a smile in Garrett's voice—joy.

"Damn straight he's Snoopy. Still going strong."

Snoopy pees on the floor a little—the highest compliment an excited dog can give.

"The last time I saw you, you were a puppy," I coo. "And look at you now, you handsome silver fox." I look up at Garrett, as Snoopy's happy whining serenade reaches a crescendo. "I think he remembers me."

"Of course he remembers you," Garrett says roughly. "You named him."

I remember that day, how it looked, smelled . . . what it felt like. Garrett, showing up at my house with a ball of fluff wrapped in his T-shirt. Taking him to the walk-in pet clinic, buying supplies at the pet store, bathing him together, and then, that night, cuddling him between us in the middle of Garrett's bed like he was our baby.

I continue rubbing my hands all over his soft fur. My smile stretches so wide, it brings tears to my eyes and Snoopy licks them away.

"I've missed you, good boy."

And for the first time I can remember, I realize with a deep stab of longing . . . that there are many things around here that I've missed.

"Do you want wine?" Garrett asks from the island in his kitchen where he's seasoning two T-bone steaks. I'm trimming the asparagus that will be wrapped in foil with a little butter and parmesan cheese, then put on the grill.

"Sure."

Garrett goes to the small wine rack beside the fridge, his movements smooth and graceful. "Red or white?"

"White, please."

When he sets the half-filled wineglass next to me, I snort out a laugh—can't help it.

"What?" Garrett asks.

"Nothing, it's just . . . funny. It feels like yesterday you were bringing me beer in a plastic cup and the most romantic thing I thought you could do was cook me a bowl of ramen. And then, boom, here we are." I hold my glass up to the light. "You have actual wineglasses and you're all . . . Rico Suave. How did we get here?"

Garrett lifts one broad shoulder. "We grew up."

"Yeah, I guess so."

"Although"—Garrett opens a cabinet door, the second

shelf stacked with the familiar orange and white packages—"I still make a kick-ass bowl of ramen."

I laugh.

"It's all about adding the extra spices."

He moves back to the counter, picking up the tray and giving me the dirtiest of smiles.

"But that's nothing compared to my steaks. Once you taste my meat, baby, it's the only thing you'll want in your mouth."

"So . . . why history? Teaching? How did that happen, exactly?"

We eat in the backyard, at a small table with a dim lantern between us and strings of bare-bulb lights hanging above the fence, framing the yard. The lake is stunning at night, still as glass, shining like a pool of moonlight.

"That's an interesting story."

Garrett bites a piece of steak off his fork, sliding it from between his lips. And I'm struck by the way he chews—it's hot. I don't think his chewing turned me on before, but now, the way his lips move and his jaw tightens, just rubs me in all the right ways.

Or, it's possible I'm really weird.

How Garrett cuts his food is sexy too. The way his sculpted forearms contract with that muscular vein on display, just asking to be licked. And he has great hands—long, thick fingers—the way they wrap around his utensils makes me imagine how they would look wrapped around his cock. How he would grip himself, if we were making love, and move between my legs, hungry to push inside me. I would lift my hips to meet him—both of us all frenzied, urgent, sweaty need.

"Are you hot?" Garrett asks.

Because I'm flushed and fanning myself.

I take a long sip of wine. "No, I'm fine. So . . . teaching?"

He nods, wiping his mouth with his napkin. That's hot too.

Holy shit, I'm in trouble.

"I went into college undecided, you know that. I figured I'd be majoring in football," he jokes. "And then it was . . . spring of my sophomore year, just after my second knee surgery . . ."

Garrett was named Player of Year and received the National Quarterback Award his first year at Rutgers. But then, early in his second season, he took a hit that shattered his knee and ended his career. I watched the replay on television only once, and then I threw up in the bathroom.

". . . I was taking US history. The first day of class, the professor—Malcom Forrester—walked in all serious and dignified, wearing a suit. He nodded to a few of us but didn't say a word, not until he stepped up to the podium to give his lecture. And when he did, it wasn't just a lecture, it was a speech—and it was mesmerizing. Like Abraham Lincoln was right there, talking to us. He made it so vivid, Cal, the battles, the politics, he made it so . . . interesting."

Garrett's own tone is mesmerizing, and it's like I can feel the excitement he felt then.

"I used to bring a recorder to class—this was before smartphones—so I could take notes from the lecture later, because when Professor Forrester was talking, I just wanted to listen. To absorb every word of history he was handing out."

Garrett takes a drink of wine, his eyes finding mine. "And that's when I knew what I wanted to do. If I couldn't play football, I wanted to coach and I knew I wanted it to be at Lakeside. But almost just as much, I wanted to do what Professor Forrester did. I wanted to make the past come alive for the kids in my class, really teach them something. Something they can take with them, that'll make a difference in their lives." He shrugs. "And the rest is history."

I put my hand over his on the table.

"I'm sorry about your knee. It shouldn't have happened, not to you."

There's no pain in his eyes, no flinching—I know it must've been a deep wound for him, but I'm relieved to see that it's healed. That it didn't scar him, change him, not the part of him that matters.

"Life happens, Callie—sometimes it's good, sometimes it sucks hairy monkey balls. But, life happens to all of us."

"I sent you a card when you got hurt," I tell him quietly, like a confession. "I put my number in it, in case there was anything I could do. I don't know if you got it."

"Yeah, I got it."

"Oh. Why didn't you call me?"

He lifts one shoulder again. "I figured it was a pity-fuck card. That you felt sorry for me. I didn't want a pity-fuck card from you."

"It was not a pity-fuck card! I was devastated for you!"

I smack his arm.

Garrett grabs my hand, holding it between the two of his.

"Careful, you'll break your hand on that steel."

I snatch my hand back from the idiot, shaking my head.

"I thought about coming to see you, but I was still talking

to Sydney then, and she said she'd heard you were dating someone new. I didn't want to complicate that for you. Make things harder than they already were. I sent the card so you'd know I cared. I wanted to cheer you up."

He smiles crookedly, and my chest feels light, breathless.

"Sydney heard wrong, I wasn't dating anyone seriously. I wish you would've visited me in the hospital. A blow job would've cheered me up—you were always really good at those."

I hit him again. "Jackass."

He just chuckles.

<hr />

After dinner, washing the dishes is a team effort—Snoopy licks the plates, Garrett washes, and I dry. Once that's done, Garrett refills my wineglass and grabs a water for himself and we head back outside, sitting in the low, cushioned chairs beside the fire pit. The air is tinged with a hickory, smoky scent, and everything has that pretty, flamey, orange glow.

"Okay, Mr. Miyagi . . . Daniel-son me."

Garrett's smile is broad, and I feel that tingling, weak sensation in my knees. Then he clears his throat and begins to school me.

"The key to controlling your class, is figuring out what each kid wants or needs and giving it to them. But at the same time, letting them know, depending on the choices they make, you have the power to take it away. For some kids it's grades—that's easy. For others it's attention or approval—knowing that you give a shit, that you're watching them. For others, it's being a listener, an authority figure who's safe, someone they know they can go to if they've really fucked up. And some of them will."

"It sounds like you're talking about being a therapist."

He tilts his head. "I've been doing this for thirteen years, Callie. All teachers are therapists . . . and social workers, friends, wardens . . . confessors. Just depends on the day."

"I don't remember being this high maintenance when we were in high school. Teachers were teachers—some of them were barely checked into the job."

Garrett shakes his head. "These kids aren't us; they'll never be us. They're more like . . . young Lex Luthors. They've never known a world without the internet. Email. Text messaging. Social media. Likes and views are king, bullying dickheads are inescapable, and genuine social interaction can be almost completely avoided. It makes them really fucking smart technologically and really fucking stupid emotionally."

"Jesus, when you put it like that, I feel bad for them." I sigh. "Even for Bradley Baker, and he looked me in the face yesterday and told me to go fuck a goat."

"Bradley's a dipshit, a showoff. And it's okay to feel bad for them—Christ, I wouldn't change places with a single one of them for anything. Even if it meant I could play football again." Then his voice goes firmer, more insistent. "But don't feel too bad, don't let them walk on you. Our job isn't to protect them from their own dumb choices; it's to teach them to make better ones. Teach them how not to be a screw-up in a screwed up world."

I gaze at the fire, letting the stark, logical truth of his words sink deep into my mind. Then I take another sip of wine and glance over at the man beside me. In the glow of the flame, Garrett's brown eyes are glittering, gorgeous warm brandy and his face is a sculpture of handsome.

"You know, that's really deep, Garrett. Grown-up you is *deep*."

He grins wickedly. "It turns you on, doesn't it?"

"I'm not gonna lie . . . it's pretty hot."

He stretches his arms above his head, flexing all those muscles. "Yeah, I know."

And that's how it goes for the next few hours. We tease and laugh, about teaching and about life.

"How do I make the kids think I'm the bomb-dot-com?"

"Never saying 'the bomb-dot-com' would be a good start."

I think back, remembering how I would roll my eyes every time my parents said "hip" or "far out" or "psychedelic." How ancient it made them seem. My face screws up as I try to guess the current teenage lingo.

"Rad?"

"Nope."

"Totally tubular?"

"Uh-uh."

"Bitchin'?"

Garrett cringes. "Jesus, no."

I laugh. "Okay, then what's the new cool word for 'cool'?"

He leans forward, legs spread, resting his elbows. "'Cool' is still cool. And if you really want to take it up a notch, throw in a 'dank.'"

I squint at him. "Dank doesn't sound cool."

"Don't overanalyze it . . . just trust me. Dank is cool."

I take a sip of wine and lean forward too—until our arms

are just inches apart.

"What else?"

"Thick," Garrett says confidently.

"Thick is good?"

He nods. "Thick is very good. Try it in a sentence."

I tap into my inner dirty Dr. Seuss. "Garrett's dick is thick."

He gives me the thumbs-up.

"I approve of this message."

And we both laugh.

A little while later, Garrett asks, "Why aren't you married, yet?"

I snort, giving him the bitch-brow. "My sister's gotten to you, hasn't she?"

A chuckle rumbles in Garrett's throat.

I turn the tables back on him. "Why aren't you married yet?

"No hard and fast reason." He shrugs easily, the way he always did. "I just haven't met someone I wanted to marry. Or who wanted to marry me."

"Same."

"So, no serious relationships?"

Now it's my turn to shrug. "I've had relationships. I don't know if I'd call them serious."

"So . . . you're saying you still like me most of all? I'm still the number one boyfriend?"

"This matters to you?"

"You've known me since I was fifteen years old. When has being number one not mattered to me, Callie?"

I roll my eyes, evading the question. Because Garrett's cocky enough . . . and yes, he's still number one in my book.

And then, even later, we sit in our chairs, facing each other. The air is quieter and so are our voices. Snoopy sleeps on the ground between us as I pet him in long, slow strokes.

Garrett lifts his hand, drawing his thumb across my top lip, over the small white scar above it.

"That's new. What happened there? Wild night out with the girls?"

"No. I got mugged."

Garrett goes still and tense.

"What? When?"

I tilt my chin up towards the stars, remembering. "Mmm. It was my last year of graduate school. I was walking home from campus at night and this guy just blindsided me, punched me, split my lip open—took my bag, my computer."

Garrett frowns hard at the scar, like he wants to scare it away.

"It could've been worse. I only needed four stiches."

"Jesus fucking Christ, Callie."

And then I tell him something I never thought I would.

"I wanted to call you when it happened."

The words float between us for a quiet moment, heavy and meaningful.

"I didn't tell my parents or Colleen; they would've freaked out. But after it happened . . . I wanted to call you so bad. To hear your voice. I actually picked up my phone and started to dial your number."

Garrett's eyes drift intently across my face. And his voice is jagged but gentle.

"Why didn't you?"

I shake my head. "It'd been six years since we'd talked. I didn't know what you would say."

He swallows roughly, then clears his throat. "Do you want to know what I would've said?"

And it's like we're in a time machine bubble—like every version of ourselves, the past and the present, the young Callie and Garrett and the older, meld into one.

"Yes, tell me."

Garrett's thumb skims over the scar again, then down, brushing my chin.

"I would've asked you where you were. And then I would've gotten on a plane or a train or a boat, or I would've fucking walked to get to you, if I had to. And when I was with you, I would've wrapped you in my arms and promised that nothing, no one, would ever hurt you again. Not as long as I was there."

My eyes go warm and wet, but I don't cry. Emotion pierces my chest, that feeling of being cared for, protected, and wanted. And the bones in my rib cage go limp and liquid with all the tenderness I feel for him.

"You were always my girl, Callie, even after you weren't anymore. Do you know what I mean?"

I nod. "Yeah, I know exactly what you mean."

We continue to talk about important and silly things. We fill in the cracks, the years, and all the missing pieces between where we were and where we are now.

And that's how we start. That's how we begin.

How we become us . . . again.

CHAPTER Nine

Garrett

I should've kissed her.

God damn it.

I wanted to, more than I wanted my next breath—and every one that would follow. And there was that moment, when I drove Callie home, and we looked at each other under the dim light of her parents' porch, when I know she wanted me to kiss her. I felt it, the pull—like the soft grasp of her hand.

But I fucking hesitated.

It's the greatest sin a quarterback can commit—the surest way to get sacked on your ass. Holding back. Debating. Pussing out.

It's not like me. I operate on instinct—on and off the field—and my instincts are never wrong. I act . . . because even a bad play is better than no play at all.

But not last night.

Last night, I waited—overthought it—and the moment was gone.

Fuck.

It bugs the hell out of me the next day, all of Sunday morning. It buzzes in my brain like an annoying mosquito during my run. It distracts me at The Bagel Shop, while I shoot the shit with the guys, and it replays in my head over breakfast in my mother's kitchen.

The full, soft pink berry of Callie's mouth—just waiting for me to take a taste. I wonder if she tastes as good as she used to. I bet she does.

I bet she tastes even better.

Double fuck.

Later in the afternoon, I make myself stop thinking about it. I don't really have a choice, because I have a driving lesson and this student requires my full attention.

Old Mrs. Jenkins.

And when I say old, I mean her great-grandkids pitched in and bought her lessons for her ninety-second birthday.

Mrs. Jenkins has never had a driver's license—Mr. Jenkins was the sole driver in their house, until he passed away last year. And there aren't any age restrictions for licenses in New Jersey. As long as you can pass the eye exam, they'll put that laminated little card in your hand and make you a road warrior. It's a terrifying thought I try not to dwell on.

"Hello, Connor. Nice day for a drive, isn't it?"

Yeah, this is our sixth lesson and she still thinks I'm my brother. I corrected her the first dozen times . . . now I just go with it.

"Hey, Mrs. Jenkins."

I open the driver's side door of her shiny, dark-green Lincoln Town Car and Mrs. Jenkins puts her pillow on the seat—the one she needs to see over the steering wheel. Usually, I take my students out in the company car, the one with double pedals and steering wheels, that's emblazoned with "Student Driver" in bright, screaming yellow along the sides.

But . . . Mrs. Jenkins and the great-grandkids thought it'd be safer for her to learn on the car she'll actually be driving, so she won't get confused. I thought it was a valid point. Besides, she's not a speed demon.

After we're both buckled in, Mrs. Jenkins turns on the radio. That's another thing—according to her, background music helps her concentrate. She doesn't play with the buttons while she drives; she picks one station beforehand and sticks with it. Today it's an '80s channel with Jefferson Starship singing about how they built this city on rock'n'-roll.

And then we're off.

"That's it, Mrs. Jenkins, you want to turn your blinker on about a hundred feet before the turn. Good."

I make a note on my clipboard that she's good on the signaling, and then I have to hold back from making the sign of the cross. Because we're about to hang a right onto the entrance ramp to New Jersey Parkway—home to the biggest assholes and most dickish drivers in the country. As we merge into the right-hand lane, traffic is light—only two other cars are in our vicinity.

And the speedometer holds steady at 35.

"You're going to have to go a little faster, Mrs. Jenkins."

We reach 40 . . . 42 . . . if there was a car behind us, they'd be laying on their horn right now.

"A little bit faster. Speed limit's fifty-five."

Over in the left lane, a car flies by, doing about 80. But

Old Mrs. Jenkins doesn't get rattled—she's like the turtle in "The Turtle and The Hare" . . . slow and steady, humming along to "Take Me Home Tonight" by Eddie Money on the radio.

We make it to 57.

"There you go, Mrs. J! You got this."

She smiles, her wrinkled face pleased and proud.

But it only lasts a second—and then her expression goes blank—her mouth open, eyes wide and her skin gray.

"Oh dear!"

Because there's something in the road straight ahead of us. It's a goose with a few tiny goslings behind it—dead center in the middle of our lane. Before I can give her a direction, or grab the wheel, Mrs. Jenkins jerks us to the left sharply, sending us careening across the middle and left lane of the fucking parkway.

"Brakes, Mrs. Jenkins! Hit the brake—the one on the left!"

"Oh dear, oh dear, oh dear . . ."

We fly across the median, with green and brown grass clipping, bursting around us and clinging to the windshield. And then we're on the northbound side, heading the wrong way into three lanes of oncoming traffic.

Holy shit, I'm gonna die . . . .to an Eddie Money song.

How fucked up is that?

I'm not ready to go. There's too much I didn't get to do.

And at the very top of that list is: kiss Callie Carpenter again.

Not just once, but dozens, hundreds of more times. Touching her again. Holding her. Telling her . . . there's so many fucking things I want to tell her.

If I don't make it out of here alive . . . that will be my biggest regret.

In a hail of screeching brake pads and swerving tires we make it across the highway without being smashed to smithereens by another car. We dip and bounce jarringly over the grassy gully beyond the shoulder and finally roll to a stop in a thick line of bushes.

I breathe hard, looking around—fucking floored that we didn't die.

Well . . . *I* didn't die. Holy shit, did Old Mrs. Jenkins die?

I turn towards her hoping she's not spiraling into a stroke or heart attack. "Are you all right?"

With almost Zen-like calm, she pats my hand on her shoulder. "Yes, Connor, I'm all right." Then she shakes her head, thoroughly disgusted. "God damn geese."

Almost dying really changes your perspective.

There's no quicker way to light a big, blazing fire under your ass than almost biting the bullet. So, as soon as the paramedics check out Mrs. Jenkins, just to be safe, and I talk to the state troopers, fill out a report, see Mrs. Jenkins back home again, and get back into my own car, I only have one thought in mind.

Only one place I'm going.

Only one person who matters to me, in this moment.

I'm out of the car in front of Callie's parents' house before I even get it in park. I jog across their front lawn, pull open the screen door, and knock on the oak one. And I don't stop, until it opens.

And then she's there. Standing blond and beautiful in the doorway, the scent of roses and vanilla surrounding her. It's what my youth, what love, smells like. Her smile is sweet and a surprised sparkle shines in those green eyes . . . the ones I want to drown in all over again.

"Garrett . . . I was just—"

This time, I don't hesitate. I don't wait.

I step closer, wrap my arms around her and kiss her with everything I am, and everything I ever was.

Her mouth is so fucking warm, and soft—new and familiar all at the same time. Callie's lips move with mine, pliant but eager. And that connection, that bond, that live-wire spark that was always there between us flares up again, bright and strong. I cup her jaw in my palm, stroking her smooth cheek with my thumb, leaning in closer, tasting her deeper.

And I was right. She tastes even better—like warm honey, melted sugar.

Slowly, savoringly, I ease out of the kiss, brushing my lips against hers one last lingering time. Callie's eyes are closed, our foreheads are pressed together, and our breaths are the same—harsh and needy.

"Did you think of me?"

Her eyes open slowly, blinking up at me in that way that makes me want to kiss her again—and then do a hell of a lot more than kiss.

"What?"

"All those years, all this time, did you think of me? Because I thought of you, Callie, every fucking day. I would hear a song or pass a spot in town and some perfect memory of us would come back. And I would wonder where you were . . .

how you were . . . and I would think of you . . . every single day."

She doesn't close her eyes, she meets my gaze head on, wets her lips with her small pink tongue—and nods.

"I would hear you in my head, whenever I needed you . . . and sometimes for no reason at all. And I would think of you, all the time."

And there it is—that same feeling I get on the field after a really great play—the thrilling, electric excitement of being exactly where I'm supposed to be, doing exactly what I was born to do.

"I missed you," I whisper. "I didn't even know how much . . . until you came back."

She smiles, her eyes going shiny with wetness. Because Callie's a crier . . . happy or sad, sometimes both at the same time . . . she always was.

"I missed you too, Garrett."

And she doesn't hesitate either. She reaches up, clasps her arms around my neck, and kisses me hot and hard and wet, with years' worth of wanting. It's almost a full-on make-out session right there on Callie's parents' front step. Her fingers slide through my hair, and my hands skim down her arms, gripping her waist, pulling her closer, rediscovering the feel of her.

The feel of us.

And we feel spectacular.

CHAPTER
Ten

Callie

High school parking lots are one of the most dangerous places on earth. I don't have statistics to back that up, but I know it's true.

I pull into the school parking lot Monday morning in my dad's giant, newly repaired mint-green Buick, with "Back in Black" by AC/DC blasting from the speakers. I feel tough, powerful—like I'm driving a tank.

I'm a badass teacher—I'll run you down even if you're a student—I've got twenty-nine more in class just like you.

The outfit helps too—leather boots, blue jeans, a starched white blouse, and a black leather jacket. It's my armor. The morning air is cool and crisp today, but I barely feel it. I'm locked and loaded and ready to roll.

As I march towards the main entrance, I spot Garrett and Dean and Alison Bellinger outside the doors. They pause when they see me, waiting.

"Damn," Dean chuckles. "Callie's got her shit-kickers on. Did you dig them out of a mosh pit from 1993?"

Garrett crosses his arms. "Somebody's channeling Michelle Pfeiffer in *Dangerous Minds*."

He looks fantastic. His hair is tousled from the breeze and kisses his brow, and he's wearing a dark-blue sweater that's snug around his biceps and soft, worn, light-blue jeans. I remember his arms around me yesterday on my parents' porch. The wonder and exhilaration of the moment.

Of him.

The intensity in his eyes, the desire and possessiveness in the grasp of his hands. The scorching feel of his mouth, his wet, talented tongue that made my stomach swirl and my head spin.

So much for not complicating things.

But I'm not going to play head games with myself or Garrett—we're too old for that shit.

I have feelings for him—I always have—our breakup had nothing to do with either of us not wanting each other desperately. But these aren't just leftover echoes of a sweet, first love—this is something new. A throbbing, breathless attraction to the amazing man he's become. I want to be near him. I want to know him, inside and out, all over again.

And he feels the same way. Garrett wants this version of me as much as he always did—maybe even more. I heard it in his whispered words and felt it in his kiss.

I don't know if we have a future, if it can go anywhere. We have separate lives on opposite ends of the country. But I'm not going to worry about that—for now, I'm going to take each day as it comes and enjoy every moment we can.

Except for now. Now is not the time for enjoying or worrying or relationship building . . . now is the time for focusing. Now is the time to be ice and steel—don't smile, don't waver.

"Little fucknutters don't know who the hell they're dealing with," I growl.

Alison pumps her fist. "That's the spirit."

Garrett opens the door for me. "Go get 'em, *Gangster's Paradise*."

The first few periods go great. This mean-teacher shit actually works.

I scowl and frown and lay down the law. I make them take notes on stage direction and famous playwrights—the boring stuff. Fun, dramatic, silly exercises? Not today, kiddies . . . maybe not ever again. I imitate the Soup Nazi from Seinfeld—no fun for you!

I tack homework passes on the wall, to be given out at my discretion. There really isn't any homework in theater—the only homework my drama teacher in high school, Mr. Pelligrino, ever gave us was practicing pratfalls. But these kids don't seem to realize that. They respond to my attitude, to the role I'm playing—I am Pavlov's bell and they're the dogs.

Until . . . fifth period. My D&B class.

They're different.

It's not just because they're the meanest of the bunch. But I see something in them, in each of them. The performer in me senses it. There's emotion simmering in this room, talent just waiting to be tapped into.

It's in David Burke—the slouching rebel, the Hamlet and leader of the pack. The other kids defer to him, wait for him, even if they don't realize it. If I win him over . . . I win them all.

It's in Layla Martinez—she's a Juliet—quiet, tragically pretty, with the most expressive eyes I've ever seen.

It's in Michael Salimander—the dark-haired, clever kid who probably only took this class to drive up his GPA. He reminds me of Puck, there's brilliance in him, and if the comic doodles that cover his notebook are any indication, creativity too.

It's in Simone Porchesky—the Medea, with her blue-black hair and blood-red lipstick, and a resentful chip on her shoulder.

They could emote. They could perform. They would draw all eyes to them.

They could be magnificent.

"What do you want?"

I don't yell the question, but project my voice through the rectangular room, grabbing their attention from the scattered chairs they sit in. When they don't answer, I take off my jacket, hang it on the back of my chair, walk around to the front of my desk and fold my arms.

"We want a striptease! I wanna see titties!" Bradley Baker yells from the back of the room.

Garrett was right—he is a dipshit.

I ignore him. "You have to be here; I have to be here. So, what do you want to do while we're here?"

"We want you to cry again." Simone sneers.

I nod. And look to the rest of them for answers.

"We want to do something that doesn't suck," Toby Gessler offers, popping an earbud out of one ear.

"We want to get out of this room," Michael says.

"Okay. Anyone else?"

"We want money." David smirks. "You get paid for coming here; we should too."

The gears in my mind go spinning. With Alison's advice and the token system my sister used with her kids when they were little, and Garrett's words.

"The key to controlling your class, is figuring out what each kid wants . . . and giving it to them . . . letting them know . . . you have the power to take it away."

"You know what I want?" I ask.

"We don't care." Bradley laughs, but no one else joins in.

"I want to put on a play. At the end of the year. With just the theater students."

Julie Shriver hadn't put on a play at Lakeside for years. Quickly, I flip through scripts in my head—something with a small cast, with catchy songs, something with an underdog . . . something they would like.

"*Little Shop of Horrors*. Do you guys know it?"

A few of them shake their heads. The others don't respond.

"It's about a plant from outer space. And a guy, a florist, who had been pushed around his whole life, finds it and takes care of it. Then . . . he chops up everyone who's ever been mean to him and feeds them to his plant."

They laugh.

"Dayum! Like *Saw* on Broadway," Toby says.

"Gruesome." David nods. "Is there blood?"

"There is." I nod.

"No way am I getting up on a stage," Simone scoffs. "I'd rather have my belly-button ring slowly ripped from my body. And my nose ring too."

Bradley flinches and covers his nose.

"You wouldn't have to," I shoot back. "Not all of you will be actors. We'll need . . . a director's assistant—someone to keep things running smoothly. A stage crew to make and move the sets. Sound crew, light crew. We'd need makeup crew and costume design."

"I'll be in your play." Bradley holds up his hand. "But only if I get to kiss a really hot chick."

I've been on enough stages to know when my audience is captivated. Right now, this one is, so I keep it going.

"The second boy I ever kissed was in a play, a stage kiss. He shoved his tongue down my throat, even though he wasn't supposed to, in front of an auditorium full of people."

"That's messed up," Simone says.

"It was. After the performance, my boyfriend kicked the crap out of him."

Layla's voice is quiet, and lilting, but I hear her. "That was Coach Daniels, right? You guys used to go out when you were in high school?"

I chuckle a little. How do they know these things? No point in denying it now. "That's right."

Then I clap my hands. "So, how about this? You work with me and I'll work with you. We start working on the play, and I'll award a one-hundred-dollar gift card to the best theater student at the end of each semester."

"Can you do that?" Michael asks.

I shrug. "We'll call it a scholarship. I won't ask Miss McCarthy if you won't. If we don't know we're breaking the rules, we're not really breaking them, are we?"

There's more than one way to skin a cat . . . and there's a bunch of ways to teach a class.

"Five hundred dollars," David says from the back, daring me with his eyes.

I lift my chin and nod sharply.

"Done."

My voice is brisk and authoritative, without even trying, as I walk back behind my desk.

"Michael, I'd like you to be my assistant. Auditions will start next week, and we'll need to get crew sign-up sheets posted. Are you good with that?"

"Uh . . ." His eyes are round behind his glasses, like an owl who has no idea how he ended up on this particular branch. "Yeah. Sure."

"Good. As for the rest of you, before auditions, there's some basic acting techniques we need to go over." I snap my fingers and point at the small elevated platform in the corner—the makeshift stage. "David, you first."

He rolls his shoulders and flips his dirty-blond hair, then he rises and hops up on the stage. He lifts one leg, like a flamingo, holds his right arm over his head and his left arm straight out to the side.

I sit back in my seat and fold my arms.

"What are you doing?"

"I'm being the tree." He grins smart-assedly. "Isn't that what theater is all about? Feel the tree . . . be the tree . . ."

The kids laugh, and I join them.

"Theater is about taking something that's been done a thousand times before—Shakespeare, Oscar Wilde, Arthur Miller—and making it feel like something new again. Making it your own. So forget the tree . . . be the leaves instead."

You got this, Callie.

And I think I just might.

CHAPTER
Eleven

Garrett

Slowly, firmly, I slide my tongue into Callie's warm, waiting mouth. Her lips are rose-petal soft, and with every inhale I breathe in the sweet, delicious scent of her.

I forgot about kissing. Just kissing.

How good it can be—how hot—all by itself. The kind of hot that feels like my heart is going to punch out of my chest and my cock is going to bust through my zipper.

I forgot . . . but with every brush of her lips, Callie reminds me.

I feel the tip of her wet tongue stroking mine and I moan. I lean forward over her, my arms pulling her closer, my hands sliding into the silk of her hair, cradling her head—holding her right where I want her. Where I need her to stay—tight, flush against me, chest to chest, breath to breath. Right here, right there.

One hand stays fisted in her hair, while the other slips

down, brushing her neck where her pulse thrums against my fingertips, and across her collarbone.

Over the years, I've touched lots of breasts. Hundreds. Probably thousands, if you count them separately. I'm a connoisseur of breasts, an expert. If tits were restaurants—I'd be fucking Zagat's.

But these . . . these are Callie's breasts.

And that makes it different. More. Better.

My fingertip circles her nipple, feather light and teasing, making it stiffen beneath the cotton of her blouse. I slide the rigid point between my thumb and forefinger, softly at first, then harder, pinching. And then I open my palm and cup Callie's breast in my hand, massaging and rubbing.

Hello, sweet friend, how I've missed you.

She's perfect . . . fucking perfect in my hand—all soft and full, warm and firm. I want to drop to my knees and worship her. Lick up her stomach, suck the hard, scorching point of her nipple into my mouth, and feast on her until she screams my name.

Callie's hips rotate, rubbing against me, searching for friction, and the sexiest purr rolls from the back of her throat.

That's it, baby. Give me those sounds. Fuck me, this is good.

It's also insane.

Riiiiiing

The bell screams outside the heavy door, disturbing our happy place—sucking face in the fucking janitor's closet. Ray's whack-job palace. This is what we've been reduced to, this is who we are—two horny teenagers stealing kisses and dry-humping the first chance we get.

Between Callie taking care of her parents and their house,

me grading papers—which is more fucking time consuming than the world will ever know—football practices and the extra one-one-one practices with Parker Thompson, our after-school availability is practically nil. We talk on the phone every night—long, good, deep conversations that end when we're yawning more than speaking. Phone sex isn't on the table just yet, so I've made do with jerking off to the memory of Callie's sultry, sleepy voice after we hang up. I also had dinner at Callie's parents' place on Tuesday. We all watched *Jeopardy* and ate KFC together while I copped a feel of Callie's smooth, bare leg under the dining room table.

It's ridiculous. Like high school all over again. I'm seriously considering sneaking through Callie's bedroom window tonight. I wonder if Mr. Carpenter still has that shotgun.

"Shit," I pant, pressing my forehead to hers, trying to catch my breath—and get the steel pipe of my dick under control.

I need to find a textbook to hide behind. Male teachers walking the halls with too-obvious-to-be-missed boners are generally frowned upon by the school board.

"Damn it, I have to go." Callie straightens her clothes and pats at her freshly fucked looking hair. "I need to be at the auditorium before the late bell and traffic in the C-wing is always a bitch."

I nod, blowing out a slow breath. "Yeah, okay. So, you're definitely not making it to the game tonight?"

"No, I can't. My dad has a cold. My mom might hurt herself trying to take care of him, because of course he says he's dying." She shakes her head, muttering, "Men."

"Hey, take it easy on us. Colds hit us harder than women; everyone knows that. Our immune systems are fragile . . . like our egos. Present company excluded, of course."

"Of course." She smiles as she kisses me one last time. "But I'll be listening to the game on the radio. Good luck tonight, Garrett."

"Thanks. We're gonna frigging need it."

I crack the door and take a quick look into the hallway to make sure it's empty. But I don't look hard enough—because when Callie and I step out, it's into the direct path of Miss McCarthy. And she's got David Burke with her, probably hauling his ass to the office for vaping in the bathroom or something.

McCarthy narrows her eyes, like a snake.

And I don't have to worry about that textbook anymore— my hard-on runs for his life.

"What's going on here?"

"We were just looking for . . ."

"Spackle." Callie finishes, her eyes wide like quarters.

She's a stage actress so you'd guess she'd be good at lying. But she's really not. She never was.

"Spackle?" Miss McCarthy asks.

"Yeah," Callie swallows so loud I think I hear her gulp. "There was a . . . crack . . . in the . . . floor . . . in my . . . classroom. And Garrett was helping me find spackle to . . . fill it. Don't want to risk a lawsuit."

David smacks his lips together. "Wow, that was lame. Are you sure you two went to college?"

McCarthy holds up her finger to David. "Zip it." Then she turns the finger on us. "You're already on my shit list, Daniels." She pins Callie with her beady eyes. "And now you're on my radar too, cupcake. There will be no filling of cracks on school grounds, am I clear?"

"As crystal."

"Yes, Miss McCarthy." Callie nods.

She shoos us with her hand. "Now get to class."

After one last glance at each other, Callie and I head off in opposite directions.

And I think I just discovered the fountain of youth—getting busted by your high school principal. Cause, god damn if I don't feel sixteen again.

Here's the thing about teenagers—they have the ability to turn even the simplest event into a major production. A life or death type of drama.

Case in point: two of my team captains, John Wilson and Anthony Bertucci, and my receiver, Damon John, approach me in the hallway just after fourth period. They're wearing their suits and ties—and serious as hell expressions.

"We've got a problem, Coach," Wilson tells me.

I step back into the classroom and the boys converge around me in a huddle.

"What's up?"

Bertucci tilts his head towards Damon John, and his voice goes low.

"DJ's gotta take a shit."

I blink at them.

Then I glance at DJ. "Congratulations. Why is this a problem?"

"I gotta go home," DJ says.

"There's a bathroom in every hallway in this building."

DJ's already shaking his head. "I can't go here. I get like

. . . stage fright . . . the pipes lock down, you know?"

"Well . . . try," I tell him.

"I have tried." He sighs miserably. "It doesn't work, and then it feels like I've got concrete in my stomach. How am I supposed to play tonight with concrete in my gut?"

Yeah, that could be problem.

"What about the faculty bathroom?" I suggest. "I can get you in there."

"Nah, Coach, no other place feels right. It's gotta be my house. That's where the magic happens."

God damn, kids are fucking helpless these days.

"Can you hold it until after school?" I ask. "Coach Walker can drive you home then."

Again, it's a negative.

"That's hours from now. The turtle is rearing its head—once it's back in its shell, there could be muscle strain—"

I hold up my hand. "Yeah, yeah, thanks . . . I get it."

Wilson presses his lips together. "But we have a plan."

Oh boy.

"What's that?"

"I go out and talk up Officer Tearney in the parking lot. My brother was in the academy with him." Wilson motions with his hands and if we had a white board, he'd be illustrating his play on it. "I block Tearney's view of the south exit while DJ goes out the bathroom window in the locker room and Bertucci stands guard to make sure he can get back in."

DJ adds, "I can sprint home in ten, do the deed, and be back here in fifteen."

Apparently, DJ shits as fast as he runs—there's something I could've gone my whole damn life without knowing.

I squeeze the bridge of my nose. "And why are you telling me this?"

"We wanted to make sure you were good with it," Wilson says. "In case things go south and we get pinched. We didn't want you to be pissed."

Now that's respect. Yes, technically they should be able to take a shit without my blessing, but still, as a coach—I'm touched.

"Text me if you get busted. I'll cover for you." I point at DJ. "Don't twist an ankle getting home. And save some energy for the field—don't sprint and shit it all out."

They all nod and we bump fists.

"Cool."

"Thanks, Coach D."

"You the man."

"Good luck, boys. Go with God." As they walk tall down the hallway, I can't help but think . . . this is my job, this is my life, this is what I do. This is the stuff no one tells you about when you're in college earning that teaching degree.

Operation DJ Takes a Shit is a success, and a few hours later, my team is in the locker room suiting up. Music is big—it helps them get in the right head space—so I play a lot of Metallica, some Bon Jovi and "Goodnight Saigon" by Billy Joel to instill that brotherhood, we're-all-in-this-together kind of feel.

Parker Thompson looks small and shaken in his shoulder pads as he stands in front of Lipinski's old locker—his new locker.

I move to the center of the room, Dean turns the music

down, and all eyes turn to me, waiting for me to say the words that will inspire them, that they can take onto the field and lead them to victory.

Speeches are serious business with me. I spend the week writing them, because they matter to these kids. Some weeks are easier to write than others.

"I'm proud of you." I look at each of their young faces. "Every one of you. You've worked hard, put in the time, put your heart into this team. For some of you seniors, this may be the last season you ever step out onto a field . . . and things have happened in the last few weeks that aren't how you thought this would go."

I turn slowly, meeting their eyes. "And I know you guys talk . . . like my mom and her club ladies . . ."

Muffled, guilty chuckles reverberate through the locker room.

". . . and I know some of you think that I let my ego get in the way—that Lipinski's not here because of some pissing contest between the two of us."

I shake my head.

"It wasn't like that. Pride's a good thing—it makes you work hard, strive to be better . . . but I would sacrifice my pride for any one of you. I would bend and I would break, in a heartbeat, if I thought it'd make us a better team, a stronger team."

I point at Lipinski's locker. "Brandon's not here because he chose not to be here. It was his choice. He wasn't thinking of you and he sure as shit wasn't thinking of the team when he made it. And that's on him. It's easy to work hard, to be proud when things are going your way . . . when all the pieces fall into place in front of you. But the true test of a man—of a team—is what happens when those unexpected hits come. When you get your teeth knocked out and you're down on your knees . . . are you gonna stay down and whine that it wasn't supposed to be this way? Or are you gonna stand up, with your head high, dig deep and move forward? Pull together all your intensity, all your strength, and get it fucking done—push the ball down that field."

I watch their gazes intensify and their heads nod as the words penetrate. I step towards Parker and tap his shoulder. "Parker made a choice too. And it wasn't easy. We've asked a lot of him—a shit-ton of responsibility is riding on his shoulders. But he stepped up for you, for this school, for this team!"

My voice rises and my players get to their feet. "So, we're gonna go out there, together, and play our fucking hearts out—together. You'll make me proud and you'll make yourselves proud and we'll leave it all on the field—because that's who we are! That's what we do!"

"Hell yeah!" someone yells.

And then they all start yelling, stomping their feet and clapping their hands—fired up, like gladiators in the bowels of the Colosseum.

Wilson yells, "Who are we?"

And the answer bounces off the walls and rattles the lockers.

"Lions!"

"Who are we?" Bertucci bellows.

"Lions!"

"God damn right you are!" I point towards the locker room door that leads out to the field. "Now go be fucking heroes."

They end up being heroes, all right. The kind of heroes who get slaughtered—*300*, Spartacus kind of heroes. It's a blood-bath.

Ninety percent of football is mental, and with the shake-up in our team's leadership, their heads are messed up. Parker Thompson only had two completions and even our defense played like dog shit.

I hate losing. It leaves a black, twisting feeling in my gut—an awful mix of frustration and embarrassment. Coach Saber used to tell us, "Losers lose and say—I can't do it. Winners lose—and figure out what they did wrong, so they can do better the next time."

It's a principle I try to live by . . . but it still blows.

The next day, Saturday afternoon, I lie on the couch with the shades drawn, the lights off, and Snoopy curled in a depressed puddle of fur around my feet.

He hates losing too.

There's a knock at the door and I know immediately it's not a member of my family—they know better than to disturb me in my period of mourning. I drag myself to the door and open it . . . to find Callie on my front step, graceful and glowing, looking like a ray of sunshine made flesh.

I sent her a text when I got home from the game last night—and it wasn't even dirty. I'm ashamed.

"Hey!" Her glossy, strawberry lips smile.

Callie was always beautiful, she doesn't know how to be anything else, but there's something extra now—a boldness, a womanly confidence that turns me right the hell on. Even in my sad, loser bubble—my cock perks up. He has all kinds of ideas on how sweet Callie could comfort us, each one filthier than the last.

I lean down, pecking her lips hello.

"Hey."

She runs her hand over the stubble on my jaw. "How are you doing?"

She's wearing snug jeans that hug her hips, high brown boots, a burgundy V-neck sweater that shows off her creamy neck, and her blond bouncy hair is held back by a thick black headband—giving her a sexy, Mod-Squad, '60s kind of look.

"Fine."

Yes, I grumble. And I'm probably pouting too.

She bobs her head, nodding. "Riiight."

Callie looks down at Snoopy. "He's still doing the post-loss pouting thing, huh? I figured as much."

I leave the door open for her, turn around, and walk back into my living room—face-planting back onto my trusty couch. He'll never let me down.

I can't see her, but I feel it when Callie follows me into the room.

"So, apparently my parents never bothered to replace the mattress in my bedroom . . . ever. And it's only going to take one more night for the springs to actually puncture my spine."

I grunt in response.

"Colleen is with them now, and while I'm sure you have lots of sulking to do, I thought maybe you'd want to leave the pit of despair for a few hours and . . . come shopping with me? It'll cheer you up."

I roll over. "Wait, let me check."

I slide my hand into my pants, cupping my junk.

"Yeah, I still have a dick. Why would shopping cheer me up?"

Callie's eyes roll behind those thick, long lashes.

"Because, McGrumpy-face, I thought you may want to help me break in the new bed, after we set it up in my room?" She throws her arms up from her sides and sighs mockingly. "Buuut, if you'd rather stay here . . ."

I'm intrigued.

"A bed, you say?"

Callie nods.

"In your room? The one with a door? And . . . without your parents?"

"Yep." She pops her *p,* making me stare at her lips, her mouth. I fucking love Callie's mouth. "What do you think, Garrett?"

And she looks so damn cute, and sexy and sweet . . . my cock's cheered way the hell up already. And my frown turns around into a grin.

"I think we're going to get you a kickass bed, baby."

I call my brother's cell, so we can borrow his pickup truck. When it goes to voicemail, we head over to my parents' house. On the way, I glance over at Callie, her hair lifting in the breeze of the open window, her eyes lighting up when I beep, and she waves to Ollie Munson. There's just something so good, so fucking right about seeing her in the car next to me— after all this time—that fills my chest with a peaceful, settled sensation. I thread our fingers together, holding her hand for the rest of the drive.

"Callie!" My mother engulfs her in a hug. They were close back in the day—sitting together at my football games, having Betty Crocker chats in the kitchen. My mom was pretty wrecked when we broke up. For years, every new girl I started hanging out with got the "not as (fill in the blank) as Callie" stamp of disapproval.

"Look how beautiful you are! You haven't changed a bit. Doesn't she look beautiful, Ray?"

"Beautiful," my dad grunts, staring at the television remote in his hands like he's disarming a bomb as he changes the batteries. "Good to see you, sweetheart."

"Thanks, Mr. Daniels."

Then he fixes his crusty, disapproving gaze on me.

Here we go.

"Your boys got crushed last night, son."

Moral support was never his strong suit.

"Yeah, Dad, thanks. I was there. I know."

"Your quarterback's playing scared. He's got no confidence."

"I'm working on it." I sigh, rubbing the back of my neck. I look to my mom. "Is Connor around? We need to borrow his truck."

"No, he went by the house to see the boys. It's not his weekend, but he had the afternoon off so he wanted to spend some time with them."

It's like a frigging scavenger hunt around here. While my mother pours Callie a cup of coffee and they start talking about all things San Diego, I try my brother's phone again. Still a bust—straight to voicemail.

So, a little while later, Callie and I pull up to Connor's stone-front behemoth of a house. His pickup is in the driveway, the blue spruce he planted the first year they moved in is growing in the front yard, and his German shephard, Rosie, is barking in the back.

But inside . . . all hell is breaking loose.

Before we get to the front door, I can hear Stacey and my brother arguing, yelling, their voices overlapping in sharp, angry verbal slashes. But their words are drowned out by the roar of a . . . *chainsaw*? Is that a chainsaw?

I look up at the upstairs window, half-expecting to see Leather Face staring back at me.

In the foyer my nephews look like they don't know where to go first—like three baby bears who've lost their momma.

"Uncle Garrett!" Spencer runs to me. "Dad's freaking out—he's chopping the house down!"

And the sound of the spitting chainsaw roars louder.

"What the hell is going on?" I ask my oldest nephew, Aaron.

"Dad took us for ice cream," he explains, his face tight and flushed. "We were supposed to go to the park after, but Spencer got a stomachache so we came home early. And Mom was here . . . with Mr. Lawson."

"He's her new friend," Spencer says, all round-eyed innocence.

"He's Brayden's basketball coach," Aaron adds quietly. "They were upstairs."

"He ran out the back when Dad got the chainsaw from the garage," Brayden finishes.

Jesus. Out of the four of us . . . Connor's the fucking calm one.

"Wait here," I tell the boys, then take the stairs two at a time.

Inside the bedroom, my brother's just finished sawing off the last post of the four-poster bed and he's getting to work on the footboard.

Stacey waves her arms, her dark hair flying around her face. "Stop it! You're acting like a psycho, Connor!"

My brother just squints behind his safety goggles. "You want to screw someone else—knock yourself out. But it's not gonna be in our bed. That's where I draw the line."

Zzzzz . . . boom . . . and down goes the footboard.

"Hey!" I cup my hands around my mouth. "You two geniuses realize you've got three kids downstairs?"

Only they're not downstairs anymore. They shuffle through the doorway, staring at what's left of their parents' bed and getting a front row seat to the Jerry Springer-level marital dysfunction.

My brother switches off the chainsaw. But Stacey still screeches, 'cause that's how she rolls.

"Tell your brother that! He's decided to be Super Dad all of a sudden, even though he was never there for me!"

"I. Was. Working!" My brother pushes his hands through his hair, making it stick up at every angle. "I'm a doctor. When I get called in—I have to go, even if it's fucking girl's night out!"

And they go back and forth, hurling sins and grievances at each other like a tennis ball at Wimbledon.

Until Aaron's quiet, lethal words cut through the air.

"You are such a whore."

And all the oxygen is sucked out of the room. Like that vacuum sealing food preserver my mother uses. No one moves, no one says a word, it's silent.

Until the smack of Stacey's palm slapping Aaron's face

rings out, sharp and cracking.

"Never speak to me like that again." She points at him, her voice trembling with fury, and heartache.

My brother yanks his safety goggles off his face. "Aaron. You can't talk to your mother that way."

Thirteen-year-old Aaron's eyes dart between his parents, filling with tears. "Are you serious right now? You're holding a chainsaw."

My brother glances down at the power tool in his hands, like he's just realizing he's holding it.

"Look at you . . . both of you . . ." Aaron's voice cracks. "Look at what you've done to us."

And this—this is why I don't have kids of my own. Why I probably never will.

Remember those egg assignments we all got in middle school? The ones where we had to carry around an egg for a week, take care of it like it was a real baby? It's a stupid assignment.

Kids are so much more breakable. Fragile. It's so easy to screw them up. With our own selfishness. Our mistakes and regrets.

I see it all the time. Every day.

My nephew swipes at his cheeks roughly and glares at the two people who gave him life.

"You're both assholes. I'm out of here."

And he rushes from the room.

"Don't leave, Aaron!" Spencer cries.

Stacey sobs into her hands and my brother moves to run after Aaron, but I cut him off.

"Let me. Let me talk to him."

Connor nods and I turn, meeting Callie's eyes. One of the

best things about being around someone who's known you forever is . . . no words are needed.

She puts one arm around Spencer and the other around Brayden, ruffling their hair.

"Hey, guys, I noticed you have a treehouse in your back-yard. I love treehouses—can you show it to me?"

Outside, I catch my nephew in the middle of the yard. He whips around, taking a swing at me. I bear-hug him, locking his arms at his sides.

"Let me go! Let me go!" He struggles.

"Easy . . . come on, Aaron, stop. You have to stop."

He fights and twists some more. But eventually he wears himself out, breathing hard and going slack in my arms, leaning against me.

"They suck," he chokes against my shirt.

"I know."

"I hate them."

"You won't always." I lean back, looking down into his eyes. Aaron's so much like my brother—smart, good, steady—when he's not hurting. "It won't be like this forever, Aaron. I promise."

He wipes his cheeks with the back of his hand, sniffling and nodding.

I hook my arm around his neck, dragging him along. "Come on, I'm driving you guys over to Nana and Pop's. You're staying there tonight."

After my family drama quota is filled for the day, Callie and I finally make it to Mr. Martinez's furniture store and find her a white wrought-iron bed. Getting the queen-sized mattress inside her room is a trip and a half, mostly because Callie's dad insists on helping me drag the fucker in.

From his wheelchair. With his right, casted leg sticking straight out like jousting lance.

"You're going the wrong way, Stanley!" Callie's mom yells from the open back screen door, with a cigarette hanging from her lips.

"I'm not going the wrong way!" he shouts back.

But, yeah, he kind of is.

Still, we manage to get the mattress into the hallway, which, thankfully, is too narrow for his wheelchair.

"Thanks for the help, Mr. Carpenter. I got it from here."

Callie's room hasn't changed a bit. Same pink walls, same flowery curtains hanging over the window I used to sneak through after her curfew—so we could screw quietly on her blanket on the floor. Good times.

Her old CD player is still here too—playing her favorite band.

"Jesus, Callie, ABBA? I see living in California didn't improve your taste in music."

She slaps my ass, scowling all fierce and protective of her bad music. It's really fucking cute.

"Leave my ABBA alone. They're classic and they make me happy." With "SOS" as our background music, Callie picks up a wrench and opens the assembly instructions, tilting her head in a way that makes me want to bite her pale, graceful neck. "Now let's get this sucker put together. Time's a-wasting, Coach."

Half an hour later, I slide the mattress on the bed frame and push it into the corner. With a naughty look on her face,

Callie slips around me to her bedroom door, opens it a crack, and listens. The only sound from the living room is the hum of the TV. She shuts the door, meets my eyes . . . and locks it with a decisive click.

Then she hops on her bed—her tits bouncing beautifully under her sweater—and my mouth goes dry. She lies back on her elbows, with one foot braced on the mattress and the other dangling off the edge.

"We've got about fifteen minutes before they start trying to maneuver the wheelchairs around the kitchen to fix dinner for themselves. Until then . . . wanna make out?"

It's absolutely crazy how much those words turn me on. All the blood in my body rushes south to my groin, making my head go light and my balls heavy. I want her. Even in the rapture of our horniest, hormonal adolescent days, I don't think I wanted her this much.

Callie's green eyes rake down over me, like she's imagining all the things we can do to each other in that timeframe—and we can do a lot. I'm efficient like that.

And I don't think about the game last night, or my brother's issues this morning—they're not even a whisper in my mind. All there is, all I see, is me and Callie alone in this god-awful pink room, with ABBA playing on the radio and her beckoning me to the bed with those smiling lips and dancing eyes.

She gives a throaty laugh when I practically pounce on her, nestling my hips between her oh-so-welcoming thighs. I take that pretty mouth in a deep kiss, and thrust slow and firm against her, feeling how hot she is for me, for this, through our jeans. Sensation races up my spine and Callie gasps into my mouth.

Things go from playful to rock-hard serious real fucking quick. Callie pushes against my chest, and I grasp her waist, keeping us tight and flushed together as we roll over. We're chest to chest, her long legs straddling my hips and her hot, sweet pussy sits on my straining dick.

Perfect . . . she feels so fucking perfect.

"Garrett," she breathes out in an airy moan.

And I groan back, low in my throat, "Callie. Jesus, Callie."

Her hips roll and rock, back and forth, slow at first . . . then in a faster . . . a more desperate slide that makes my eyes roll back in my fucking head. My fingers dig into the flesh of Callie's ass and I thrust up quick and hard against her.

"Fuck me . . ."

Roughly, I yank the neck of her sweater down, baring one breast covered in a pale pink bra. I break my mouth from Callie's and blaze a trail of licking kisses down her chest. Callie sucks at my shoulder, biting at the base of my neck, rotating her hips in glorious circles, rubbing her clit on my thick cock, jerking us both off with the pressure.

I dip my head and wrap my lips around her, taking in a mouthful of delicate lace and gorgeous tit. I suckle her hard . . . then harder . . . flicking my tongue relentlessly over her perfect pebbled nipple. Callie's back bows, arching, giving me more of her breast. God damn delicious. She yanks at my hair, holding me tight, writhing in perfect, shameless abandon.

But times flies. And life's not a bitch . . . it's a cockblocker.

Because just as Callie starts to chant my name in that beautiful, high-pitched, keening voice—always a telltale sign she's about to fall apart in my arms . . . Mrs. Carpenter's raspy voice punches through the bedroom walls.

"Callie! Is Garrett staying for dinner?" There's a crash of pots and pans, like a full set of cymbals got knocked to the ground. "I'm making sloppy joes!"

We freeze, mid-hump. And the fiery lust fusing us together gets doused with a big bucket of arctic seawater.

"Fuck," Callie pants against my hair.

I release her breast with a pop of my lips. "That was the idea."

She laughs, but it's more of a painful, choking sound. "This is awful."

I breathe slow against her, working to get my shit under control.

"No. No, it's okay. It's better this way." And I try and make myself believe that, which is hard when your cock is achingly . . . well . . . *hard.*

I brush her cheek with my fingers. "I want to be able to take my time with you, Callie." My voice goes harsh, low, as I give words to the fantasy unfurling in my mind. "I don't want clothes between us or your parents on the other side of the wall. I want to feel it when you come all around me. And when I'm inside you, I'm going to want to stay for a hell of a lot longer than fifteen minutes."

Callie's eyes are glazed, lust-drunk, and I wonder if I can make her come like this with words and promises alone.

"I want to be above you, beneath you, behind you . . . I want you weak, drained from coming, hoarse from screaming my name. I'm going to need hours, baby . . . fucking days . . ."

Her hips lift, rubbing against me, starting us up all over again. "Yeah . . . God, Garrett, I want that too."

"Callie!" Mrs. Carpenter yells again. "Did you hear me?"

I give up. I collapse back on the bed.

"Yes!" Callie yells at the wall. "Yes, I'm coming."

And then she groans while smiling, looking down at me. "Except I'm really not."

I laugh, even though it hurts. And my dick starts thinking of new, inventive ways to kill me for toying with him this way.

Callie takes a deep, cleansing breath. Then she drags herself away from me, standing next to her shiny new bed. "Do you want to stay for dinner?"

"No, thanks." I glance down at the massive bulge straining my pants. "I'm going to just head home and spend the night rubbing one out. Or maybe . . . five."

She leans down, her hair falling around us as she pecks my lips. "Same."

CHAPTER
Twelve

Callie

On Monday, I start showing the '80s movie *Little Shop of Horrors* to my classes, and, as if the semi-bribery weren't enough, it seems to make them like me more. I guess an in-class video day never gets old.

Then we start auditions. I bring them all down to the big stage in the auditorium, because on a stage, with a spotlight in your face and endless rows of seats staring back at you . . . the whole world looks different.

I sit at a table, just beyond the orchestra pit, with Michael beside me and the other students congregating in the back, talking quietly and staring at their phones. I call them up one by one—each student who didn't sign up for a crew spot. James Townden, a senior with plans to attend Juilliard next year, gets excused from his classes to accompany the auditions on piano. Once they're on stage, I have them sing "Happy Birthday." It's quick, everyone knows it, and it gives me great insight into their vocal range.

Bradley Baker goes first.

"I wanna be Audrey Two," he declares from the center stage. "He's the star of the show, and he's got a big head—I was born to play this role."

"Noted," I tell him, folding my hands.

Then Bradley proceeds to jump around the stage, wave his arms, howl out the birthday song. His voice is terrible . . . but he's entertaining. Completely over the top.

"The dentist," I tell Michael. "Orin Scrivello, DDS. Bradley's perfect for it."

Next up is Toby Gessler. Apparently, he's a "SoundCloud" rapper with the stage name "Merman." I recently learned SoundCloud is like self-publishing for music—kids post their songs on the site hoping to build up a fan base, maybe get discovered by a studio. Most of them . . . are *not* good. And Toby's no different. He stands on the stage with a backwards baseball cap on his head and oversized white sunglasses on his face and thick gold chains rattling around his neck, and he raps the birthday song.

It's . . . unique. Some would say, brave. And I know the perfect role for Toby.

"He'll be the chorus. Crystal, Ronette and Chiffon," I tell Michael.

He writes it down on his iPad, but scratches behind his ear. "In the movie, they were girls. Aren't they supposed to be girls?"

"Remember what I said about theater? We put our own stamp on it." I glance back up at Toby as he dives into some breakdancing moves. They're not good either. "Maybe we'll have him rap the songs."

I put my hand up to my mouth and throw down a little beat-boxing of my own. Then I rap, "Li-li little . . . ssshop of horrors," ending with the classic hip-hop arm cross.

"What do you think?" I tease. "Does it work?"

Michael looks like he's afraid. "Don't . . . ever do that again, Miss Carpenter."

I laugh, then think of something else, snapping my fingers. "We should have Toby wear a tuxedo. Mr. Ramsey, Kayla's dad, has a place in the mall that rents tuxedos, right? Maybe he'll rent it to us for free in exchange for advertising space in the playbill."

"That's smart." He nods.

"That's why I make the big bucks." I tap my temple. "In the coming months, I'll take Simone to check out the local thrift shops for possible costumes too."

And Toby's still rapping.

"Thank you, Toby," I call out.

He gives the peace sign to the empty auditorium. "Merman lives! Whoo! See you next tour!"

"Next . . . Layla Martinez," I announce.

And like a ninja, David Burke slides into the empty chair next to me.

"Is this seat taken?" He winks.

Then his pale blue eyes stay on Layla as she slowly, stiffly, walks up the side steps, like she's walking to the guillotine. David nods encouragingly, and she stares back at him, as if his gaze is the only thing keeping her standing. Once she's center stage, the brisk notes of the piano float through the auditorium. But Layla misses her cue. She wets her lips, her face paling, like she's going to hurl.

James stops playing, then starts the song again.

Layla squeezes her eyes closed. "I changed my mind. I can't do this."

"She's just scared, Miss Carpenter," David says softly. "But she's good, you gotta hear her. Layla's really good."

I stand up and hold out my hand for James to stop playing.

"Hey," I call to Layla. She fixes her tortured eyes on me. "It's okay. It's stage fright; it happens to everyone. When I was in high school, I used to throw up before every performance."

"For real?" Layla asks.

"Yeah. I kept a toothbrush and toothpaste with me at all times." I keep my voice steady and confident. "But I know a trick. It helped me and I bet it'll help you too. I want you to turn around and close your eyes. Block out everything, so it's just you and the song."

Layla's eyes dart to David, then back to me. "Will you be able to hear me if I'm facing the other way?"

"That doesn't matter. All that matters is that you're able to stand up there and get through it. One step at a time. Will you try that for me, Layla?"

She runs her teeth over her bottom lip. "Okay. Yeah, I'll try."

"Good."

Layla turns around and I nod to James, who starts to play again.

Then, after a few moments, Layla begins to sing. Holy shit, does she sing. She's hesitant, scratchy at first, but then her voice smooths out and rises. Her pitch is perfect, her voice smoky and smooth, like thick, fresh honey. She's got range, reach, hidden power in those pipes—it's so clear, even in just the few simple notes of the song. But more than that, every word is filled with emotion, the kind of singing that tells its own story, the kind of voice that can break hearts, and lift souls.

"Wow," I whisper.

David smiles up at me, his whole face lighter, younger looking. "I told you."

When Layla finishes, I applaud—everyone does—even the kids in the back who weren't paying attention before she started to sing.

Layla's tight curly hair flies as she turns around, laughing. "I did it!"

"Audrey," I tell her, excitement bursting like crazed Pop Rocks in my stomach. "You're our Audrey."

And just like that, the hurling look is slapped back on Layla's face.

"I . . . can't do this in front of people, Miss Carpenter."

"Not yet." I agree. "But by the time I'm done working with you, you will."

This kind of talent deserves to be heard.

"I want to be Seymour."

I turn towards David—not really surprised. Garrett and I talked about him the other night. We both agreed he has potential, that he could do amazing things if only he had the motivation . . . if only he cared.

David doesn't care about theater or the play or school. He cares about Layla.

He asks to borrow Michael's glasses, and my dark-haired assistant hands them over, curiosity pinching his features.

David Burke slips them on his face, then flinches. "Damn, man, you're blind."

Then he leaps up on the stage, his gray trench coat flying out like a superhero's cape. He musses his dirty-blond hair . . . and then he starts to sing "Grow For Me," one of Seymour's songs. I don't know if he remembers the lyrics from when I showed the movie in class or if he looked them up and practiced, but he knows every word. His voice isn't the miracle Layla's is, but it's pleasant. More importantly, David possesses that unteachable but essential characteristic of any star. Charisma. Stage presence. Personality.

I glance around the room—every eye in the auditorium is on him as he sings a capella and . . . makes Layla smile beside him.

And hot-diggity-dog, I've got my cast.

In the days that follow, something incredible starts to happen. It's a genuine Christmas miracle at the end of September. My students start to have fun. They get interested, invested—in the sets, the costumes, the music . . . the whole idea of the show. They begin to want it to be good—and that's the first step towards greatness.

It makes me feel like David Copperfield and Khaleesi all rolled into one.

It makes me feel . . . like a teacher.

"Bigger!" I yell, climbing onto the stage and pointing towards the back row. "Everything on the stage has to be exaggerated, brighter—the makeup, your movements. They have to see you from all the way back there."

We're doing our first script read-through and will begin blocking on the same day. Normally, these would be separate—but since my after-school availability is limited, I have to double-time it during class.

"And louder!" I raise my voice and stamp my foot, shaking dust bunnies down from the rafters. "I told you guys, projection is key. If you're speaking in your normal voices, no one in the audience will hear you." I look at Layla, "Don't be afraid to be loud. Ever. On stage or off."

"That's good advice," Garrett says, walking down the main aisle with a few of his players behind him. "Louder is always better."

And I have to make a conscious effort to keep my tongue from falling out of my mouth. He's doing the preppy look today—a collared button-down beneath a sky-blue sweater. My heart flies and my skin tingles remembering the feel of his weight on top of me, on that new mattress, the sound of his groans, those powerful arms surrounding me, the hard relentless swell of his cock between my legs.

Was it really just a few days ago? It feels like months, years. The janitor's closet has been a no-go zone since McCarthy busted us. I've taken my parents to physical therapy appointments every night this week, so the only time Garrett and I have had together is on the phone, by text, and a few hot and heavy kisses against his Jeep when he swung by my parents' house late Monday night just to be able to see me alone for a few minutes.

It's so weird how life can change, how fast. You've got your five- or ten-year plan all laid out and then, overnight, everything you thought you wanted shifts, and all the places you'd planned on going don't seem so important anymore.

I don't remember how I lasted sixteen years without Garrett Daniels in my life. Now that he's back, I'm like a junkie—

I crave him, think about him, all the time.

"Coach Daniels?" I try to sound professional, while every cell in my body is screaming for inappropriate.

Our eyes meet, then Garrett's eyes drag subtly and slowly down over my black turtleneck, dark-blue skinny jeans, and leather pumps. It's only a few seconds, but when his gaze rises back to mine, his eyes are heated—hungry—and I know he's thinking the same thing I am: get me, him, *us*, out of these fucking clothes.

"Miz Carpenter, Ray said there were some heavy set pieces you needed pulled out of storage?" He hooks his thumb over his shoulder. "This is my free period, so I figured I could give you a hand . . . or whatever you need."

He could give me a hand, all right . . . a hand, a finger . . . two of Garrett's fingers was always my favorite.

"Thank you, yes. That would be . . ."

Fuck-hot? Incredible? So mind-blowing my hair will turn white?

". . . great."

Garrett smirks, raising an eyebrow—like he can read my mind—and at this point, I have no doubt he can.

I look to Michael. "Can you show them what we need from the storage closet?"

Garrett and his boys follow Michael out of the theater.

Then Toby flips through the script in his hands, shaking his head. "I don't know about this anymore. The idea of doing some of this stuff is pretty weird—they're gonna laugh at us. I don't want to look like a frigging idiot."

Classic case of cold feet. They want the play to be good . . . but they don't trust me to show them how to *make* it good. Not fully, not yet.

"You're only going to look like idiots if you hold back, if you try to play it off like you're too cool for school." I slouch and shrug the way David sometimes does, garnering soft giggles from the class. "But if you let it all go, throw yourself into your part—the only thing anyone will see is how amazing you are. That's why trust between the director and the performers is so important. If you trust me, I promise . . . I won't let you look like idiots." I meet their eyes and swear, "And I sure as hell will never let anyone have a reason to laugh at you. Not *ever*."

"You should show them the thing." Garrett's voice echoes in the theater, surprising me. I spin around to find him leaning against the stage-left wall—all mesmerizing, cocky confidence.

I know "the thing" of which he speaks. It was a trick I used to do for him to show off—back after our sophomore-year class trip to Manhattan to see *Les Miserables*.

I shake my head. "I don't want to do the thing. I don't even know if I still can."

He scoffs. "Of course you still can."

"What's the thing?" Simone pipes up.

"The thing," Garrett answers, "is why you should listen to Miss Carpenter. Why you should trust her. She knows her shit."

David grins crookedly. "Okay, now you have to show us the thing."

I sigh dramatically. "All right. But it's been a while, so be kind."

I shake out my hands and crack my neck—and do a few vocal warm-ups.

Garrett cups his hands around his gorgeous mouth. "Stop stalling."

I stick my tongue out at him and the whole class laughs.

And then I begin. I perform the full cast version of "One Day More" from *Les Miserables*—I step to the side, turn to the left or right, cross my arms, pound my fist into my hand, change my posture, the key of my voice, my facial expression—to differentiate each character. I'm just one person, but with each line, I become—Jean Valjean, Cosette, Marius, Eponine, Inspector Javert—I become them all. I don't look at my audience, but past them, towards the back of the theater, until I close my eyes on the very last rousing note.

Slowly, I open my eyes and every one of my kids is staring at me like I have four heads. Until David starts to clap— loud and quick—and like baby ducks, the rest of them follow, until a full-on applause rings out. Garrett puts his fingers to his lips and whistles.

And it's ten times better than any standing ovation I've ever received.

"Holy crap." Bradley stands up. "That was sick!"

It's okay—sick is good.

"Can you teach us how to do that?" Toby asks.

"Yeah." I nod. "Yeah, actually, I can."

The bell shrieks from the hallway and the kids grab their stuff and head towards the door.

"We'll pick this up tomorrow," I call after them. "And it's never too early to start memorizing your lines!"

In the midst of the shuffle, I make my way over to where Garrett's still standing against the wall, arms crossed, waiting for me. I lean in towards him, as much as I can without setting the high school gossip mill on fire . . . or jumping him.

"That was sexy as fuck," Garrett growls low, making me blush like the virgin I was before I met him.

"You always did have a thing for *Les Miserables*," I tease him.

And his smile hits me right in the center of my chest, making feel giddy and silly and light—like my feet aren't on the ground. He makes me feel that way.

"Thanks for helping me with them—for trying to get them to trust me."

He tucks a rogue strand of hair behind my ear. "Anytime."

Garrett stares at my mouth, his brown eyes intense and swirling—filled with carnal thoughts and desperate, delightful ideas. "Come over tonight, Cal. Even if it's just for an hour or ten minutes, I don't care. I'll feed you ramen and do dirty things to you."

I laugh. How could any girl say no to an offer like that?

CHAPTER
Thirteen

Garrett

No, no, no—as if this season wasn't already a flaming bag of dog shit . . . as if being 0–3 wasn't humiliating enough to make me want to burn the school down . . . now this, on game day.

"Walk away, dude," Dean whispers to himself, because he gets it too. "Keep your mouth shut and walk away."

Damon John—my star receiver and his long-term girlfriend, Rhonda, are having an argument—a loud, public, right in the middle of the fucking D wing-break-up, kind of argument. The crowd's about six students deep, but Dean and I can hear every word.

"You broke my heart. You only get to do that once."

I like Rhonda; she's a good girl for DJ—sweet, smart, doesn't take any of his stupid shit. But it would seem Damon John has forgotten that fact.

"Whatever, baby." He shrugs, looking right through her.

"Been there, done that. I'm over it."

What a little asshole.

But that's high school boys for you—back them into a corner and they turn ugly—like Gremlins fed after midnight.

Rhonda lifts her chin, holding back tears. "Do not text me, do not call me, do not show up at my house. You are dead to me."

When DJ swallows hard and his eyes flair with uncertainty—I catch it, but I'm probably the only one who does. To the rest of the world, he laughs, blows it off . . . but I know him—studied his every move, so I know better.

"Works for me. In a few hours, I won't even remember your name."

Dean covers his eyes. "Dumbass."

With that, Rhonda turns around and walks away, and doesn't look back. The late bell rings and the crowd disperses.

I glance at Dean. "DJ and Rhonda were together for two years, man."

In high school years, that's like twenty.

"Yeah." He shakes his head. "It's gonna be bad."

And bad it is.

I hear just how much as I walk down the hall towards the locker room after school. The mixture of despair and regret that sounds like a mortally wounded animal . . . but is really a seventeen-year-old boy who's been dumped on his sorry ass.

I open the door and sure enough, there's DJ lying on his back across the bench, with his forearm across his face, covering his eyes.

Crying.

For even the staunchest supporters of the "boys don't cry" rule—a locker room is the exception. A thousand disappointed, heartbroken tears have been shed here.

Six of my starters surround DJ, without a single clue between them about what to do. If he'd twisted an ankle or cramped a muscle, they'd know. But a busted heart? That's out of their league.

"I don't get it," Sam Zheng says. "If you still like her, why did you say all that crap to her in the hallway? Why didn't you just say sorry?"

Ah . . . Sammy, he's a sophomore—still innocent.

"I don't know," DJ moans. "I didn't mean it." He turns on his side, moaning, "How am I supposed to play tonight? How am I supposed to live without my bae?"

"Oh damn," Kyle Lanigan gasps. "What if she bangs someone else to get back at you? Or two people . . . a threesome? Dude, she could be doing it right now! Like *right now*!"

DJ's face crumples.

I walk to the bench, move his legs, and sit down.

Then I sigh. "You screwed up, Deej."

"I did," he sniffles. "I screwed up so bad, Coach."

I look around at the faces of my players. "But, this could be a good thing. It's better you all know the truth now, while you're still young."

They move closer, gathering around, staring at me like I'm Jesus Christ on the mount, about to preach.

"What's the truth, Coach D?" Wilson asks, wide-eyed.

I lean forward and lower my voice. "The truth is, when it comes to guys and girls, men and women? We need them, more than they will ever, *ever*, need us."

I've passed on a lot of life lessons to these boys, but this may be the most important of them all.

I mean, Stacey wasn't even that great of a wife, but my brother's a fucking basket case without her. Ryan without Angela? I don't even want to know what kind of disaster that would look like. Hell, my old man can't even make microwave popcorn without my mom telling him what buttons to push.

And me . . . it's only been a few weeks . . . and the thought of Callie walking out of my life again makes my stomach fold in on itself and twist around in my gut.

I'm so incredibly screwed.

"Holy shit," Wilson whispers, his teenage mind utterly blown. "You're right."

I nod my head. "Damn skippy."

DJ sits up, wiping his eyes. "I gotta get her back, Coach. I love her, for real. I know we're young, but . . . she's the one . . . the only one for me . . . you know what I mean?"

I think about green eyes, soft lips, and sweet laughter. I think about the voice I could listen to forever—how I'm captivated by every thought and wish and idea in her fascinating mind. I think about the feel of her arms clinging to me, wanting me—strong and delicate, fire and lace—and the scent of roses and vanilla.

Oh yeah . . . I know *exactly* what he means.

"Okay, then here's what you're going to do . . ."

He huddles down, the same look on his face as when I'm breaking down a play.

"First, you kick ass tonight on the field—show her you're a winner. Girls like winners. Then you're gonna admit you acted like a jackass, and tell her you're sorry. Because that's what real men do when they fuck up—they own it."

"A grand gesture may be in order," Dean suggests, leaning against the wall near the door.

DJ's face scrunches in deep thought. "What kind of gesture? How?"

Jesus, have these kids never seen a John Hughes movie? It's times like this I worry about the future of our youth.

"Do something big, something she won't expect—dedicate a song to her or a Facebook post or one of those Snapgram story things—whatever the hell you kids do now."

"You get extra points if it involves begging and humiliation," Dean adds.

I put my arm around his shoulder. "And then . . . maybe Rhonda gives you a second chance. You earn another shot."

He wipes his nose. "What if she doesn't? What if I really lost her?"

I pat his back. "It'll hurt like a hell, I'm not going to lie. But you'll get through it. You'll know you gave it your all and that your relationship with her was a moment in your life that you'll never forget. You learn from it, let it make you better. And maybe, down the road, you'll meet someone else and that's how it's supposed to go. Or maybe, one day if it's really meant to be . . . you'll get another chance with her. And if that happens . . ."

Even if it's twenty years later . . .

"You make damn sure you don't screw up again."

Friday night-home games are always big in Lakeside—and not just because the parents of the players and students are in attendance. The whole frigging town shows up. My parents are here, my brothers, Callie's here with her parents and her sister too. I saw Callie outside my office before the game.

She let me cop a feel for good luck.

And then, I took the field with my team.

No matter how old I am—fourteen or thirty-four—football games all sound the same. The crunch of the pads, the grunts, the war cry, the vicious shit-talking that would reduce grown men to tears, the drumbeats of the band, the chants of the cheerleaders, and shouts of the crowd. They look the same—the glare of the lights, the smoke of our breath, the streaks of dark mud on white uniforms. They smell the same—grass and dirt, popcorn and hot dogs, adrenaline and victory almost within reach.

But not every game feels the same. Actually, every single one feels different.

Tonight, there's something extra going on—an electricity in the air that feels like life is about to change. A pressure pushing down on my shoulders and a current of excitement sparking through my veins.

We're playing North Essex High School. Their defense is top-notch, but tonight my boys are kicking ass and taking names. They're monsters—unstoppable—all their fucks surrendered in the last three losses, with no more left to give. Nothing and no one is getting past them. By the fourth quarter, with only twenty seconds left on the clock, the scoreboard is still 0 to 0. It's the best game we've played all year. The ball is ours and if we don't lock it down with a field goal or touchdown now, we go into overtime.

"Yes! Nice hit, Dumbrowski!" I clap my hands as the players jog off the field. "Good hustle."

Parker sprints off the bench to me as the offense moves

onto the field. But before I open my mouth to give him the play, he calls it himself.

"Wishbone forty-two."

Well, what do you know.

"That's right. Good call." I smack his helmet encouragingly. "You look different tonight, kid—did you grow last night or something?"

He snorts, lifting a shoulder and grinning shyly. "I don't know."

He does look different, but it's not because he grew. It's the way he's carrying himself, the way he walks. Hard work and focus will do that to you. Parker stands straighter, head higher, with a solid surety to his steps. Our extra practices have started paying off—being entrusted as the starting quarterback of a varsity team that has your back is starting to take effect.

There's an air around him that wasn't there before—Parker Thompson knows where he's going, and more importantly, he knows exactly how he's getting there.

"No? What'd you eat for breakfast this morning?"

He shrugs again. "Cereal . . . I think."

For some kids, direction is all they need. Someone to help them focus, to bring their talents to the forefront. Like a pencil—the lead's already there inside, it just needs to be sharpened.

"Well, keep it up." I clap my hands. "Come on, let's go."

Parker nods, his face scrunched and serious. He pops his mouthpiece in and slides his helmet on and yells to the offense as they jog onto the field, "Come on, guys, get on the ball!"

The players line up and the ball is hiked, but North Essex anticipates our play. The line holds and Parker adjusts, stepping back, dodging, scanning the field, searching for an opening. We've been a running game the last few weeks, so the coverage on our receivers is weak. I know what's going to happen; I can practically see it before the chance comes . . . but more importantly, Parker can too.

Time stretches, the seconds drag, and everything moves in slow motion. It's like I'm seeing the field through Parker's eyes—every route, every angle. And then it all clicks, snaps hard into place.

"Wait, wait for it . . ." I whisper as the players push and clash.

Down field, DJ cuts left at the thirty-yard line, breaking free of the cornerback who's right on his heels.

"Now." My voice is low and urgent. My eyes dart from Parker to DJ and back again. "Come on, Parker, you got this. Throw it."

He looks left, steps back, pumps his arm, reaches back, and throws.

And god damn, it's pretty.

The ball spirals through the air, high and long and straight, before arching down . . . right into DJ King's hands.

There's a rush of sound—the cheers of crowd behind me—and my own blood roaring in my ears.

"Yes! Go, go, fucking run!"

I hop down the field, like an idiot—it's a coach thing—waving my arms, telling DJ to run. But I don't need to—he's already hauling ass.

And just a few seconds later, he sprints into the end zone.

He spikes the ball and points at me. Christ, I love that kid. I point right back at him. And the ref raises his hands, just as the clock runs out, signaling a motherfucking touchdown for the Lions.

The first of our season . . . our first win. Hell yeah.

You'd think we just won the Super Bowl—that's how it feels. The kids go nuts, rushing the field, hugging each other, bumping chests and smacking helmets.

DJ tears off his helmet, hops the fence, sprints up the stands to the announcer's box. There's the squeal of feedback, and then his breathless voice yells out of the speakers.

"I love you, Rhonda! I'm sorry I'm an asshole, but I love you, baby! That was for you!"

Dean appears at my right, pounding my shoulder. "That's how we do it! Back in the saddle, D!"

And I smack his back. "Damn straight, man."

I jog out to the field and shake Tim Daly's hand, the North Essex High School coach. And as I turn around and jog back towards the bench, I spot Callie, on the other side of the fence, watching me.

She stands beside Mrs. Carpenter's wheelchair. She's wearing a black Lakeside football T-shirt under a puffy gray coat. She has a white knit cap over her blond hair that's fuck-hot in a really cute kind of way. Her eyes are like two shiny emeralds beneath the bright field lights, and as she lifts her hand and waves to me, her pretty lips slide into a bursting, ex-hilarated kind of smile.

And just like that . . . I'm gone all over again.

I don't stop jogging until I'm at the fence.

"Hey."

Callie tilts her head. "Nice game, Coach."

"Yeah . . . yeah, it was a good one." I smile down at Cal-lie's mom. "Mrs. Carpenter, can I take Callie out tonight? You can have my cell phone, keep it right next to you, and call us if there's any problems."

If that doesn't work, I'm prepared to offer my little brother a thousand dollars to babysit them for the night.

Mrs. Carpenter waves her hand. "We'll be fine. You kids worry too much. Go have fun; have her home by lunchtime tomorrow."

Just when I thought this night couldn't get better—it blows better out of the frigging water.

"I can do that." I nod.

That's when the little bastards I coach decide to dump a cooler of Gatorade down my back. It's cold, like a thousand icicles stabbing my spine at once, and I have a sense of how Caesar felt when he got taken out by his Senate. *Et tu, shitheads?* But I take it like a man. I push a wet hand through my hair and lick some of the liquid off my top lip.

I hook my thumb back over my shoulder, holding Callie's gaze. "I gotta go do a football thing." She laughs, nodding. "I'll pick you up in a little while."

And she waves, smiling. So beautiful it almost hurts to look at her.

"I'll be waiting."

CHAPTER
Fourteen

Callie

Back in high school, after good football games—Garrett was always . . . well . . . horny. He was a teenage boy, so horny was pretty much the default setting—but after a big win, he was hotter, hungrier, more aggressive. I could practically smell the testosterone on his skin—which made *me* horny. I remember, when we'd make the requisite appearance at the after-party, how he'd keep me close, always touching me . . . his hand in mine, his thumb stroking my palm, his arm around my shoulder, rubbing my back. If I had to leave his side, his eyes would follow me around the room, over the rim of his cup of beer, like I was the only person who mattered. Like I was the heart, the center of his whole world.

We would never stay at the after-parties for long.

That same familiar anticipation fills me now, while I wait on my parents' front porch for Garrett to pick me up. I pace, I fidget with the knit cap on my head, and toy with the zipper on my coat. My muscles are strung with excitement, so tight I feel like a rubber band that's ready to snap. A horny rubber band.

I still don't know where this is going with Garrett—and that scares me a little. Because Garrett Daniels is back in my life, in a way I never saw coming . . . winding his way around my heart. And it's like a tragedy—like Romeo and Juliet—we already know how this ends. With goodbye. We both have these great, awesome, separate lives—far, far away from each other. We have careers, friends, homes, and neither one of us is going to turn that upside down. I know I'm being reckless—stupid—I'm going out on that diving board, about to cannonball into the deep end of hurt and heartache. But an ever-growing part of me just doesn't care—and that scares me even more. That part will take what she can get, for as long as she can, heartache be damned.

It's after eleven, late for this neighborhood. The residents on my parents' street have already gone to bed, the windows dark and the air quiet. I hear the Jeep coming down the street before I see it, and by the time it stops at the curb, I'm already running across the lawn to meet him.

I don't wait for Garrett to open the door; I do it myself and climb in. His hair is damp, and the cab is heavy with his clean, ocean, after-shower scent.

Garrett's eyes are black velvet and his voice is dark silk, caressing me. "Your nose is pink. How long were you waiting out there?" He holds my hands in both of his, blowing against them, making my hands warm and my heart trip.

"Not too long. My parents are down for the night . . . and I was excited to see you."

His eyes drift over my face, touching the hat on my head, my eyes, my mouth.

"I couldn't wait to get to you too."

He holds my gaze for another beat, and then nods, dragging his eyes to the road.

"Are you hungry?" Garrett asks as we drive down the empty, street-lamp-lit roads.

"No."

I watch his hands on the steering wheel. Garrett has beautiful hands—strong, graceful—quarterback hands. They hold the leather wheel loosely, and his posture in the seat is relaxed and easy. Confident. Capable. I feel an indescribably calming sensation in the presence of such self-assurance. I always knew, if I were ever unsure or confused, it was okay—because Garrett would know what to do. I could put myself in those skilled hands, follow his lead, and it would all turn out fine.

We pull up to his house and get out of the Jeep without saying a word. Garrett holds my hand on the way up the walk, rubbing his thumb back and forth slowly against my inner wrist. The living room is dim—the light above the clean kitchen sink the only illumination. Snoopy lifts his head from where he's curled up on the recliner, but after a second he lies it back down. Garrett tosses his keys on the corner table, then turns to look at me. His mouth—that gorgeous, mouth that I have dreamed of—settles into a casual smile.

"Do you want something to drink, Callaway?" he asks softly.

My breath catches when he says my name. No one says it like he does—I've dreamed of that too.

"No."

My heart picks up speed, and that full-body tightness that started on the porch pulls at me harder. Like my muscles are thinning, stretching, reaching. For him. Another second ticks by, and Garrett continues looking at me, watching me. He knows what's going to happen; we both do. It's unspoken, but thick in the air between us.

He reaches for me, cupping my cheeks in his two large hands and drawing me closer. I close my eyes and lean against him, nuzzling his throat, feeling the rough scrape of his stubble against my cheek. And I want to feel the scratch of it every- where . . . my stomach, my breasts, between my legs.

"I missed you, Callie." Garrett kisses my forehead, my temple, my hair, breathing me in. "God, I missed you."

Everything inside me clenches at the need coiled in his confession. And I nod, because it's the same for me.

Garrett slips my hat off my head and unzips my jacket, sliding it down and off to the floor. His hands skim up my arms, and he whispers, "Are you nervous?"

A quick, light laugh bubbles from my lips, and I tilt my head to find his eyes.

"I wasn't nervous the first time; why would I be nervous now?"

I remember that night . . . every detail. It's my favorite memory.

It wasn't planned—there were no candles or flowers. But it was still romantic . . . it was still beautiful. The two of us, in Garrett's Jeep, parked in the still darkness beside the lake. I remember the smell of the leather seats, and the scent of our desire—I felt high on the want for him. For more. I remember the hot, hard press of Garrett's bare cock against my thigh and the raw, scraping sound of his voice against my ear.

"Callie . . ."

It was a prayer and a plea—a question, asking permission. *Are you with me? Do you feel this? Do you want this as much as I do?*

And I clung to him.

"Yes . . . yes, yes, yes . . ."

He was gentle, slow, so worried about hurting me. But when he was buried deep inside, when we were finally connected and joined, we were too far gone with how good it was to ever go slow. It was unpracticed, wild, and perfect—and I finally understood why they called it making love.

The touch of Garrett's hand brings me back to the moment, back to his eyes.

"You're trembling," he whispers.

And I am.

I lay my hand on the center of his chest, feeling the thrum of his heartbeat.

"I just . . . I just want you so much."

And then there are no more words.

Garrett kisses me deeply, hungrily. He lifts me and we fold together, my ankles locking across his lower back. His fingers hold, flex against my ass, greedily clasping me against him, holding me strong and secure as he carries me up the stairs to his bedroom.

Our heads turn, our tongues delve, never breaking the searing kiss as my feet slip down his hips to the floor. I slide both hands under his T-shirt, feeling all that delicious, smooth, hot skin and ridged muscle. He grasps the hem of my shirt, our mouths parting just long enough for him to lift it over my head. My bra falls away next, Garrett's expert fingers effortlessly releasing the back clasp. I tug at his shirt and he yanks it off. And then our bare chests collide and the feeling—the sensation—of our bare skin, my heavy breasts against his hard, hot chest is glorious. Breathtaking.

He pushes at the waist of my leggings, bends to drag them down my legs. My fingers work at the button of his jeans, pulling them down his hips, both of us still kissing and kissing—nibbling and feasting on each other's mouths.

There's no awkwardness, or hesitation. We've been here before. Our lips, our hands, and our hearts remember.

We move together across the room until I feel the bed against the backs of my knees. Garrett's hands knead my breasts, slide down my stomach, slipping between my legs, rubbing and petting my soft, slick lips.

"Callie," he groans. "Fuck, you're so wet." He kisses me hard, sipping at my lips, then drinking deep, murmuring. "So hot."

And then my fingers are wrapping around him, sliding and pumping the hot, silken steel of his erection in my hand. He's so hard, so aroused. My thumb caresses the head of his cock, rubbing the fervent moisture at the tip.

And it makes me feel beautiful. Sexy and powerful . . . and wanted.

We fall back on the bed. I spread my legs wide for him, open and offering everything to him.

Take me, love me. Anything he wants . . . it's always been like this between us.

His lips slide down my throat to my nipple and my head digs into the pillow, my back arching, as Garrett suckles me hard. His hair is silk between my fingers as he moves to my other breast, and my head spins with the sensations. My pulse pounds with the weighted pleasure of his hot mouth on me.

My memories of loving Garrett are pale and flimsy compared to this. This is real and solid . . . and us. How did I breathe without this? How will I exist without it?

That dark thought is swept away when Garrett lifts onto his knees, between my thighs. He stretches his long arm to the nightstand, grabbing a condom. I run my hands up and down his torso while he rips open the square foil package—I like the way my hands look on him. Garrett takes his cock in his hand—and I love the look of that too—the way he touches himself, rolling the condom over his thick erection, pinching the latex at the tip and running a hand over his heavy balls. Every movement is sure and confident and so erotically male.

My tongue peeks out to lick my lip—I want him everywhere at once. I want to take him in my mouth, swallow him down, deep in my throat. I want him buried inside me, thrusting hard and rough—I want to feel his hot come on my skin, on my breasts and my stomach and my ass. There is no off-limits, there is no wrong for us—there's only insatiable and desperate, dirty and deeper—more and yes and good.

Garrett grabs my hip, jerking me downwards, and he slides the blunt head of his cock through my lips, where I'm slippery and hot. My muscles clench, feeling empty. He rubs himself against my clit, circling and stroking, sending waves of white bliss screaming up my spine.

I brace my feet on the bed and lift my hips, begging him without words for more.

For him.

"Callie."

His rough voice pulls me through the fog of lust, bringing my eyes to his. His jaw is tight with anticipation and his chest rises and falls in ragged breaths.

"Callie, baby, watch. Watch me . . ."

I nod jerkily. I'll do anything, give him anything he asks, as long as he doesn't stop touching me.

He pushes against my opening and I moan, my knees spreading wider, aching for him deeper. I'm small, narrow, and there's something so mesmerizing about watching Garrett's hands on his big cock—watching him slowly push inside me.

He inhales sharply at the sensations, the feelings.

And, dear God, I feel it too. My tight muscles clench around him, making just enough room as he slides in—so hot and hard. So . . . so *good*. Our pelvises meet and Garrett's chin drops to his chest as he's nestled, buried fully inside me.

"Fuuuck," he moans. "Fuck me . . ."

And then he's dropping to his elbows on either side of my head, kissing me roughly. He pulls his hips back, then slides all the way back in. And we moan together. He begins a rhythm, a smooth, thrusting glide in and out. A constant forward movement and retreat, fucking me steady.

I breathe jagged, nonsensical words into his open-mouthed kiss.

"Garrett . . . Garrett . . . it's so good."

"I know," he groans, flexing his hips, touching me so deep inside. "I know, baby."

"It's so right." I grasp at the strong, taut muscles of his back, sliding my hands down, pressing against his hard, clenching ass. "So . . . right."

Every touch, every kiss that wasn't his felt . . . different. Not bad, not uncomfortable—but *different*. Not the *same*. Not this.

It's only ever felt right with him.

Time ceases to exist. There's only Garrett above me, inside me, surrounding me. My arms stretch up over my head and his fingers wrap around my wrists. I raise my hips, giving myself to him . . . giving myself over to the pleasure that pulses through my body with every thrust of his hips.

Garrett's gaze is hot and heavy-lidded with how good it feels. He moves harder, faster, rougher . . . pushing me higher. It's like my soul is climbing, rising.

"Garrett . . . Garrett . . ." I keen in a whimpering voice I hardly recognize.

And then I'm falling, arching up against him as my orgasm takes me, twists me, and wrings his name from my lips. I contract around his hardness, clenching him inside me, never wanting to let go, never wanting it to end. Garrett's face presses against my neck and he fucks me hard, groaning as he rides through his own pleasure and comes with hot pulsing jerks within me.

For several long moments we stay just like that, chasing our breath, holding each other with heavy, satiated limbs. I run my fingers through his hair, across his back that's damp from exertion. Garrett presses a kiss against my ear, my jaw, my mouth—gentle now—and my heart feels swollen with tenderness for him.

"We're so fucking good at that," he whispers.

"We were always good at that," I tell him.

His lips slide slowly into a cocky, arrogant smile that also happens to be gorgeous.

"We got better at it."

I laugh. He slips his hands beneath my head, cradling me in his arms.

And it's perfect.

There's something so incredibly sexy about watching a man walk naked across a room. Especially a man like Garrett Daniels—with his self-possession, his control of every long, sinewy movement. A man who knows his body—knows what it's capable of and just how to use it.

I roll on my side and enjoy the view of Garrett's hard, sculpted ass when he walks to his adjoining bathroom and takes care of the condom. And I enjoy the show even more on his way back. He's still semi-hard—his cock a stunning spike of thick flesh against a bed of dark hair. I want to kiss him there, lick every inch. My eyes trail down his legs, to the wide, white scar that's slashed across his knee. I want to kiss him there too—thousands of kisses—one for every day I missed from when that scar was made.

Garrett rolls onto his back on the bed next to me—a graceful lion returning to the pride. He tugs me against him, his arm around my shoulder, my chin on his chest, our damp skin molding and our bodies aligned. We don't stop touching each other—caressing with fingertips, sliding palms and brushing lips. We talk in hushed, secret, sacred tones.

"What's your favorite memory?" I ask him. "Something I don't know about yet."

Garrett squints at the ceiling as he thinks.

"One year, when I was . . . twenty-seven, it was the last game of the season, we didn't go to the playoffs . . . and Bailey Fowler, a senior with Down syndrome, was on the team. He'd only gotten a few seconds of field time all year—I treated him like any other third string player. I thought it was important to treat him the same. Anyway, the last play of the game, Bailey was in and . . . James Thompson, our quarterback, passed him the ball. They must've worked it out with the other team, because a few of the kids went after him, but nobody touched him. And he ran that ball all the way to the end zone. Bailey was so frigging happy; everyone in the stands was cheering. It was such a *good* moment."

He glances down at me. "What about you?"

Mine isn't as uplifting, but it's a joyful memory. I tell him about *Twelfth Night*, the first production I was involved in after graduation, with the Fountain Theater. How I'd prepped for the audition, wanted it so badly . . . and got the part.

"I finally got to play Viola."

"That was your dream role."

I tilt my head, looking up at him. "You remember that?"

"I remember everything, Callie." He picks up a strand of my hair, brushing it with his fingers. "Every one of your dreams . . . your laughs"—he cups my cheek—"and the tears too."

A memory rises in my head—a rainy day, senior year, in Garrett's bedroom—when he held me, rocked me in his arms, and I soaked his skin with tears.

I close my eyes, brush it away. I don't want to go down that road, not when we're making this new, precious, happy memory. I turn the corner instead.

"What's your favorite song?" I ask, wanting to absorb every detail of him.

"'Undone—The Sweater Song'—by Weezer is still my favorite. It was our song."

My face scrunches. "Ah . . . that wasn't our song, Garrett."

"Sure it was. It came on in my Jeep, right before the first time we had sex. We discussed it afterwards. Totally our song."

I roll my eyes. "Nooo . . . our song was 'Heaven' by Bryan Adams. It was our Junior Prom song."

"I have no idea what you're talking about."

I laugh, teasing him. "I thought you remembered everything?"

"I do. And I can't believe you had our song wrong all these years. It commemorated a fantastic fucking moment in our relationship."

I bite his chest. "I can't believe *you* had our song wrong."

He moves quick, making me gasp—flipping me onto my back, hovering over me with a wicked look in his eyes.

"Your memory needs refreshing, babe. Let's retrace our mouths."

"Our mouths? I think we're supposed to retrace our steps."

"Nope." Garrett glides his wet mouth across my neck, over my breasts, licking his way down my stomach, settling his dark head between my thighs. "When *our song* was on in the Jeep . . . I was doing this with my mouth . . ."

He drags the tip of his tongue through my slit, circling my clit, sending a jolt of simmering heat through my body.

"And your mouth was busy moaning."

He laps at me, laves me with the flat of his wet tongue. And I moan.

"Yep, just like that. Ring any bells?"

"No." I manage to shake my head, my heart racing.

"Hmm." He hums against me and I see stars. "Guess I'll have to try harder."

He kisses me between my legs—wet, searing, open-mouthed kisses. He eats me, devours me, worships me. He groans against me, telling me how good I taste, how hard I make him.

"Is it coming back to you now, Callie?" Garrett teases hotly.

He spears me with his tongue, over and over. He swivels his mouth, sucking on my clit, fucking me with his fingers.

Until I'm gasping, agreeing to anything—everything.

"Yes . . . yes . . . yes . . ."

And I shatter, break into a thousand points of pleasure. And when I'm boneless—possibly dead—Garrett kisses my pubic bone and glides up my body, all self-satisfied smirking.

"That's what I thought."

<hr>

After that . . . things get wild. We go through three more condoms before the night is over.

And Garrett was right—we are better at it now.

I ride him with a boldness I didn't possess when we were young. I roll my hips and scrape my nails down his back—making him beg, groan with pleasure.

He puts me on my hands and knees and pounds into me from behind—rougher than he ever dared when we were teenagers. He pulls on my hips, tangles his hand in my hair, and whispers dark, dirty promises and filthy words.

The last time is slow and unhurried. Chest to chest, entwined, we sink into each other, come together, and lose ourselves in each other's eyes. Afterwards, Garrett envelops me in the tender safety of his arms, buries his face in my hair, and we fall into sated, exhausted sleep.

I open my eyes to the sound of inhaling and exhaling—a light, serrated rumble—breathing that's not my own. It's not your grandpa's, blow the roof off the house kind of snore, but more of a nice, rolling reverberation.

Huh—grown-up Garrett snores. That's new.

I like it. Manly but also cute.

He lies on his back with me tucked against his side, my head on his chest, his arm across my back.

And we're not alone.

On his other arm, with his nose in the crook of Garrett's neck . . . is Snoopy, his eyes closed in peaceful, puppy slumber. Sunlight streams through the window, and I take a second to glance around the bedroom—I wasn't exactly interested in the décor last night. It's a nice room. Like the rest of the house, it reminds me of Garrett—neat, simple—all bachelor blues and beiges.

I also soak up the chance to look at Garrett while he sleeps. His strong jaw, his relaxed brow, so handsome—a filthy-mouthed Greek god. My eyes drop to the dark hair that dusts his chest, and the trail below his belly button that dips beneath the sheet—coarse and devastatingly masculine. I really like that too.

I shift slightly, stretching gently without disturbing the other occupants of the bed. I'm sore all over—my arms, my thighs, slightly aching between my legs—my muscles overworked from being so thoroughly well-used. And I can't stop grinning.

But . . . if my students hadn't chased me off Facebook, I would definitely be changing my relationship status to "it's complicated."

Is it fucking ever.

Over the years when I imagined running into Garrett again—because everybody imagines running into their ex—I always thought he'd be married. To a supermodel, with kids—half a dozen boys, on his way to populating his own football team. And the image always came with a heaping helping of heartache. But he was a catch. I knew that. He was too amazing to not get scooped up by some lucky, undeserving bitch.

I figured he'd be off-limits. No longer mine.

But here we are.

This wasn't part of the plan—not what I thought would happen when I came home weeks ago. But I'm not sorry about it—not even a little.

I just have to figure out what to do. How this works when I go back to San Diego.

If it works.

Or maybe . . . maybe I'm getting ahead of my boobs here. I look around the room again—a single man's room, through and through, and not by accident. Does Garrett even want it to work? Sure, we've been talking, texting, humping like dust bunnies in the janitor's closet . . . but we haven't talked about a future. About what happens when I go back to my real life . . . and he stays here. Maybe it's just a hookup of convenience? Temporary, like a vacation hookup—the kind that was fun but forgettable as soon as you leave the island.

Jesus, I'm having my very own morning-after Oprah "ah-hah" moment.

It was easy not to think about it before last night. To keep it light, flirty—to just go with getting to know Garrett again. But here, now, lying beside him with nothing between us but warm sheets . . . shit just got real.

I ache when I look at him. Ache to stay, ache for him to follow . . . ache to keep whatever this is between us long after the end of the school year. But does he want that too? And if he does . . . what does that even look like with Garrett in New Jersey and me in California?

Ugh . . . I need coffee. This is too much thinking without coffee.

I shimmy down the bed, under the sheets, and out the bottom. I scoop Garrett's T-shirt up from the floor, but before I put it on . . . I smell it. Inhale deeply, practically snorting the cotton up my nostrils.

Then I open my eyes . . . to find Snoopy staring at me. He tilts his head, in that doggie way, that says—*Girl, what the hell are you doing?*

"Don't judge me," I tell him softly, then slip the shirt over my head.

Snoopy hops down off the bed, his little nails clacking on the hardwood floor. And Garrett shifts, mumbling, throwing his arm up over his head before settling back into slumber.

And God . . . even his armpit hair is arousing.

I look down at Snoopy. "Okay, you're right . . . I have issues. Come on."

I scoop him up because Garrett said his legs aren't great and he has trouble with the stairs, and I carry him down to the kitchen. I let Snoopy out the back door, leaving it open, the

cool morning air blowing on my legs and up Garrett's shirt—
giving me goose bumps. I fill the stainless steel coffeemaker
with water and grounds and get it brewing. I check my phone,
to make sure I didn't miss any texts or calls from my parents.

By the time Snoopy returns and I pour a scoop of dry dog
food from the bin into the corner bowl with his name on it, the
coffee is ready. I pour myself a steaming cup, blowing gently,
and gaze out the kitchen window at the golden, shining streaks
of sunlight rising up on the lake and the flock of five geese in
V formation flying through the morning gray sky—honking
like cranky commuters in rush hour traffic.

And the whole time, one thought runs through my mind
and one feeling thrums through my heart—over and over
again: *It would be so easy to get used to this.*

I turn around to grab a mug for Garrett—and then I
scream.

"Holy shit!"

Because I've seen one too many *Children of the Corn*-like
horror films in my day, and there's a pair of big brown eyes
staring at me just above the counter, on the other side of the
center island.

They're Spencer's—Garrett's five-year-old nephew's
eyes.

"Hi!"

I press my hand to my chest as my brain conveys this information and calls off the impending heart attack.

"Hi."

"You're Uncle Garrett's friend, right?"

"That's right. I'm Callie. We met the other day at your
house."

"Yeah. Dad's sorry he almost chopped the house down."
He shrugs. "Adults lose it sometimes; it's no one's fault."

"That's true." I grin.

Until he peers around the counter and his little brow furrows.

"Why don't you have pants on?"

I almost tell him adults lose their pants sometimes too—
but I'm afraid that could lead down the wrong road. So I slap
my forehead instead.

"I forgot to put them on!" I hook my thumb over my
shoulder. "I'm gonna go do that now."

Then I pull Garrett's T-shirt down to make sure I'm covered and I scoot out of the kitchen. Right into Connor Daniels's path, with his two other boys behind him.

"Hey, Callie." His eyes graze downward, taking in my
bare bottom half. He rubs his neck bashfully. "Sorry."

"No worries!" I scurry past them, boobs jiggling because
I'm not wearing a bra either. Yikes.

Garrett's walking out of his bedroom—shirtless with
black sweatpants hanging low and delicious on his hips—as I
make a dive into it.

I can hear him talking to his brother and nephews downstairs as I search for my clothes.

"Sorry, Gar—I got called into the hospital and Mom
wasn't feeling so hot."

"What's wrong with Mom?" Garrett asks.

"Just that cold that's going around, but I wanted to let her
rest. Can the boys hang with you today?"

"Yeah, no problem."

"Can we go fishing?" Brayden asks excitedly.

"Sure, buddy."

"Your girlfriend has a nice ass." The older one—Aaron—comments.

"Watch it," Garrett warns.

"You would prefer I said her ass wasn't nice?" the teenager asks.

"I'd prefer we leave her ass out of the conversation altogether."

The opening and closing of cabinets and drawers fills the pause in conversation. Then I hear Garrett's voice again. "Get yourself some cereal, I'll be right back."

I'm sitting on the edge of the bed, just hooking my bra, when the bedroom door opens. Garrett walks straight to me and climbs onto the bed—onto me—pushing me back, straddling my waist, keeping his weight on his knees, holding my wrists loosely above my head and gazing down into my eyes.

"Hi."

"Hi."

He leans down and kisses me, sucking at my bottom lip. "You taste like coffee."

He tastes like mint and smells like . . . home.

"I made a pot."

He leans back, watching me, eyes trailing over my face.

"Stop freaking out, Callie."

"I'm not freaking out."

"I can hear you freaking out, from here." He tilts his head, his dark hair falling into his eyes. It's not a cute-tilt, like Snoopy. It's a sexy, hot-tilt . . . a manly-tilt. "The question is, why?"

I swallow and lift my chin and just . . . put it all out there.

"Am I Cancun?"

Garrett laughs. "What?"

"Am I that girl in Cancun . . . the one you do shots with, and go to clubs with, and have sex on the beach with . . . and then never see or think about ever again?"

He squints at me. "What the hell are you talking about? Were you drinking something else besides coffee?"

I shake my head and sigh.

"I'm not staying in Lakeside, Garrett."

A shadow falls over his features. "I know that."

"I have a life. A whole life in San Diego that I plan to get back to."

"I know that too." He reaches out, tracing my bottom lip with his thumb. "But for this year, your life is here."

"And what happens when I go back to San Diego?"

"I . . . don't know. But I know I want to figure it out. And we will, Cal, we'll figure it out."

Those are good answers. I like those answers. But I have to know, I want us to be clear—no misunderstandings or mistakes.

"What is this to you . . . what are we doing? What do you want?"

Garrett smiles that easy smile that makes me want to lick every single inch of his skin.

"This is . . . you and me . . . the reboot. We'll talk and laugh, and fuck until we can't move and probably fight at some point too. And we'll . . . *be*."

I reach for him. He releases my arms and rolls us to the side, my hands around his neck, my leg draped across his hip. "As for what I want . . . I want you, Callie. For as long as you're here, for as long as you'll let me have you. I want all of you."

CHAPTER
Fifteen

Garrett

On Monday, I start picking Callie up in the morning, so we can drive to school together. I don't know why I didn't think of it before—all those post-fantastic-screwing endorphins pumping through my bloodstream must be giving me brilliant ideas. Although no one sees us pull into the parking lot or walk in together, by midmorning talk around the school hallways is already rampant. It's like the kids can smell the attraction on us—nosy little bloodhounds. They whisper and point, and by Tuesday they ask me about it, because privacy and personal boundaries mean nothing to them.

Are you and Miss Carpenter hooking up?

Is Miss Carpenter your OTP?

Miss Carpenter's hot, Coach. You gotta lock that down. Give a chick a mile and she'll take the whole nine inches from somebody else, you know what I'm saying?

OMG, Coach D! You and Miss Carpenter should totally

go to prom! It's sooooo cute when old people date!

OTP is One True Pair, by the way . . . and I hate myself for knowing that.

By Wednesday, they invent one of those celebrity, name-mashing nicknames for us. "Darpenter," Dean tells me, barely managing to keep a straight face.

I sit back in my office chair. "You're screwing with me."

He's pulled some pretty twisted practical jokes in the past.

He holds up his empty hands. "Afraid not. Kelly Simmons told me it's all over the girls' bathrooms and Merkle said two of her art kids engraved it on keychains."

"Keychains?"

"Yep, you and Callie are officially relationship goals." He makes the hashtag sign with his fingers. "Congratulations."

Then he cracks up.

"Great—thanks."

Darpenter . . . sounds like a chemical you use to strip off paint.

"It could've been worse, D. Could've been . . . Carret." He reconsiders, "Carret's kind of cute, actually."

I give him the finger.

"So it's official then?" My best friend asks, sobering slightly. "You guys are giving it another shot? I've lost my wingman?"

All this time, all these years, when it comes to dating I've been fixated on keeping my life my own—keeping it uncomplicated and drama-free. But it's different with Callie—so easy to slip into that steady groove because we mesh . . . seamlessly fit together. We always did. She knows me, she gets me—and there's not a single thing about her that I don't adore.

My life is still simple, still easy . . . but it's just so much better with her in it.

"Yeah, man. I mean . . . it's Callie, you know?"

And I don't need to say anything else. Dean gets me too.

"I'm happy for you. I hope it works out . . ." Then he snickers, ". . . Gallie."

Dickhead.

"You're the only person I know who doesn't eat fruit to be healthy, but actually enjoys it."

It's kind of nuts the things you find attractive about someone when you're really into them. Callie was always a fruit salad kind of girl, even when we were kids. Right now, we're in The Cave, the teachers' lounge, as our classes attend a first period anti-drug assembly in the auditorium. And she's popping giant, radioactive-sized green grapes in her mouth. Watching her slip them between her gorgeous pouty lips is turning me on something fierce.

She giggles, shrugging. "Fruit is good." She holds one out to me. "Want one?"

My eyes dart between the grape and her mouth.

"No . . . I just want to keep watching you eat them."

Her pretty green eyes narrow wickedly. She takes the next grape and gives it a nice, slow lick and I can't help but picture her doing the same to my balls. Then she closes her eyes, gives a little hungry moan before making a lovely, wide O with her mouth and popping the big round grape through her luscious lips.

I smother a groan. Looks like a trip to the faculty bath-room for some "private time" is in my future. Jesus, how old am I again?

"Get a room, you two," Donna Merkle teases as she sits down at the table next to Callie. And then I catch her staring at Jerry's ass as he pours himself a cup of coffee across the room. They've been markedly less vicious with each other during the staff meetings, though they still hate-fuck each other with their eyes.

It's not an uncommon thing for relationships to develop between teachers—no matter how weird or incompatible it may look from the outside. It's like costars on a movie set or soldiers on deployment—we're all stuck in this building to-gether for hours a day, and only other teachers really under-stand what it's like. Things are bound to happen. And some-thing is definitely happening with Merkle and Jerry. Callie sees it too.

"You and Jerry first, Donna."

"Leaving now," Merkle says, rising. And Jerry's eyes fol-low her right out the door.

I lean forward, resting my elbows on the table.

"So, you're coming over tonight after the game, right?"

Callie's parents have made some good progress on the re-covery front. The hospital bed has been taken down—they're using walkers and crutches to get around now. They still need Callie to do any heavy lifting, but their progress has given her just a bit more time out of the house . . . and over at mine.

"Definitely." She nods. "Can't mess with a streak."

God damn, she's perfect.

We've won every game since mine and Callie's first night together, and I have no doubt we'll win again tonight. Her pussy is my gorgeous good-luck charm and I make damn sure I give that beauty the gratitude and worship it deserves.

Later that day, in third period, Miss McCarthy comes on the loudspeaker and announces the nominations for homecoming queen, who will be crowned next week. When she reads Simone Porchesky's name, Nancy and Skylar and more than half the rest of the class bust a gut laughing.

Nancy shrieks and grabs her phone. "OMG, Simone is up for homecoming queen! Hilarious!"

I know Simone—she's in Callie's theater class. Blue hair, piercings, tattoos—she's designing the sets and the costumes for Callie's play.

"Why is that hilarious?" I ask.

But my gut curdles with the suspicion that I already know why.

"It's a joke," Nancy tells me. "A bunch of us got together and put her name in as a joke. I posted about it but I didn't actually think she'd really get nominated! This is amazing."

I think about that scene from *The Breakfast Club*, where Andy the jock talks about the humiliation the kid whose ass cheeks he taped together must've felt. I think about Callie, and the care and affection she feels for her students—how hearing about this is going to crush a piece of her.

And I think about Simone, just a girl trying to figure herself out—and the isolation and embarrassment and the fucking hurt she's going to feel. Because kids know when you're laughing with them, even if they don't see it. They know when they're a punchline. And it's soul shattering.

"Why would you do that?"

Nancy shrugs. "I don't know."

I believe her—and it's horrifying. That she would inflict this kind of cruelty on someone else without any real reason at all.

Her mouth twists. "Simone's a freak—have you seen her? She tries too hard to get attention—to get noticed. So, we gave her what she wanted . . . we noticed her."

"That's genius!" someone in the back—I don't even know who—calls out.

David Burke's not laughing, but he's the only one. Even DJ joins the party—they sneer and giggle—a room full of pitiless little monsters.

I slam the side of my fist on the desk. "That's enough!"

The chatter cuts off quick when they see I'm pissed, when they realize this is not fucking okay with me. They go wide-eyed and silent.

"I have never been more disappointed in you than I am right now." I shake my head. "All of you."

They're supposed to be better than us. More accepting, more open, more understanding—a green generation, with hands reaching across the world, and love that always wins. They have more advantages, more resources and benefits than any who've come before them—and they still put so much energy into tearing each other to shreds.

Sometimes it feels pointless—like we're trying to hold up a dam that's crumbling beneath our fingers. Because kids are kids—no matter the century. They'll always be so *young*. Too young to know what matters, what's important, and how fast it all goes. Too young to not be selfish and stupid and sometimes just straight-up mean. They haven't lived long enough to know how to be anything else.

But that doesn't mean I'm going to stop trying. Trying to make them better—everything I know they could be. By any means necessary.

So, I bring the hammer down.

"Research paper."

And they groan.

"The topic is, propaganda and the 'othering' of groups in the lead-up to World War II. Five pages—minimum."

"Nice fucking job, Nancy." Dugan, a flannel-wearing, long-haired member of the skater crowd, throws a balled-up piece of paper at her.

"Knock it off," I tell him.

Then I up the ante. "And I want you to write it by hand."

Skylar Mayberry's arm rises like a rocket.

"I don't understand. What does that mean?"

I pick up a pen and a piece of notebook paper and demonstrate. "I want you to *write* . . . a research paper . . . *by hand.*"

She squints at me. "Why?"

"Because I want you to actually think about what you're writing. The words and ideas you're putting down."

David Burke's hand goes up next. "They didn't teach script in my elementary school."

"Me neither," Brad Reefer joins in.

"You can print." I point at them. "And use white-out or a pencil. If you hand me an assignment that's filled with scribbles, I'll give it back and make you write ten pages."

They moan in agony again.

And it's music to my ears. Growth is painful; change is hard. So, if they're unhappy—it means I'm doing my job right.

During the weekend, on Sunday, Callie and I hit the grocery store together—because even something as boring as grocery shopping is better if I can look at Callie's ass while doing it.

"Pork rinds?" I ask as she puts a massive bag in the cart.

"My dad loves them. Colleen and I have been rationing them, hiding the bag, or he'll eat them until his stomach pops."

She looks especially hot today, with her hair pulled up into a high ponytail, a touch of pink shine on her lips, wearing snug black jeans and a royal-blue sweater that highlights her creamy skin and hugs her round tits perfectly.

I come up behind her when she bends over the cart, rubbing my ever-hardening dick against her ass. "I've got some pork for your rind right here, baby."

And I'm only half-kidding.

She turns, her face scrunching, and pushes me away. "Ew . . . you're disgusting."

I grab her hips and pull her flush against me.

"You know you like it."

She peers up at me, biting her bottom lip.

"Yeah . . . maybe I do."

She reaches up and pecks my lips—and I taste the promise of more to come. If we ever finish fucking grocery shopping.

I move to the back of the cart so we can get on that, and almost crash into another cart.

A cart that's being pushed by Tara Benedict.

Tara looks back and forth between us. "Hey, Garrett. And . . . Callie . . . hi . . ."

"Hey, Tara."

"Tara . . . hey. How's it going?" Callie smiles.

And because Tara's cool, there's only a hint of awkwardness.

"It's good. I heard you were back in town. Welcome home."

A dark-haired little boy comes up behind her, Joshua, holding the hand of a light-brown-haired guy with glasses.

Tara gestures to the man beside her. "Matt, this is Garrett and Callie—old friends from high school."

I shake Matt's hand and the four of us talk for a few minutes about nothing in particular. Eventually we say goodbye and Callie and I walk over to the next aisle.

"So . . ." Callie says, walking next to me, "you and Tara Benedict, huh?"

I toss a box of corn flakes into the cart. "It was a casual thing. Not serious."

"Right."

"Was it that obvious?"

She shrugs. "A woman looks at a guy that she's slept with in a certain way. I could tell."

I slide my hand into the back of her jeans, giving her plump, pretty ass a squeeze.

"You jealous, Callaway?"

She takes a second to think about it. Then she shakes her head.

"You know what . . . I'm not. Lakeside's a small town, we were bound to run into someone you've dated—probably won't be the last time. Whatever happened through the years, it brought us both here. And I like here." She takes my hand out of her pocket and holds it in her smaller one. "Here is good."

I lean down and kiss her, softer, longer this time.

"Here is very, very good."

Callie smiles, then resumes pushing the cart. After a minute, she laughs. "Besides, it's not like you hooked up with Becca Saber or something."

Becca Saber . . .

The back of my neck goes itchy and hot.

Becca is Coach Saber's daughter—she was in the same grade as us, and the splinter under Callie's fingernail all through high school. She was on my dick like white on rice, and not subtle about it. She'd drop by the locker room after practice, always making sure I knew she was available and up for anything. She got off on doing it in front of Callie. I told her to cut it out, that I wasn't remotely interested, but that didn't stop her from trying over and over.

And Callie . . . pretty much just sucked it up, let it go, ignored it, and kept her mouth shut. For me.

To not cause problems between me and the football coach I idolized, who thought his daughter was an angel straight from heaven.

"That would be a different story." Callie shrugs, still smiling.

I open my mouth to tell her, because—like I've said before—a guy gets to a point in his life when he knows that straight-up, brutal honesty is simpler. The best way to go.

Except . . . when it's not.

I look over at Callie again—and she's so happy—gazing at me with the perfect combination of playfulness, tenderness, and heat.

Here, where we are now, really is good. And it could all go away at the end of the year when Callie goes back to San

Diego. Distance was the reason we ended the first time . . . one of the reasons anyway. And if history is bound to repeat itself . . . well, fuck . . . this could be all the time I get with her. The only time I get.

I think about what I tell my kids every Friday . . . *"Don't be idiots."* And I take my own advice. Because only an idiot would waste a minute—a second—with Callie explaining and rehashing shit that happened years ago. That shouldn't affect us at all here, now, in this moment.

So I nod. "Yeah, totally different story."

Then I put my arm around her, kiss the top of her head, and we head off together to the frozen food section.

CHAPTER
Sixteen

Garrett

Mrs. Carpenter, with Colleen and Callie's help, has decided to cook up an epic spread for Thanksgiving. Callie's friends from San Diego, Bruce and Cheryl, are coming to Lakeside for the holiday. The day before Thanksgiving, I drive Callie to Newark to pick them up from the airport.

We're waiting near the baggage claim when a piercing war cry rings out and a blur of beige sweater and dark-red hair comes streaking around the corner—all but tackling Callie.

"Girlfriend!" The blur squeals. "I've missed you! Damn, you look great—the Jersey air agrees with you."

This must be Cheryl. Callie's told me about her—the loud, quirky bookkeeper of the theater company Callie will be returning to at the end of the year.

She bounces with delight in her tall friend's arms, hugging her back. Then she introduces me to Cheryl and I get a hug slammed into me too—knocking me back a step. Cheryl would've made a great lineman.

Then the redhead pumps my arm in a vigorous hand-shake. "It's so great to finally meet you, Garrett! Callie's been telling me all about you." She does a double-take. "Wow, you really are handsome, aren't you? Hello, Mr. Adonis."

I like Cheryl already.

Bruce the Deuce, on the other hand—the tall, blond guy in the navy sport coat and beige ascot, who walks up beside Cheryl . . . not so much. I admit it—I'm not as mature about Callie's dating history as she seems to be about mine. I'm a guy—it's my god damn prerogative to want to rip the dick off of any other man that's come within striking distance of my girl.

Callie and Bruce hug—a calmer, gentler hug than the smack-downs Cheryl's giving out. According to Callie, Bruce is an actor—and yeah, it bugs the shit out of me, in a totally unreasonable way, that they share a common love of the thea-ter. Callie said they dated briefly, but didn't have sex—so I guess I'll let him live. I'll even be nice to him, for Cal's sake—but I won't ever fucking like him.

Cheryl brings Callie's attention back to her. "So, before we get the bags, I have news!"

She claps her hands, vibrating in her black boots.

"What's up?" Callie asks.

Cheryl holds out her left hand—the one with a big, spark-ly diamond on the ring finger.

"We're engaged!"

And it's like Callie's brain short-circuits. Confusion mars her pretty features as her eyes dance between her two smiling friends.

"Engaged to who?"

Bruce laughs and loops his arm around Cheryl's broad shoulders.

"Each other."

"Wait . . . whaaat?" Callie points her finger at them. "You and Bruce? Cheryl and you?"

The happy couple nods in unison.

"Do you guys even *like* each other?"

Bruce grins. "Turns out my penis loves her vagina and the feeling is mutual. Once those crazy kids got together, our hearts went along for the ride."

"Wow. I am . . ." She runs her hands through her hair, pushing it back. ". . . so confused. When did this happen?"

"It happened while we were boxing up your stuff to ship here," Cheryl says. "One minute we were arguing about whether to use Bubble Wrap or newspaper to pack your shoes . . . and the next minute we were tearing each other's clothes off. And it was glorious—just like a romance novel!"

Bruce picks up the story. "It was so good, we kept meeting up to do it, every day. For weeks."

Callie's eyes widen. "In my apartment?"

"Yeah." Cheryl's head toddles apologetically. "You may want to get a new couch when you come home."

I laugh—Cheryl's kind of awesome.

"Why didn't either of you say something to me?"

The last few months have been a tornado for Callie time-wise, but I know she's been touching base with her friends a couple times a week.

"It was so new in the beginning, we barely talked about it to each other. And there was something exciting about keeping it on the down-low. Clandestine." Bruce wiggles his eyebrows.

"Like we were doing something wrong that felt oh-so right."

"And then, last week, Bruce put his balls on the table and let it all hang out."

Callie grimaces. "Which table?"

Cheryl waves her hand. "I mean, figuratively." She turns to Bruce, her voice going mushy and mesmerized. "He told me he loved me and asked me to marry him."

"And she said yes." Bruce stares at Cheryl, brushing a hair back from her face, the very picture of total and complete pussywhippedism. Infatuation and devotion practically ooze from his eyeballs.

And I get that—respect it—it speaks to me. It's how I picture myself in my head, every time I look at Callie Carpenter.

Okay . . . *maybe* I'll end up liking Bruce. A little.

They both turn their heads to Callie.

"And here we are," Bruce says.

"We want the wedding to be in the spring, so . . . since you're going to still be here, you're gonna have to up your data plan because I'm going to need help with flowers and a dress . . . and everything." Then, slightly hesitantly, because Callie's opinion obviously matters to her, Cheryl asks, "What do you think, Callie?"

Callie's eyes drift back and forth between them. And then she flings her arms around them, hugging them both at the same time. "I think it's amazing! I'm so happy for you!"

After the hugs and congratulations settle down, we grab Bruce and Cheryl's bags and head back to Callie's parents' house. Dean's band is playing at Chubby's that night—an unusual mid-school-year performance for him—so the four of us go there for drinks.

The next day, I eat Thanksgiving dinner at the Carpenters'—Callie's dad hobbles around but still manages to slice up a mean turkey. Bruce and Cheryl are comfortable with Callie's parents and her sister and brother-in-law, so after dinner, she leaves them at the house and stops by my parents' place with me for dessert. We split the holiday between our families . . . the way couples do.

The Lakeside Lions finish their season with an 8–4 record. It's not states, and it's not anywhere close to how I envisioned the season playing out—but all things considered, it's not bad. I'm damn proud of my boys and I make sure to let them know it.

On the first Tuesday in December, I'm in my office, after school, going over tapes from the last game. On the desk, a text message pops up from Callie on my phone.

Callie: Come to the auditorium. I want to show you something.

I rise from my desk and text her back as I walk.

Me: A naked something?

Callie: Lol, no. Come through the side to the stage left loft—be stealthy.

Ah, the stage left loft. The legendary student body makeout spot. Our own little slice of seven minutes in heaven—Callie gave me our first blow job there. Though you never would've guessed it was her first time—even back then the girl had skills that could blow my frigging head off.

Me: Good times in that loft—we going for a redo?

I know she knows exactly what I'm referring to, when she texts back.

Callie: Not tonight . . . but maybe another time ;) Are you coming?

Me: Not at the moment—hopefully soon. But only after you come first.

I imagine that sweet blush rising on her cheeks, as she shakes her head at her phone.

Callie: You have a one-track mind.

Me: No, I have a three-track mind. Your mouth, your ass, and that pretty, pretty pussy—are always on it.

I walk down the side hallway, outside the theater, and quietly go through the side door that leads backstage. The overhead lights are on and there's some student chatter happening out front. I climb the black, metal ladder to the loft, where Callie is waiting.

She offers her hand as I climb the last of the way up, smiling softly.

"Hey."

She's wearing a black formfitting turtleneck today, sleek black skirt, and high black boots—gorgeous.

"What's up?" I whisper.

There's a black sofa along the back wall of the loft. The concrete walls are also painted black, with tons of graffiti left by students through the years, in chalk and white marker. It's a quiet, private space—with probably more body fluid on that old couch than I ever want to fucking contemplate.

Callie leads me by the hand to the railing that overlooks the stage below.

"David and Layla are working on their big song. They've been practicing so hard."

In the last few weeks, Callie's really hit her stride teaching-wise. She's a natural, and I'm so proud of her.

Soft piano notes float up around us, and she turns her eyes to the stage below.

David and Layla are center stage. He starts first, singing as Seymour, offering Layla his hand and telling her to wipe off her mascara—singing about how things were bad, but now everything is going to be okay. Layla gazes up at him, like he's her hero, and the music climbs and her stunning voice rises. They sound good together—stronger and softer, complementing voices.

"Look at them, Garrett. Aren't they amazing?"

But all I can look at is her. The way her hair shines and her face glows in the halo of the stage lights, her pink lips parted and her eyes wide and full of wonder and awe.

She takes my breath away.

I slide my hand across her back, covering her hip, tucking her against me.

"They're amazing, Callie . . . because that's what you are. You made them that way."

She lets out a little sigh, wraps her arms around my waist, and rests her head on my bicep, and we watch her students sing.

Some guys would worry that they could be falling too hard and fast for a woman they've technically only been dating a few months. But not me. Because I know the irrefutable truth.

It's too late—I already fell, a long time ago.

Callie can't come over to my place that night—her mom is hell-bent on bringing all the holiday decorations up from the basement and getting the house set for Christmas. It shouldn't be a big deal—but tonight, I'm antsy about it. Just . . . hungry for her. Maybe it's the realization that she's just across town, so close, when for so many years, I'd think of her but she was far out of my reach. Or maybe it's the last, cute text she sends about decorating:

Callie: Looks like I'm the elf for the night.

And doesn't that get me thinking hot, deviant thoughts about sexy, Christmas themed outfits—thigh-high white stockings, red velvet thongs, silk bows, and fur-trimmed handcuffs . . . these are a few of my favorite things.

Just before midnight, I'm sitting on my couch, still all charged up—rock hard with thoughts of her.

I look over at Snoopy. He stares back at me.

"Fuck it, right, buddy? I should just go over there?"

He lifts his nose and lets out three shrill, rolling barks.

Translation: *Damn straight, dude. Why are you still here with me?*

My dog is a genius.

I give his belly a rub and kiss his head. Then I grab my keys.

It's pouring rain outside and colder than a polar bear's cock, but that doesn't stop me from hopping in my Jeep and driving to Callie's parents'. The house is dark except for the front porch light that illuminates the evergreen wreath on the door. I wonder if Callie put it there with her pretty hands, and the thought makes me smile. I park at the curb, a little ways down the street so I don't wake her parents, and jog through the rain, across the lawn. I hop the chain-link fence into the backyard and slide up to Callie's bedroom window in the back. It's a route my feet remember well.

The pink-shaded lamp on her nightstand is on and she's turned away from the window, bent over, putting laundry away in her bottom dresser drawer.

And even though it's frigging freezing, the gorgeous view of her creamy, curvy ass peeking out of those tiny sleeping shorts is more than enough to warm me—from the crotch up. I tap the window with my knuckle, softly, so I don't scare her. But Callie still jumps, yanks a medal she got in tenth grade off the wall, and spins around, holding it over her head like a sling shot. Her eyes are wide and her mouth is round in a tight, surprised O.

Yep—makes me want to jam my cock in there—just to feel her gasp and hum around it.

When she realizes it's me her face collapses with relief, and she grabs at her chest. Her blond hair swings across her shoulders as she marches that tight little ass over to the window, slamming it open.

"You just took five years off my life! Are you nuts? What the hell are you doing here?"

I shrug. "I wanted to see you."

Callie's cheeks are flushed and her eyes are that bright, sparkling green—it's like she gets fucking prettier every time I see her.

"You would've seen me tomorrow morning."

"Nope, couldn't wait that long."

She moves back as I lift myself through her window—and shuts it behind me. Then I stand up, dripping on her cream carpet.

Callie pulls at my shirt. "Take this off. Your lips are turning blue."

Together, we lift it over my head and Callie gasps when

she touches my icy chest. The sound goes straight to my dick.

"Garrett, you're freezing!"

I step closer, putting my arms around her, feeling all her sweet, soft warmth, nuzzling my nose with hers, wanting her so damn much.

"Warm me up, then, baby."

Her hands slide through my hair, down my neck, and across my shoulders, rubbing heat into my skin.

Her voice is husky. "My parents are in their room. We have to be quiet."

How many times has she said those words to me, in this room? A dozen times, maybe a hundred.

"I can be quiet," I remind her. "You're the screamer in the group."

I slide my hands up her rib cage, taking her pajama shirt with me, baring her pale, perfect breasts. If I went blind at this moment and those beauties were the last sight my eyes would ever see? I'd be good with that.

I walk us back until Callie's pressed up beside her door—wedged between the wall and my hard place.

I kiss her mouth, her neck, down between her tits, sinking to my knees in front of her. She plays with my wet hair as I pull those tiny shorts down her legs, revealing even teenier white bikini panties underneath. *Fuck me*, cotton on Callie is just as sexy as leather or lace—possibly sexier. I brush my nose against her cunt, over her panties, feeling her heat, getting dizzy—high—off the scent of her.

Then I slide those panties down her legs too—leaving her bare except for that neat, blond patch between her legs.

Callie looks down, watching me, her lids heavy and her chest panting.

I lift her leg and put it over my shoulder—opening her up for me. And then I lean in and lick her slow and firm and deliberate, just like I was thinking about . . . dreaming about all night. I stroke her with my tongue, up and down, unhurried, taking my time. I fucking love the taste of her. I love the smooth, soft, wet feel of her against my tongue. I love all her sounds, her breaths, every move she makes—especially when she's like this—hot and begging and squirming for my touch.

I go in for another lick—deeper this time, sliding between her plump, juicy lips. Fucking delicious. Callie's head lolls back against the wall, eyes rolling closed, moaning too loud above me.

I *tsk* at her, teasing, because I can be a real bastard sometimes.

"You have to be quiet, sweetheart." I flick Callie's clit with the tip of my tongue. "I'll have to stop if you're not quiet. Do you want me to have to stop?"

She whimpers, shaking her head.

I thrust my tongue inside her, fucking her with it, in and out, slow. Her hips lift in time with my tongue and she pants out hard, harsh, moany breaths.

"I can make you come like this, Callie," I tell her quietly, never taking my mouth from her perfect flesh. "Do you want me to make you come, baby?"

A high-pitched purr comes from the back of her throat.

I open my mouth and suck at her lips, dragging my tongue inside, licking every fucking inch of her like I own this pussy—like I own *her*. And some dark, possessive part of me wants to hear her say I do.

"Tell me you're mine."

I slip two fingers inside her, pumping and groaning at

how hot and wet and perfectly snug she is.

"I'm yours, Garrett," She moans softly. "Oh God . . . I'm yours."

I lift Callie's leg higher, adding a third pumping finger and grazing her swollen, rigid little clit with my teeth.

"Always?" My voice is demanding, harsh.

Slowly, Callie opens her eyes and gazes down at me.

"Always," she whispers, touching my cheek, my jaw. "I've always been yours."

And I smile against her skin. "Good answer."

Then I give her what she needs, what we both want—I suck and feast on her, fucking her with my fingers and rubbing firm, constant circles on her clit with my tongue. She comes so hard, clamping down around me, her head against the wall, back arching, her mouth open, gasping silently.

When it's over, I kiss her thigh, her hip and stomach, reverently. I stand up and kiss her pouty mouth. She laughs against my lips, sounding a little silly, a lot satisfied.

The kiss deepens and she makes that purring sound in the back of her throat that drives me crazy. We turn together, like we're dancing, and fall on the mattress, nipping at each other, laughing because it feels so good.

Callie rises up on her knees, tugging my sweatpants down my legs. My cock springs up, thick and so ready.

"Your turn." She wiggles her eyebrows.

She crawls over me, ass in the air—so I smack it. Callie giggles, dips her head and licks her way up my dick like it's her favorite flavor Popsicle. She sucks at the head and pumps me with her hand—making my vision go fucking white behind my eyelids. She takes me in her mouth, nudging the back of her throat, and bobs her pretty head up and down—sloppy and sucking and so god damn good.

Nope . . . nope . . . too good.

I pull her up, under her arms, bringing her face up to mine.

"I don't want to come in your mouth tonight." I kiss her harshly. "I want to fuck you, baby." I kiss her again, lashing with my tongue. "Can I fuck you, Callie?" I want to pound into her, ride her pussy until she forgets her name and only knows mine. "Will you let me fuck you, baby?"

She moans, breathing hard.

And then she smiles.

"Well . . . since you asked so nicely."

I roll her under me. Her legs are spread and her sweet lips glisten with how much she wants me. And my cock is *right there* at her opening, ready to push and slide into all that slick tightness.

But I stop. Because my dick is bare . . . and we really need a condom. And because I wasn't exactly thinking with the brain above my shoulders, I left my wallet in the Jeep.

"God damn it," I growl. "Do you have condoms?"

She shakes her head.

Going outside half-naked in the icy rain is going to be hard on my hard-on. But, in the end . . . worth it.

"I left my wallet in the Jeep." I press my lips to her forehead. "I'll be right back."

I go to move, but Callie holds my wrist.

"Or . . . or we could not use anything."

I freeze. Because this is a big deal for us. We were here before, a thousand years ago, when we were young and stupid and invincible. It didn't end well.

"Callie?"

"I'm on the pill, Garrett." Her eyes are big and vulnerable. It makes me shake with the need to protect her, from everything and for always. "And I trust you."

And suddenly, what was playful and dirty . . . becomes something different. Something more and meaningful, and loaded with more emotions than I can name.

Everything I feel for her is right there on my face. How much I want this, how I would die before I ever did anything to hurt her, how I need to know that she means it.

"Are you sure, Cal?"

"I want to . . ." she whispers, taking my hand and bringing it to her breast. "I want to be close to you like that again. Feel you . . . just you and me."

"It's only ever been you."

She smiles softly, understanding. "Me too."

Callie tugs on my arm and I cover her with my body. The slide of our skin is like the strike of a match, reigniting all that heat—making us burn even hotter. But there's gentleness now too.

I need her to know how much she means to me, want her to feel it with every move I make.

I cup her face in my hands, then I kiss her soft and I kiss her long. Callie's hips rise, gyrating, sliding her slick pussy all along my hard shaft—calling to me. I shift back, then drag the head of my cock to her opening. I watch her face as I nudge my hips forward, sinking all the way in, in one full push, until I'm buried to the hilt. Callie's mouth opens, gasping for air, and she clamps down all around me, clasping me inside her.

And the feel of her . . . Jesus . . . she's so snug around me, so wet and hot. I feel everything—every breath and beat of her heart. I flex my hips, shallow at first, then longer strokes, pulling almost all the way out, just so I can slide back in.

And it's so fucking good.

It's like I lose the ability to form sentences—there are only words, grunts, and gasps. *Deeper, yes, harder and more . . . always more.* There's only her gripping heat, my pounding hips, and our moaning, kissing lips.

I thrust faster, harsher, our bodies slapping—and Callie takes it all, clinging to my shoulders until she's going tight all around me. Squeezing and contracting—she comes whimpering my name against the shell of my ear. And that's all it takes to push me over. I stroke one last time and then I'm filling her, coming in thick, hot pulses, deep inside her.

We're silent for a few moments, just holding on to each other, quaking with the aftershocks.

Slowly, I lift my head, finding her eyes, reaching for the words so I can give them to her. "Callie, I . . . I—"

"I love you too, Garrett." Shiny tears rise in her eyes, making them glisten. "I never stopped. I think I'm going to love you forever."

I'm already nodding, kissing her. And my voice is thick with all that I feel for her. "I love you, Callie—I always have. Always."

Later, we lie quiet and content—I've set the alarm on my phone, so I can take off in a few hours, before morning. I'm just about to drift off when Callie scrapes her teeth along my shoulder. "Hey, you know what I was just thinking?"

I don't open my eyes. "How happy you are that I couldn't wait until tomorrow to see you?

"Yes, that's true." There's a lovely smile in her voice. "And you know what else?"

"What?"

"We should've gotten me a new bed years ago. So much more comfortable than the floor."

I chuckle. "God bless beds with springs that don't squeak."

Callie settles in against me, warm and languid, brushing a good-night kiss against my chest.

"Amen."

CHAPTER
Seventeen

Callie

In December, the days seem to speed up—rolling, blurring, blending—into each other, a wonderful swirl of school, my parents, and Garrett.

Garrett.

We're going strong and steady—embedding ourselves into each other's lives with every passing day. It's exhilarating—fantastic—I love him, want him, think about him all the time. Some nights I dream of him—sultry, gliding dreams—where I swear I can feel the drag of his lips, the touch of his hand and the hot press of his body. And when I wake up, I get to see him—act out every decadent moment of those dreams.

I know we have to talk about what happens at the end of the year, but we don't—not yet. Right now we're just enjoying each other—reveling in this beautiful limbo of the now, with no regrets.

The kids really throw themselves into the show. And with

my parents more mobile and on the mend, I have a little more time than I did at the start of the school year. I play music for the kids while we work on painting the sets—the soundtrack to *Mamma Mia* and another one of my forever favorites, *Grease 2*. I hear them talk to each other, but more, they talk to me— open up about their home lives, their friends, their dreams, their fears.

Layla's parents are having money problems and she's worried their furniture store will go out of business and they'll have to move. She couldn't handle being a new girl at a new school, where she doesn't know anyone. David's grandmother kicked him out of the house—he didn't have a real room there anyway, just the couch, he tells me, trying to play it off like it doesn't bother him, like it doesn't hurt. But his eyes tell a different story. He swears he's lucky—he has good friends who let him crash at their places—friends who treat him more like family than his own family ever did.

After the homecoming queen nomination prank, it was a rough few days for Simone—she shut down, withdrew, stopped participating. I took her aside one day in class and told her I was devastated for her, livid on her behalf. I told her I would give anything to body swap with a random seventeen-year-old girl—*Freaky Friday* style—so I could get back at every one of the little shit-bastard-assholes who was trying to make a joke out of her. And I think that conversation helped, because Simone told me she knew what she was going to do, that she was going to homecoming. I drove her to the Consignment Closet, in Hammitsburg, where we found a black lace and tulle dress that was beautiful and badass . . . just like her. Toby "Merman" Gessler escorted her onto the field the night of the homecoming game—and every one of my students was there with me, shouting and clapping and cheering her on. Simone didn't win the crown that night, but she won the respect of every student in Lakeside—even the ones who tried to break her.

These days, Simone is taking cosmetology classes at night, at the local Vo-tech, and she plans to take business classes there over the summer. She doesn't want to go to college, but hopes to work at and eventually own her own salon here in town when she graduates high school. Michael's older brother had to drop out of college to go to rehab—his second stint. His love-hate of heroin started right here in high school, because, at least according to my students, there's no drug they can't get within five minutes in this building. You just have to know who to ask, and apparently, the entire student body seems to know who those people are.

It's fascinating to me, how there's this whole other teenage universe that operates in the shadows of adult awareness. It's a school, but it's also its own society, with its own rules and rituals—a condensed, mirror reflection of the outside world.

One night, while I'm sleeping at Garrett's, we're awakened by the sound of screaming fire trucks and police cars. It's across town, but Lakeside is small enough that the commotion feels close—just a few miles away. Snoopy spins in circles and barks in panicked warning at the door. I call my parents, and Garrett calls his. It turns out there's a fire—at Baygrove Park—a big one. The park, the swings, and the surrounding trees are reduced to ash. It doesn't spread to the nearby houses, but it's a close call.

By morning, everyone's heard the news . . . the fire wasn't an accident. It was set on purpose—someone in Lakeside is an arsonist.

Two days after the fire, I'm in the main office with Mrs. Cockaburrow, who is helping me make extra copies of the *Little Shop of Horrors* script for my class. The kids have school issued iPads, and the district has a Go Green policy, but for blocking and notes—only a hard copy script will really do.

"Thanks, Mrs. Cockaburrow," I say.

She smiles and shuffles back behind her desk, eyeing Miss McCarthy's closed office door the way researchers watch a volcano that's overdue for an eruption.

I walk back to the auditorium, just as the school police officer, John Tearney, is approaching the door. I remember John from high school—not fondly.

"John? What's going on?"

He pauses at the door, eyes raking over me, making me think of the medical shows my mother watches—the ones where patients always end up with some exotic worm crawling under their skins.

"Is David Burke in this class?"

I step in front of him, putting myself between him and the door.

"Yes. Why?"

"Gotta bring him in for questioning, about the fire."

My stomach turns to a lead ball in my abdomen.

"Are you arresting him?"

"Not yet. For now, I just want to question him."

I delve deep into my legal knowledge—most of which comes from watching *Law & Order* through the years.

"He's a minor . . . do you have his grandmother's permission to question him? She's his guardian."

Tearney's jaw twitches with annoyance. "What are you, his lawyer?"

I square my shoulders and lift my chin. "No. I'm his teacher. And David's in class right now, so you can't have him."

"This is a police investigation, Callie. Don't tell me who I can and can't have. Move out of the fucking way."

I don't move. I lean in.

"I know you. I remember you. I remember when you were a senior trying to slip roofies into freshman drinks at after-parties." I get right in his face, hissing like a momma cobra snake. "I know you."

His mouth twists and he leers down at me. "Wow. I guess you can take the girl out of Jersey, but you can't take the bitch out of the girl, huh."

"Hey!"

I turn at the sound of Garrett's voice. His *furious* voice. He's standing in the hallway, a few feet away, with a group of students behind him.

"Watch your mouth, Tearney."

A rumble of whispers, a few giggles, and one "Oh shit" come from the teenagers behind him.

"Garrett, it's fine."

He shakes his head, jaw clenched and eyes on fire.

"Nope, not fine. Not even a little."

"Do we have a problem?" Tearney asks, puffing out his chest like a meathead monkey.

Oh, for Christ sakes.

"Yeah—you talking to her like that is a major problem for me."

And out come the kids' phones. A cacophony of clicking shutters and pinging recording buttons echo through the hall. It's possible we're on Facebook Live.

"Stop it." I glare at them. "Put your phones away!"

Tearney steps towards Garrett. "I don't like your tone. You threatening a police officer?"

Garrett doesn't have it in him to back down—it's not how he's made. "Only if you want to hide behind your badge. Otherwise . . . I'm just threatening *you*."

"What in the holy hell is happening around here?" Miss McCarthy yells, marching up to us, slicing through the tension with her presence alone.

Tearney steps back from Garrett, his shoulders falling just a bit.

"I want to question David Burke about the Baygrove Park fire. Miss Carpenter is taking issue with me pulling him out of her class."

"He doesn't have a warrant," I explain. "He doesn't have permission from David's guardian."

Miss McCarthy nods. "I'll bring David to my office. We'll talk there." She looks hard at Tearney. "All of us."

"But, Miss McCarthy—"

"Callie," she cuts me off. "In all the years you've known me, have I ever given you the impression that I'm a pushover?"

"No. No, you haven't."

"Do you honestly think I would let one of my kids be mistreated? By anyone?" Her gaze drifts around the hallway, then comes back to me. "These little shitheads are my whole life."

I take a breath and let it out slowly. "Okay."

I open the auditorium door and the group of us walk down the aisle. I scan up and down the seats.

"Where's David?"

Layla's eyes are wide and worried.

"He . . . he left."

And so begins the manhunt for David Burke—Lakeside's very own Billy the Kid. Parents are called, a search warrant is issued for David's grandmother's house, even though he doesn't live there anymore. More officers show up at the school, pulling David's friends down to the office to question them. Rumors flare, and spread and grow—like the fire itself.

There's posts on social media that say David was spotted in New York City, pretending to be a homeless man. Another says he killed someone in the park and started the fire to burn the body. There are subtweets and retweets, suspicion about police stakeouts and undercover cops infiltrating the school. But for days . . . there's no David.

The following Saturday, I stay over at Garrett's and in the morning we go to breakfast at his parents' house. All three of Garrett's brothers are there.

"Have you heard anything, Callie? David's in your class, right—do you know where he is?" Ryan asks me across the kitchen table.

"She hasn't heard anything," Garrett answers for me.

"Callie?" Ryan nudges—seeming less like Garrett's older

brother at the moment and more like a cop than ever before.

Ryan's wife, Angela, feels it too. "You're not on the clock, babe."

"Leave her alone, Ry," Garrett answers again, holding my hand under the table. "She cares about the kid. She's upset."

"If she cares about him, she needs to tell me where he is," Ryan shoots back. "This is serious shit. The whole street could've burned down . . . homes . . . people could've gotten hurt."

"I don't know where he is, Ryan," I tell him simply, because it's the truth. "I haven't heard anything."

Ryan takes a bite of his bagel and turns his brown eyes on Garrett. "Do your players know where he's at?"

Garrett shrugs. "Probably. But I'm not going to ask them."

"Why not?"

"Because I'm not going to make them lie to me."

Garrett leans forward over the table. "You can't be that old Ryan—you have to remember what it was like in high school. It's them against us. Deny until death, teenage honor code. I guarantee you every kid in that school knows where David Burke is right now . . . and I can also guarantee not a single one of them is going to tell us. Period."

That night, after my parents have gone to bed and the dishes are done, around ten o'clock, I get a text. I'd given all the kids my cell, because they're my performers—I told them to text me if something came up, if they couldn't make rehearsals or needed a ride.

It's David. I'm in the backyard. Come outside?

I'm not shocked that he knows my parents' address. I've been back long enough to remember that everyone knows where everyone lives in small towns. I go out the sliding glass doors, onto the patio, and David emerges from the darkness of the bushes that line the yard. He looks tired, his dirty-blond hair lying limp and too much tension for someone his age tightening his eyes.

"David . . ." I sigh. "Are you all right?"

He shrugs, forcing a smile. "I'm all right. But listen, I need a favor. I can't trust my friends . . . they're morons. But, I'm gonna be gone for a while . . . so . . . can I leave my hedgehog with you? Will you take care of her for me?"

David lifts the carrier in his hand—a hamster cage—and sets it on the patio table. I spot the telltale ball of black and beige quills in the corner, peeking out from the pile of shredded newspaper bedding.

"Her name's Pisser."

"Pisser?" I ask.

David lifts one shoulder. "It seemed right. She pisses on me every time I hold her."

"Oh." I nod. "Okay. Yes, of course I'll take of her for you." I sit down in the chair and gesture for him to sit next to me. "Do you want something to eat?"

"Nah, I'm good."

"Where . . . where are you going?"

"Where they can't find me. North Carolina maybe or—"

"No. No, listen to me, you don't have to do that. I'll stay with you, okay? We'll go together and we'll explain to the police that you didn't do this. We'll make them understand."

David looks at me, and the floodlight above him gives his

face a pale, ethereal glow, making him seem even more fragile. Childlike.

"But I did do it, Miss Carpenter," he confesses softly. "I set the fire."

And it feels like I've been punched in the stomach. Because . . . that never occurred to me. I was so sure they had it wrong, just rounding up the usual suspects. The David I've come to know is kind and talented—protective of his friends. I can't imagine him being so . . . destructive.

"Oh." I shake my head. "David, why?"

He looks down, kicking a pebble with the tip of his sneaker, looking small and lost.

"I don't know. I wish I didn't. I don't know why I do the things I do sometimes."

And I just want to hug him. Keep him safe, tell him it will all be okay and not have it be a lie.

He rises. "I gotta go, now."

I dart out of my chair. "No—wait—listen to me. David, there will an after . . . an after this. This will pass. But the choices you make right now will affect the rest of your life." I hold out my hand to him, begging. "Please, trust me. We can get you a public defender or a pro bono attorney—that means they'll work for free. I can help you. Let me help you."

"They're going to send me to jail, Miss Carpenter."

"I know you're scared, but you can't run. You can't run away. That will only make it worse."

He shakes his head. "Miss Carpenter—"

"There's so much you can be, David. So much you can do with your life. It's not too late, I swear. Please don't throw that away. The other kids look up to you—I saw it the very first day. They believe in you . . . and I believe in you too."

His eyes jump to mine. And I wonder if anyone in his life has ever said those words to him. Did anyone stick with him, support him, or did they all just cut and run?

"You do?"

I nod. And my voice is firm, insistent . . . willing him to believe it too.

"I do. I think you are capable of doing wonderful things. Some incredible things with your life. You just have to . . . wait, take a breath . . . and make the right choice. To do better. And I'll be there to help you."

"Do you promise?" David asks hesitantly. Hopefully.

I take his hand. "I promise."

David comes inside after that. I make us sandwiches and tea, and we talk. And then an hour later, I call Garrett. He comes to pick us up, and together we drive to the police station.

Garrett calls his brother and Ryan meets us in the lobby of the police station. Before Ryan takes him in the back, David turns to me.

"Miss Carpenter?"

"Yes?"

"I just want you to know . . . you're a really good teacher."

There's a pressure in my chest that makes my bones bow, like I could break open at any moment.

I hug him, wishing I could do more. "Thank you, David."

"Watch out for Layla, okay?" he says against my shoulder. "She gets sad sometimes."

I nod. "I will."

Then we part. Garrett puts his hand on David's shoulder, squeezing. "You're doing the right thing, David, and I know it's not easy. I'm proud of you."

David nods, his face tight.

Ryan smacks his brother's shoulder and Garrett nods. "I'll talk to you soon."

I take a step towards Ryan, dropping my voice so only he can hear. "You make sure he's okay."

His eyes are kind, understanding. "I'll do everything I can for him."

Then he turns around, takes David by the arm, and guides him through the door.

I stare at the spot where David just stood and my vision goes blurry. Garrett is right behind me—I feel the heat of his chest, his presence . . . his strength.

"Callie?"

"I didn't think it would be like this." My throat is closing, my voice raspy and strangled.

"Like what?" Garrett asks gently.

"I thought teaching would just be a job. I'd do the year and go back to California. Simple." My chest tightens, crushing me. "I didn't think I'd care about them so much."

Garrett holds my hand, threading our fingers together. "Kids sneak up on you. They have the uncanny ability to be amazing . . . when you least expect it. They're easy to care about."

The tears come then, scalding and heavy behind my eyelids. And my lungs swell with too much feeling. Because David's not a bad kid, not even a little. He's a good kid . . . who did a really bad thing. And he doesn't even know why.

And that's so much harder. So much sadder.

"I didn't . . . I didn't think they'd break my heart."

And I sob, the grief of all that's happened breaking loose and flowing from me.

Garrett pulls me against him, pressing my face against his shoulder, rubbing my back and kissing my hair.

"Yeah. Yeah, they'll do that too."

The next morning I walk into the auditorium and am met by thirty somber, dejected faces. The news about David turning himself in, that he's sitting in a jail cell at this very moment, has already torn its way through the school. I put my bag down on a chair in the front row, and my rib cage is filled with concrete.

"We have to finish blocking today. Turn to scene seventeen in your scripts."

For a moment, none of them move. They just look at me.

"That's it?" Michael asks quietly. "That's all you're gonna say?"

I clear my throat, fumbling with the pages of the script in my hands. "Um . . . Bradley, you're the understudy for Seymour. You need to start learning those lines. I'll have to pick someone from one of the other theater classes to play the dentist."

"No." Layla stands up, her voice unusually firm. "I'm not doing this with him. I'm not kissing him."

Bradley scoffs. "I don't want to swap spit with you either, loser."

"Shut up, dickface!"

"Screw you!"

"Stop it!" I slap the script down on the chair. "Don't do this."

"What about David?" Simone asks softly. "Don't you care about him at all?"

The quiet question slices me to the bone. And all the sorrow that I locked down, locked up tight last night, crests, threatening to spill over.

"The show must go on." I look at each of their sad little faces. "Have you ever heard that expression? It's true—in theater and in life. The show is bigger than any of us—bigger than you or me . . . or David. He can't be a part of this anymore, but we'll go on and do it without him."

Toby stares like he's never seen me before. "That's cold, Miss Carpenter."

"Life is cold, Toby."

And I try, I try so hard to be *cold*—to be strong. But my eyes burn and my heart aches.

"Life is going to knock you down, every one of you. Some way, at some time, something unexpected is going to come and hit you right in the knees. Knock the wind out of you."

Memories of me and Garrett wash through me, saturate me—submerge me in the remembered feeling of my whole world being turned upside down and shaken out.

"And I wish I could protect you from it." My voice cracks. "I would do that for you—for each of you if I could." I shake my head. "But I can't."

I wipe at the moisture filling my eyes, breathing deeply. "So, if I teach you nothing else this year—let it be this: the show goes on. *You* have to go on, because *life* goes on. Even when you're hurting, even when it's hard—you have to pick yourself up, lean on the people around you . . . and go on."

They're still and subdued for several long moments after that. Absorbing the words.

"I'll do it." Michael raises his hand. "I can do David's part. I already know the blocking and lines." He shrugs, smiling self-deprecatingly, adjusting his glasses. "I'm practically the real-life Seymour anyway."

My smile to Michael is grateful . . . and proud. I glance at Layla. "Are you okay with that?"

She looks at Michael, and then her eyes rise to me. "Yeah. Yeah, that works for me."

"Good." I nod. "Okay . . . scene seventeen."

And together . . . we go on.

CHAPTER
Eighteen

Garrett

"**W**hat the hell do you mean you didn't put up a tree?"

We'd gone to Foster's cut-down-your-own-tree Tree Farm this afternoon and spotted a nice eight-foot Douglas fir for Callie's parents' house. Then Callie kissed me next to it, one thing led to another—and later we walked out of there with the tree and soaked jackets and pine needles in our hair from getting busy in the new-fallen snow.

Now we're strolling down Main Street, checking out the tables of baked goods and crafts at the annual Lakeside Christmas Bazaar—talking about her holidays in San Diego. She glances sideways at me from beneath her red knit hat—the tip of her nose all cute and pink from the cold. Makes me want to bite it.

"Well, it was just me—seemed like a lot of work for one person. I put out a table tree."

"A table tree?" I'm disgusted. "What a sad little life you

had. Thank God you've got me now to rescue you from it."

She rolls her eyes. Then tugs me over to a table of graphic novels based on the classics. She buys *The Count of Monte Cristo* and a few others for David. I'm taking Callie down to visit him tomorrow—three days before Christmas—at the Jamesburg Home for Boys. She's talked to him on the phone a few times and he seems like he's doing okay—sitting tight while his public defender negotiates a plea deal for him.

"Hi, Coach D; hey, Miss Carpenter!"

"Hey, guys."

"S'up, Coach Daniels! Looking good, Miss Carpenter!"

"Hi, kids."

It happens every few minutes—we're spotted and greeted by gaggles of our students as we thread our way through the crowd. It's an occupational hazard—as is being cornered by an overeager parent and subjected to an impromptu conference.

"Darpenter forever!" a faceless voice calls from behind us. And Callie and I both laugh.

She stops on the sidewalk for a moment, threading her arm through mine, leaning against me, gazing down the street. The wreath-laden street lamps and strings of twinkling white lights make stars in her eyes.

"I forgot about this," she says softly, watching coat-and hat-covered families—pretty much the whole town—bustling around, talking and laughing, drinking spiked eggnog and hot chocolate. "I forgot how this feels. Being home for Christmas."

There's something different, warmer, about Christmas in a small, old town. It makes you feel like Norman Rockwell's paintings and *It's a Wonderful Life* are real—like you're living inside them.

"It's magical." Callie sighs.

And she looks so pretty, I have to fucking kiss her. I press my mouth against hers, tasting winter on her lips. Then I whisper wickedly in her ear, "Come back to my house tonight, and I'll give magical a whole new meaning."

She giggles . . . and later, comes back to my house where I make hot, sweaty good on that promise.

Over winter break, Callie spends the day with her parents, then switches off with her sister and spends most of her nights with me. The Thursday night before Christmas, we're at Chubby's. "Dancing Queen" by ABBA is on the jukebox, and Callie's leaning over the bar, singing along with Sydney, her old theater friend. They've been talking again, rekindling their friendship, and I'm not going to lie—I'm glad. Because there's been a voice, buzzing around my head for the last few weeks, that says the longer Callie's here, the more roots she revives . . . the more likely she is to stay.

For now, I shake my head, kicking those thoughts away—focusing on the here and now and what's in front of me.

And what's in front of me . . . is Callie's perfect ass. Round and bitable in snug jeans. The things I can do with that ass—I take a long drag on my beer—can't wait to get her back to my place tonight.

The ABBA song ends, and "Should've Been a Cowboy" by Toby Keith takes its place. Callie comes back to our table, carrying another round for herself and me and Dean. She plants herself on my lap, singing with Dean about California, women, whiskey, and gold. She's smiling, laughing, and it all feels so damn good.

Until it all goes straight to shit.

And Becca Saber approaches our table, her blue eyes trained right on me. And I swear to Christ she sounds exactly like Maleficent, from that Disney movie I watched with my niece Frankie a couple weeks ago.

"Well, well, well . . . Garrett Daniels . . . it's been a long time."

Fuck.

This isn't gonna be pretty.

Callie stops singing and looks up at Becca—an open, innocent expression on her face.

"And Callie Carpenter. I didn't know you were back in town. Isn't this just like old times."

The last I heard, Becca had married a businessman and was living in North Jersey. I think she's a mortician or something.

"Hello, Becca," Callie says.

There's a wicked gleam in Becca's narrowed eyes, something sharp and dangerous. "How funny is this?" She hooks her thumb back towards the bar. "My husband's in real estate; we own the parking lot outside. I was in the area and decided to pick up the rent check from Sydney . . . and I run into you two. Are you guys like . . . back together again?"

Callie smiles, cool, calm, and totally collected. "Yeah, we are."

"That's adorable. God, Garrett, I haven't seen you since that night . . . up at Rutgers, remember?"

Callie goes stiff on my lap.

"We were so drunk . . . we got pretty wild that night. Good times." She tilts her head towards the door. "Well, I have

to get going." Her eyes graze over me, and it feels cold . . .
slimy . . . like an alien invasion. "Make sure you hold onto him
this time, Callie. He is just . . . incredible."

Her head swivels away from us.

"Oh, hey, Dean."

Dean dips his chin. "She-devil." He wags his finger. "You
make sure you watch out for those priests now. One good
splash of holy water and it's"—he waves his arms—"straight
back home to hell for you."

"Bye, Dean," Becca says dryly. Then she walks away.

The table is silent then. I watch the emotions scatter over
Callie's face. Her forehead scrunches and a little line appears
between her brows that I want to smooth away for her.

"Did . . . did you fuck her?"

There is no good answer to that question.

Okay—*no* would be a good answer . . . but that's not an
answer I can give.

"It was a long time ago."

Callie turns away from me, staring down at her hands on
the table. Then she stands up. "I'm gonna go."

I rise from the chair, but Callie puts up her hand. "I don't
want to be around you right now."

And she walks the fuck out.

I look at Dean, who waves his hand. "Go, Romeo . . . go.
I'll take care of the tab."

"Thanks, man."

And I'm following Callie out the door into the empty
parking lot.

"Callaway! Hey, where are you going?"

She doesn't turn around. "Home."

"I'll drive you."

The light of her phone casts her face in a pale, bluish glow.

"No—I'll take an Uber."

I snort. "That'll take an hour. The closest thing to an Uber around here is the back of Mickey Kadeski's bike." I step closer and she doesn't move away. "Come on, Callie. Get in the car."

She looks up at me and it's all there in her eyes—anger and betrayal and so much hurt it knocks the breath out of me. But then she nods tightly and gets in my Jeep.

Callie

*B*reathe . . . *just breathe* . . .

A part of me knows I'm being silly—stupid. I'm a thirty-four-year-old woman. An adult. This shouldn't be wrecking me like it is.

Garrett slept with Becca Saber. He fucked her, touched her. His mouth kissed her; her hands touched him. All of him.

I fold my arms around myself and a groan slips from my lips. Because it hurts. Hurts just as much as it would've if I'd found out when I was seventeen. And it's like that seventeen-year-old girl has possessed me—like she's running the show.

"You lied to me."

From the corner of my eye, Garrett shakes his head while he drives.

"I didn't lie."

"Oh, give me a fucking break!" I turn to him. "Do you

think I'm an idiot? I brought up her name in the grocery store weeks ago! And you didn't say anything—*that's* a lie."

His hands tighten on the steering wheel. "It doesn't matter."

"It matters to me! And you knew that—and that's why you lied."

"It was seventeen fucking years ago! You're being totally ridiculous right now."

"Don't do that! Don't you dare minimize my feelings. You knew I'd be upset so you took the chicken-shit way out and you lied. I'm allowed to be pissed off about that."

A minute later, we pull into Garrett's driveway.

"You said you'd drive me home," I hiss.

Garrett's eyes are two hard black stones and his jaw is granite. "We need to talk about this. That's not a conversation I'm going to have with your parents in the next room."

Fine. Fine—I feel like yelling anyway.

I yank open the car door and stomp up the walkway. Garrett opens the front door, and Snoopy's already there to greet us in the foyer. The little dog's presence gives me a moment of calm, of rationality. I pet him under his chin.

"Hey, Snoopy. It's okay."

Garrett walks to the kitchen and Snoopy and I follow. He opens the back sliding door and lets the dog out. Then he turns to me, and his eyes are softer. Regretful.

"I'm sorry, Callie. You're right. I should have told you." He shakes his head. "It just . . . it didn't matter to me and after all this time, I didn't want it to matter to *us*. Not when we were happy and rebuilding what we have. I didn't want it to screw things up between us."

My seventeen-year-old self is not impressed.

"How would you feel if it was me . . . if I'd screwed Dean?"

"That's not even the same thing! Becca wasn't your best friend. That would only be the same if I hooked up with Sydney."

Something flashes on his face—a memory. Guilt.

"Oh my God! Did you screw Sydney too?"

Garrett shakes his head. "No! No . . . there was this one night when we ran into each other at the bar. And we talked—talked about you, actually—and it was late and we were drunk and there was this one moment when it seemed like . . . but nothing happened."

I tear my hands through my hair and yell, "Jesus Christ, Garrett!"

Then Garrett is yelling back. "Nothing happened! Why are you being like this?"

"Because, every single time we were together, it was beautiful and it meant something to me. And to know, that after I left you just spread that around and became this . . . whore . . . that kills me!"

He points his finger at me. "You don't get to do that! You don't get to call me a whore because of what I did to fix what you broke."

My anger makes me jump up and down. "That's a line from *Grey's Anatomy*!"

"It's a good show!" Garrett shouts. Then he shakes his head. "Except for how Derek went out—that was fucked up. It'll never be okay."

And a part of me inside wants to laugh. But I can't.

"Don't be cute," I tell him harshly. "Not now."

Garrett's shoulders go loose, slumping. "What do you

want me to do here, Cal? I can't go back and undo it. How do I fix this?"

The air rushes from my nose, like I'm a scorned dragon.

"Was she the first girl you were with after we broke up?"

Garrett nods, stiff and tight, and the knife in my stomach twists in a little bit deeper.

"When? Where? Where did it happen?"

He grabs my shoulders and looks me in the eyes. "I'm not doing this with you—I'm not doing a play-by-play recap. It's useless and it'll only hurt you. It was after California, after we broke up. If I could go back and change it, I would, but I can't. The end."

I let out a shuddery breath. And I know he's right; I know I'm being crazy.

I close my eyes and breathe, my voice coming out small and thin. "It hurts that it was her."

"I'm sorry, Callie."

"Anyone else I could . . . but why did it have to be Becca?"

His brow furrows and his voice is tight. Pained.

"Because she was there."

I shake my head at him. "You're you—lots of girls would've been there for you. Why did you sleep with *her*? Did you . . . was it . . . to get back at me?"

His brow furrows, like he's only now considering the question for the first time.

"Maybe. Yeah."

"But why? Our breakup was mutual."

He laughs then . . . and it sounds bitter.

"No, Callie . . . it wasn't. Nothing about it was mutual."

The moments replay in my head. That morning in my

dorm room in California, when Garrett and I said goodbye.

"I don't understand. We talked about it. You agreed—you said the distance was too hard. That we'd grown apart."

"What else was I supposed to say? What was I supposed to do? Cry? Beg? I wanted to—I could see you dumping me from a mile away. But I was an eighteen-year-old kid; I had some fucking pride."

Then Garrett touches my face, his hand cupping my jaw. "When I came out to California to see you, you were happy. It was the first time I'd seen your smile—your real smile—in months. And I couldn't . . . I wasn't going to take that away from you. Not for anything. So, I lied, said it was better if we broke up—that it was okay for you to move on without me. And I'd do it again."

When I left Lakeside for college I was depressed. I had been for a while. I didn't know it then, but now, as an adult, looking back, I can see the signs. And I had my reasons. Reasons that Garrett and I didn't talk about then. But we need to do it now—there are things I need to say. So I look up into his eyes and rip off the scab.

"I wanted the baby. I wanted it so much . . . and I couldn't tell you that."

"You could've told me *anything*."

I got pregnant in January of our senior year. We didn't tell anyone—not Dean or Sydney, not our parents or Coach Saber, not Colleen or any of Garrett's brothers.

It was *ours*. Our secret . . . and then, just a few weeks later . . . our loss.

"No. I couldn't tell you that. Not after we lost it . . . and you were happy."

"I wasn't happy, Callie." Garrett shakes his head, his jaw

grinding.

"Yes, you were."

"No, I—"

"I remember, Garrett! I remember what you said, in your room that day." I close my eyes, and I'm right there again. "I remember what the rain smelled like."

The window was open in Garrett's bedroom and a curtain of rain was coming down outside. He was behind me, his warm, solid body pressed against every inch of mine—holding me, rocking me—his palm on my stomach. He kissed my neck and whispered in my ear.

"This is a good thing, Callie. It's the best thing that could've happened. It's out of our hands. We don't have to decide if we're going to have it, or keep it, or give it up for adoption. We have our whole lives now."

Tragedies are supposed to bring couples closer or tear them apart. That's not how it was for us. We didn't break up. We still went to prom, took graduation pictures, we still loved each other.

But for me, it was like . . . that tiny shard of glass stuck in the most tender part of your foot—you can't see it, but you feel it there.

"When you said adoption, I didn't know what you were talking about! It was like I didn't even know you. Because I had it all planned out, Garrett. You would play football and I would go to night school and our parents would help us raise the baby. And we'd get married and buy a house on the lake."

It was the first time—ever—that I felt like Garrett and I were going in different directions. Like I couldn't count on him.

On *us*.

Our future wasn't set in stone. It could change. It could all go away in an instant, and what would I be then? Who would I be? I didn't even know who I was without him. If I wasn't Garrett Daniels' girl . . . I wasn't anyone.

"Callie, look at me." Garrett's voice is raw and his eyes are red-rimmed. "I was an idiot. A young, stupid kid . . . who loved you more than anything in the whole world. And you were so sad. And there was nothing I could do . . . I just wanted to say something that would make it better for you. I didn't know it was the wrong thing. That's all it was, all it ever was."

Hot, heavy tears streak down my face. For all we felt. For all the things we didn't say.

"I couldn't shake it, Garrett. I tried, but I couldn't let it go. It was with me all the time." I grasp his wrists, holding on to him. "And we were so lucky—both of us . . . we didn't even know how lucky we were. We had everything—we were healthy and smart and beautiful, with amazing families and friends who loved us. We were blessed. And it was the first time that something bad had happened. Out of our control. And I couldn't let it go . . . it turned everything upside down.

"And then, when my mom brought up going away to school, when I looked at the pictures and the sunshine and the buildings and so many different faces, it felt . . . better. Like I could do anything, be anyone. I didn't have to remember how much it hurt, or be afraid of losing you because I could be someone new, someone stronger . . . a fresh start."

My chest shudders and my voice breaks. "And I had to go. I had to go, Garrett."

He strokes my cheek, his voice aching.

"I know. I know you did."

"But it was never about not loving you. Not for a day . . .

not for a minute."

Garrett pulls me against him, hugging me, holding me, rubbing my back. And I feel relieved, lighter in his arms, to have gotten it all out. After all this time.

Then Garrett presses his lips against my hair and rips off his own scab.

"I bought you a ring."

I feel my face pale. And I step back, looking up at him.

"What?"

"Remember when I sold my Joe Namath football?"

"You said you were going to buy a new computer for school."

He nods. "I sold it to buy you a ring." He looks into my eyes. "Because I wanted the baby too. And you. I wanted all of it, Callie."

He takes a step away from me, his voice rough, weighted down with memories. "I carried it around in my pocket, waiting for the right time to ask. I didn't want you to think it was because of the baby—I mean it *was* because of the baby, the timing of it—but it wasn't *just* because of that."

I nod, staring at him.

"And . . . after . . . I didn't want you to think I was asking because we'd lost it." He shakes his head. "There was never a good time. I hesitated. And then . . . you were gone. And it was too late. And I still had that ring in my pocket."

I wipe my face and push a hand through my hair, and focus on something simple.

"What . . . did it look like?"

"Do you want to see it?"

The air rushes from my lungs.

"You still have it?"

The corner of Garrett's mouth inches up and he looks down at the floor.

"Yeah."

He waves his hand for me to follow, and we go upstairs to the spare bedroom. He goes to the closet, shifting boxes around, then takes one down from a shelf in the back. Inside, there are pictures of the two of us, cards and notes . . . the dried, brown-edged boutonniere I pinned to his tuxedo the night of our prom.

Then he's holding a box—small, black leather, with "Zinke Jewelers" embossed in gold.

Slowly, he flicks open the box, and holds it out me. And inside is a tiny, round diamond with a silver band. There are smaller gem chips embedded in the band—all the way around. Light-blue aquamarine and violet alexandrite—our birthstones.

One hand covers my mouth, and my other hand trembles as I take the box from him—my vision blurring with fresh tears as I stare.

"I used to wonder," Garrett says softly, "if you would've liked it. If you would've thought I was crazy." I feel the warmth of his eyes drifting over me, searching. "If you would've said yes."

I inhale a shaky breath.

"I would've loved it. I would've thought you were crazy." My voice cracks. "And I absolutely . . . would've said yes."

I put a hand over my face as it crumples, and I cry. For all our years, our sorrows, and our joys. And I cry with a sweet, piercing relief . . . that somehow we found our way back to each other again.

Garrett's strong arms come around me, pulling me close and safe into his chest. I press my face to him and twist my hands in his shirt . . . holding on to him with everything I have.

"We're going to be all right this time, Callie. I promise. I swear."

Later that night, Garrett and I lay bare beneath the blankets in his bed—him on his back, my cheek on his chest. Snoopy's curled up down near our feet and it's quiet and dark . . . and there are no more tears.

Garrett skims his hand down my spine, and his deep voice splits the silence.

"In the spirit of complete honesty, there's one more thing I have to tell you."

I lift up on my arm, so I can see him. "Okay."

He looks deep into my eyes. "Our entire relationship was based on a lie."

I squint at him. "What?"

Garrett looks up at the ceiling, smiling.

"Remember when I asked you to borrow a quarter, for a soda from the vending machine?"

"Yeah . . . ?"

Garrett's thumb strokes my cheek. "I had like ten bucks in change in my pocket. I just wanted a reason to talk to you."

A laugh bubbles from my lips. And I kiss his warm skin, right over his heart.

"Well . . . you're forgiven. That lie was the best thing that ever happened to me."

He leans up, pressing his lips against mine.

"Me too, Callie. Me too."

CHAPTER Nineteen

Garrett

After New Year's—the school year chugs forward, like a locomotive hurling towards spring. One early Saturday morning, in February, Callie pounces on top of me, in my bed, her bra-less tits bouncing beneath the fabric of one of my Lions T-shirts—her lips peppering my face and neck and chest with hot, quick kisses.

Not a bad way to start the day.

"Wake up . . . wake up, Garrett . . . wake up, wake up, wake up!"

Snoopy hops up next to her and joins the party—licking my face and blasting me with the foul stench of his shit-breath.

I turn my head. "Ah . . . dude. You been eating your turds again? I told you to stop that."

He looks me dead in the face—regretting nothing.

Callie stops kissing me. "Snoopy eats his turds?"

I rub a hand down my face and my voice is scratchy with

235

sleep.

"Yeah. But only in the winter. He thinks they're frozen meat-logs or something."

Callie gags.

I don't know why she's up so early—the sun isn't up yet, and only a slice of light gray streaks the sky. So I take the opportunity to drag her back under the covers with me, pressing our lower halves together, ready to kick Snoopy out and take the kissing to a whole new level.

"Wait, no, don't." She covers my mouth with her hand, blocking me. "There's a reason I woke you up."

"For the fabulous fucking we're about to do?"

She laughs, pecking my lips. "After. But first . . . the green flag's up! I forgot about the flag, Garrett. Isn't that crazy?"

The park service puts a flag out on the lake, letting people know when it's frozen all the way through and safe to skate. When the green flag comes out, practically the whole town shows up—kids play ice hockey and race, couples hold hands, and Girl Scout troops sell cider and hot chocolate on the sidelines.

Callie's eyes are so wide and joyful—her excitement becomes mine.

"Do you think your parents still have your old skates?"

"Are you kidding? They're one step above hoarders—they don't throw anything away."

I tap her ass and sit up. "All right. Let's go get them then—we'll be the first ones out on the ice."

And that's how it goes—our life, here, together—for now.

We work, Callie helps her parents, we go to the movies and dinner. We go out for drinks with Dean and play Cards Against Humanity with Callie's sister and her brother-in-law. Callie drops by the weight room when I'm working out with the team, just to say hi, and I swing by the theater during rehearsals, just to look at her. We cuddle with Snoopy on the couch and spend practically every second we can together.

One Sunday, I go out for my run and leave Callie sleeping warm and pretty in my bed. When I come home, she's dusting the living room, wearing my old football jersey—and seeing my name across her back does things to me. She's got her phone playing "Out in the Street" by Bruce Springsteen, and she's bouncing and dancing and singing—as Snoopy barks along with her, running up and down the couch.

And seeing her—my amazing girl—here in my house, dancing with my dog . . . that does something to me too. And the words tear out of me, clear and true, and straight from my pounding heart.

"I love you. I really fucking love you."

I don't know how I lived without her for all those years and thought it was okay.

Callie's head is tilted, watching me, and the sweetest smile plays over her lips. She throws the dust rag on the floor and jumps onto the couch, using it as a trampoline . . . to jump into my arms. She wraps her legs around my waist and her hands around my shoulders.

"I really love you too, Garrett Daniels."

And then she kisses me.

Running her hands through my hair, making the best sounds. Things get hot pretty quick, and just a few minutes later Callie's back is against the wall and I'm pulling the front of my running shorts down, freeing my cock, and sliding her silky underpants aside. And then I'm pushing inside her.

There's the tight, wet squeeze that makes my lungs seize up and Callie's breathy little voice as she sucks and bites my earlobe.

"Love me, Garrett. Love me, fuck me . . . love me forever."

"Forever," I swear.

My fingers dig into her ass as I pound into her—shaking the pictures on the walls. And Callie writhes against me, rolling those hips, going for it, getting herself off on me. She bites my bottom lip when she comes and the pain and high-pitched whimper in her throat send me flying over the edge with her. I curse as my ass clenches and my cock jerks, spilling deep inside her.

Afterwards, my heart gallops like a racehorse . . . I gotta work on my cardio more.

Callie looks up at me with glazed, satiated eyes . . . and then they flare, widening to the whites.

"Oh shit, you're bleeding! I'm sorry."

I run my tongue over my bottom lip, tasting copper. And then I smile. "Best way to start a Sunday."

Callie

B y March, my parents' soft braces are off their legs. They're still going to physical therapy to strengthen their muscles, they still need to be careful and take it easy around the house, but they're mobile again, driving again—doing God knows what in the Buick again.

The second week in March, Garrett and I fly to San Diego for the weekend for Bruce and Cheryl's wedding. And there's a wonderful, excited pulling sensation in my chest when we get off the plane and make our way through the airport. I love San Diego—the sun, the warmth, the smell of the ocean, the laidback friendliness of the people. It feels invigorating to be back.

Coming back to my apartment is a little stranger.

It's a lot like coming back to your college dorm room after the summer break. It looks the same, but feels different—because you're a little bit different than when you left it. I open the door and Garrett puts our bags down in the small living room, looking around, taking in the brand-new, plastic-covered beige couch—courtesy of Bruce and Cher—the white walls and throw pillows, a few matching gold frames, and the vase of glass lilies on the corner table.

"Looks like you bought out the whole Pottery Barn catalog, huh?" he teases.

I gaze around the room, trying to see it through his eyes. I've always liked a streamlined décor—neat, simple, elegant. But coming from the mishmash warmth of my parents' house all these months, or even Garrett's homey lakeside bachelor-chic place, my apartment feels bare in comparison.

Empty. Cold.

But there's one thing that turns my insides sizzling hot. And that's the view of Garrett's broad, gorgeous body standing in my living room. I love the way he looks here, surrounded by my things—that could become *our* things. I can see us living here together—I can see it so clearly, I practically taste it on my tongue.

Actually making that a reality on the other hand . . . that's more complicated.

Garrett knows Lakeside in and out and over the last few months, I've rediscovered it with him. But now's my chance to show him my city. I bring him to the Fountain Theater, with its giant crystal chandelier, old polished leather seats, and grand red-curtained stage. We hold hands and throw a penny, making a wish, in the magnificent white marble fountain out front that gave the theater its name. I introduce him to my coworkers, the actors and the crew—even Mr. Dorsey comes out of his office to shake Garrett's hand.

And to tell me they can't wait to have me back.

I bring Garrett to Sambuca's, my favorite Italian bistro, downtown and Grindstone Bakery that makes the most orgasmic croissants. We spend all day Saturday in La Jolla—shopping in the boutiques, visiting the gardens, walking along the coast. I show him my dream apartment building that still has vacancies waiting for me, and we spend an hour watching my seals sun themselves on the jetty.

On Sunday, Bruce and Cher get married in an intimate ceremony, in the Japanese Friendship Garden near Balboa Park. Though I've been an absentee best friend, Cher still has me as her maid of honor. I wear a backless silver dress, and

Garrett's eyes burn for me as I walk down the aisle and stand at the altar. I cry when Bruce and Cher say their vows and kiss—they're two of the best people I know. I love them and am so happy they have each other.

The reception is held on a rooftop terrace of the Andaz, in the Gaslamp Quarter. White Chinese lanterns illuminate every table, and glass-enclosed, water lily candles fill the rectangular pool in the center of the terrace. The bright, bursting stars in the midnight sky are our ceiling and the sound of the ocean fills the air. Garrett and I drink and laugh—the last song of the night is "Remember When" by Alan Jackson, and Garrett holds me so close while we rock softly to the music—and I tear up a little then too. What can I say . . . I'm a crier. And love is beautiful.

Garrett is quiet on the ride back to my apartment. I don't turn on the lamp when we walk inside. He loosens his tie, and leans against the window sill, looking out—the city lights glowing on his handsome face and turning the color of his eyes to dark brandy.

"What do you think of San Diego?" I ask him.

But there's so much more in the simple question than just those words.

What I really mean is, could you live here? Would you be happy here? Could you, would you give up the whole amazing life you've built, to come be here with me?

How can I ask him that? To give up his kids, and probably coaching and the things he loves so much? The things that make him who he is?

I can't.

I would never. Just like he won't ask me to stay in Lakeside.

We're stuck.

"I like it," Garrett says. "It's a beautiful city."

He turns and walks up to stand before me, sweeping my hair gently off my cheek. "It's even more beautiful with you in it, Callie."

My blood turns to liquid sugar, and I melt at the sweetness of his words.

I take a breath and push away any sad thoughts. Because we still have time. Garrett and I can still pretend for a little bit longer that we can have everything. Have each other and still keep the lives on opposite sides of the country that we love.

In the meantime . . . *sex.* We can focus on sex. Making love and filthy, fabulous fucking.

Sex with Garrett makes everything better.

I wrap my finger around his tie—reeling him in towards me.

"You know what's super awesome about this apartment?"

His mouth nudges into his sexy grin.

"What's that?"

"The shower—it has a great shower. Specifically, the floor of the shower . . . it's super comfy to kneel on."

I slide my palm to his crotch and stroke his big, thickening cock through his soft, black dress pants. And I run my tongue up his neck slowly, licking over his stubble to his jaw—so he has no doubt what I'm thinking about doing to him.

"Want me to show you?"

"Yes, please," he practically squeaks. I've never heard Garrett squeak—it's hot.

Then he grabs me, caveman style, and throws me over his shoulder, smacking my ass as he carries me down the hall to the bathroom.

Where I give him a very thorough demonstration.

CHAPTER
Twenty

Callie

Sometimes teachers have to learn their own lessons. Sometimes . . . we forget.

For all my bold talk to my students about the unexpected parts of life that will knock you down and steal your breath away, an unspoken part of me figures that Garrett and I are on easy street now. We'd found each other again, worked everything out, and are ready, willing, and able to build a future together.

It's so good between us—so right, so meant to be. Subconsciously, I feel like our love will keep everything around us good too. Happy and light. Like a couple in a fairy tale . . . nothing bad ever happens to them once they get their happily ever after. They ride off into the sunset, always kissing, always smiling, immune to any darkness.

But life surprises you. It shouldn't—we all know the rules—but when loss comes to your door, it's always a heart-breaking surprise. The hardest lesson to learn.

The Sunday after we fly back from San Diego, Garrett and I are at his house, and the night's like any other—unremarkable—no different than the dozens, maybe hundreds now, that we've shared over the last eight months. We eat dinner on the back patio, looking over the lake. We watch ESPN . . . well, Garrett watches it, while I read . . . on the couch, with my legs draped across his thighs, as he rubs and massages my calves and feet, just touching me, with Snoopy curled up between us.

Later, I take my makeup off, we brush our teeth. I climb into bed wearing one of Garrett's T-shirts and he comes wearing nothing at all. We make love, and it's hot and hard and beautiful at the same time. We fall asleep spooned together—Garrett's arm around my waist, his chest against my back, his chin resting on top of my head.

And it's all perfect . . . exactly like it's supposed to be.

And then, a few hours later, it all goes wrong.

It starts with a sound, a crying whine, a long, high-pitched whimper—that wakes us both up, our eyes opening and finding each other's at the same time. It's Snoopy. Out in the living room, stretched out on the floor . . . he's panting hard and unnaturally and he can't stand up, his legs won't hold him.

Oh no . . . oh no . . . please no.

Garrett swallows hard, the pain already rising in his eyes, because both of us know, something is very wrong.

I put my hand on his shoulder. "Get a blanket. I'll get the address for the emergency vet. You hold him while I drive."

We throw on clothes, and Garrett wraps Snoopy in a blue, fleece blanket, murmuring soothingly to him while I drive two towns over to the 24-hour animal clinic. Colleen's taken her pets here, and so have two of Garrett's brothers, all with good things to say about the staff and treatments.

And that's a comfort—to know we're not bringing Snoopy to some shyster veterinarian.

It's a comfort Garrett's going to need.

Because an hour later, after an ultrasound and an exam and blood work, an older, white-haired doctor with kind, weary eyes comes to talk to us. Snoopy lies on the exam table, breathing hard, but more comfortable after the sedative the doctor gave him.

The veterinarian explains that Snoopy has a large tumor in his stomach.

Garrett's brow furrows and he shakes his head. "But he's been fine. He's been eating, running around, everything has been normal."

The doctor nods. "Sometimes, especially with a dog Snoopy's age, these things aren't a problem . . . until they're a problem."

I hold Garrett's hand. "So, we can operate, right? To remove the tumor?"

The doctor's eyes catch and I know what he's going to say before he does.

"I'm sorry. Surgery is not possible."

Garrett shakes his head. "But I'll pay for the surgery. Whatever he needs, it's not—"

"Garrett," the doctor says softly. "Snoopy's eighteen years old. He won't survive an operation."

"I don't . . . what are you saying?"

"I'm saying that I understand how difficult this is, but I believe the best course of action is to put Snoopy to sleep. That is the most humane thing. He won't suffer, you'll have time to say goodbye, and he'll just go to sleep. It will be more peaceful than letting him expire on an operating table or endure the pain or the tumor."

Garrett's eyes pinch as he gazes down at Snoopy, shaking his head. "I don't . . . I need some time to think about this."

"Of course."

The doctor leaves and Garrett rests his head against Snoopy's—petting him gently, whispering to him. I wrap my arms around this amazing man I love, lay my cheek against his back . . . and we talk about it—a hard, teary-eyed conversation about possible second opinions and hope and wanting to shield Snoopy from any pain.

When you're an adult, you're supposed to know how to handle things like this. Pets get old—*people* get old—and eventually, everything dies. It's a brutal, basic part of life. As a grown-up you understand that, recognize it, accept it . . . but that doesn't mean, for a single second, that it doesn't still hurt.

And God, does it hurt. Like your heart is being torn out from your chest.

"Can I hold him?" Garrett asks, in a ravaged voice, when the vet comes back in.

He nods and drags a cushioned chair out from the corner, closer to the table, and nods to Garrett. So gently, Garrett lifts Snoopy in his arms and Garrett sits down in the chair. Snoopy pants hard and lets out a weak whine.

"It's okay, it's okay, buddy," Garrett soothes in a sure, steady voice. Gently, he strokes Snoopy's white fur. "You're gonna be okay . . . it's not gonna hurt anymore, I promise."

I try to hold it together. I try to be strong. But I can't stop the flood of tears that fill my eyes and flow down my cheeks. Because there's nothing harder than watching someone you love in pain and knowing you can't take it away. You can't make it better, no matter how much you want to. I sit on the arm of the chair, squeezed up next to Garrett. I put my hands on his shoulders, his arms, loving him, holding him.

"You're such a good boy, Snoopy. I love you so much. You're such a good boy." Gentle and steady, Garrett's hand slides down Snoopy's back, calm and soothing. The sweet boy dips his snout and presses his nose against the crook of Garrett's arm, his eyes closing.

Garrett's throat sounds tight, clogged with wetness as he talks to the puppy who's been with him for half his life.

"Remember when you found that dead skunk and you left it under my bed, as a present for me and Callie? Good times. Remember all those summers in the boat on the lake—you and me together. Remember . . . remember when Tim snuck you into the hospital after I hurt my knee? You stayed with me, under those blankets, you wouldn't leave my side." Garrett inhales, his voice trembling . . . then breaking. "You're my best friend. Thank you for always being there when I needed you—every time."

From the corner of my eyes, I see the doctor move around. He puts the tip of a syringe into the IV connected to Snoopy's leg, then slowly injects a thick, white liquid. I press my face to Garrett's neck, and hold him tight.

"You're gonna sleep now, Snoop, you're gonna rest," Garrett soothes, his voice rhythmic. "And when you wake up, you're gonna be healthy and happy—running through sunshine and chasing the geese. And there won't be any pain. It's okay, my good boy. I love you. It's okay . . ."

I watch Snoopy's midsection expand and contract with each of his breaths. It rises and falls. Again, and again.

Until it doesn't. Until it stops.

And the best dog in the whole world goes quiet and still.

Garrett lets out a soft groaning whimper and gathers Snoopy closer, hiding his face in the downy white of Snoopy's fur. His shoulders shake and his back shudders. I wrap my arms around him, enfolding him in my embrace, squeezing and clasping him to me. I kiss his hair and rest my forehead against his neck, and I sob.

Together, we both do.

A few hours later, we walk into Garrett's house. He lays Snoopy's collar on the hook next to the door, smoothing it reverently over the dark-blue leash that hangs there, below the metal plate etched with Snoopy's name. Our movements are heavy, weighted and slow. Mournful.

I don't let go of Garrett's hand or arm. I don't stop touching him. As deep and wrenching as my own sadness is, I know his is a hundred times more. Silently, we walk to the bedroom. Garrett sits on the edge of the bed, his feet braced on the floor. I unbutton his shirt and strip it from his arms. I skim the white cotton shirt beneath it up his torso and over his head. I unbutton his jeans and slide them down his legs, leaving him bare except for black boxer briefs.

It's not sexual, but . . . intimate. Comforting someone in their grief is an act of love, being allowed to do it is a gift of trust. To see someone at their most vulnerable, to know their bare, unhidden pain.

Garrett lies back on the pillow, folding it in half beneath his head, tucking his arm under it, staring at the ceiling. His eyes are still wet, shiny in the dim moonlight that reverberates off the lake and through the window. I strip off my sweater and step out of my black leggings. I unhook my bra and slide it off my arms. I place Garrett's clothes and mine on the corner chair, and then I slide under the cool sheets with him. Our bodies are aligned, every inch touching, and my arm is draped across his waist.

Words scrape up Garrett's throat. "This sucks."

Fresh tears spring into my eyes. I stroke his chest and curve my leg around his hip, weaving myself around him.

"I know."

His fingers brush my shoulder and his arm tugs me even closer.

"I'm glad you're here. It makes it better."

I lift up on my elbow, gazing down at him, crying for him while I swear, "I love you, Garrett. I love you so much. And I'm never letting you go again. There is nowhere in this world I want to be, except next to you—wherever you are."

Sadness strips away the extra—leaving only what's important, only what matters. They're not just words I say—they're words I mean, to the depths of my soul. I want to share it all with Garrett—every joy, and every pain too. I want to walk through life with him at my side—face whatever comes with him.

We couldn't do that when we were young. The love was there, but we weren't ready . . . we couldn't deal with the painful parts, the unexpected. We can now. We're older, wiser—stronger together. We can be by each other's sides, be each other's solace, through the good and the bad.

Garrett raises his palm against mine, pressing our hands together, watching as our fingers fold and entwine together. He looks at my face, and brushes back my hair. "I love you too, Cal, so much. Everything else . . . is just details."

I slide up and shift, so I'm on my back and Garrett's head can rest against my breast. I hum softly, because he's always loved my voice. And he lets me stroke his hair and hold him— we hold onto each other—all through the night.

Garrett

The first day after Snoopy dies is hard. The pain is still fresh and raw, a wound that's still bleeding. On a logical level, it's weird. My brain tells me that Snoopy was a dog—my pet—that he had a good run, that I'm lucky to have had him for so long. But my heart doesn't get that message. It's fucking wrecked . . . shattered . . . like I've lost a member of my family, almost like one of my brothers has died.

When my class shuffles in for third period, I know they already know. It's in their subdued, somber demeanors as they take their seats—a sea of sympathetic expressions that can only briefly meet my eyes.

After the last, late bell rings, I close the door, and as I walk back to my desk, Nancy says quietly, "We heard about your dog. We're sorry, Coach Daniels."

I manage a tight smile. "Thank you."

"It's messed up," Brad Reefer adds, in the back.

"It sucks, man." Dugan shakes his head.

"Yeah." I nod. "Yeah. It does."

"If there's anything we can do," DJ tells me from the front row, "tell us, okay?"

I clear my throat, their unusual kindness and empathy twisting my lungs into a knot.

"Thanks, guys."

Then I focus on today's lesson plan and get through it.

The second day is harder. I feel bruised all over when it settles in that Snoopy's gone. I have these crazy, split-second moments when I expect him to come around the corner barking or jump on me when I walk in the front door. And every time I realize he's not there . . . it hurts all over again.

Callie's with me every day, almost every minute. Hugging me, loving me, keeping me busy, distracting me . . . making it all just a little bit easier because she's her, and she's here.

On the third day, I walk into third period, and my whole class is already there, in their seats. This is odd for them. There's a cardboard box in the middle of my desk and at first I think it could be a prank—a stink bomb or a paintball grenade.

"What's this?"

"It's for you," Skylar says.

And they're all watching me . . . waiting . . . smiling like creepy clown children in a horror movie.

"O-kay," I say suspiciously. Then I take the lid off the box.

And I stare.

At the sleeping ball of golden fur curled up in the corner.

It's a puppy—a golden retriever puppy—about eight weeks old judging from his size. Gently, I pick him up, and hold him close to my face. His legs dangle loosely, and his snout stretches into a wide, sharp-toothed yawn. Then his black eyes creak open, and stare back at me.

The air punches from my lungs—all of it. Making my voice raspy and choked.

"You guys . . . you got me a dog?"

And they brought it to school—so much better than a rooster.

They nod.

And I'm completely knocked on my ass. My eyes burn—and my dick is big enough to admit, I may actually fucking cry.

"Do you like him?" Reefer asks.

"I . . . *love* him. It's one of the best gifts anyone has ever given me."

And it's not just about the dog. It's that it came from them—these selfish, short-sighted, amazing, awesome kids. That they were kind enough, giving enough to do this . . . it makes me feel like just maybe, I'm doing something right with them.

I shift him to the crook of my arm, and pet his soft fur and scratch behind his little ears. "How did you afford this?"

He looks like a purebreed—we're talking eight-hundred dollars, easy.

Dugan raises his hand. "I wanted to steal him."

"Don't steal shit, Dugan."

He tucks his shoulder-length hair behind his ear. "I wasn't gonna get caught."

I shake my head. "Doesn't matter—don't steal. It'll mess up your life."

He shrugs.

"We all chipped in," Nancy tells me. "All your classes."

"And the football team too," DJ says.

Nancy nods. "We remembered when you'd bring Snoopy to school sometimes."

"And to practice," DJ adds.

"And we knew it wasn't right that you didn't have a dog anymore," Skylar says.

"And we wanted to do something for you," Nancy finishes.

I choke out a laugh, shaking my head. "I can't believe you guys bought me a dog. Thank you, for real, this is . . . it's incredible. It means the world to me."

"What are you going to name him?" DJ asks, grinning broadly.

"Good question." I look down at the little guy in my arms—already asleep again. Then I get the best idea ever.

I jerk my head towards the door. "Let's go. Class trip. Way before any of your times, Miss Carpenter named Snoopy. Seems only right that she comes up with something for this bad boy too."

I throw my jacket over the puppy, in case Miss McCarthy is patrolling the halls, and lead my class down to the auditorium. Callie stands up from the front row, crossing her delicate arms, somehow looking even hotter now than when we left my house this morning.

"Coach Daniels. To what do I owe the pleasure?"

I lift the jacket, revealing the bundle of adorable in my arms. And any illusion of professionalism goes out the window.

"Oh my God!" She coos and squeals. "Who is this?"

I hand the little guy over and gesture to my class.

"A present from the kids."

She meets my eyes and her face goes soft. Because she knows—she knows what this means to me. She knows me, through and through.

"What should we call him?" I ask Callie.

And for a second, when our eyes meet, it's like we're the only two people in the room.

She gazes at the puppy, her forehead scrunching, thinking it over. Then she looks back at me.

"Woodstock. With this beautiful yellow coat . . . definitely Woodstock. And we can call him Woody for short."

I laugh, nodding.

"You pick the best names. It's perfect. Woody—awesome."

"Can I hold him?" Nancy asks.

I nod, and Callie hands him over. The kids swell in around Nancy as she sits down, drifting far enough away from us for Callie to whisper so they can't hear, "I really, really want to kiss you right now."

And I smirk, because—fuck yeah.

I point at Nancy, using my coaching voice—the one that's always followed. "Keep an eye on Woody. There's an issue Miss Carpenter and I have to deal with backstage."

If they're quick enough to pick up on what we're doing, they don't show it. I lead Callie up the side stage steps, and brush the heavy curtain aside. We step behind it and then, just in case, I tug her into a dark little alcove to the right of the stage. It's like this place was designed for making out—those naughty theater people.

I lean back against the wall, lifting my hands, gazing down at my girl.

"Have at me, babe. I'm all yours."

Callie reaches up, tugging at my shirt, bringing my mouth closer to hers. "Yeah . . . you really are."

Then she presses those sweet lips against mine and kisses the hell out of me.

CHAPTER
Twenty-One

Garrett

On the first Friday night in May, I'm wearing my gray suit, leaning against the wall outside my downstairs hall bathroom. I hear the water running inside, then silence. And a few seconds later, Callie comes out.

Her skin is a mixture of pale white and green—like mint chocolate chip ice cream, minus the chips.

"Did you puke?"

The question brings a little pink to her cheeks.

"Yeah. But just the one time." She tucks a tiny pouch, with a miniature toothbrush and toothpaste inside, into her purse.

Athletes have rituals before games. Callie has a ritual before a performance—she pukes up a lung. She always did, even back in high school. And apparently that ritual now extends to her students performing too.

Because tonight is the opening night of *Little Shop of*

Horrors by the newly christened Lakeside Players Group, at Lakeside High School.

In spite of the recent heave-ho-hurl, Callie looks stunning in a cream-colored skirt and jacket, with her hair pulled back in a low, loose bun that manages to be elegant and sexy as fuck. It makes me want to bite her neck, suck on it . . . preferably while she's riding me.

But—the happy times will have to wait until later. It's almost show time.

I call Woody into his crate and he trots in happily.

"Be good, Wood—we'll be home in a little while."

He attacks the rubber goose chew toy Callie got for him last week, with a vengeance. The pain of losing Snoopy still lingers—we kept his ashes and they sit in a simple silver urn on the fireplace mantle. But like the grief of all losses, time and good memories make it easier to bear.

I hold out my hand to Callie and she slides hers into it. Then I kiss her cheek.

"Let's go, sweetheart. Time for you to break a leg."

A few weeks ago, David Burke's plea deal was finalized. Me and Callie and Jerry Dorfman wrote letters to the prosecutor on his behalf. And they were literary masterpieces if I do say so myself, because the prosecutor agreed to let David plead as a youthful offender. If he stays out of trouble for the next two years, completes his probation and community service, his record will be expunged.

He was also allowed to come back home and return to school . . . contingent on the active participation and supervision of a legal guardian he could live with.

Anda oh man—he got a doozy of a foster parent.

She's showing him how to tie his necktie right now . . . or trying to strangle him with it.

"No, Burke, the rabbit goes in the motherfucking hole! In!" Miss McCarthy yells at him. "Jesus, are you deaf?"

Yep, David lives with her now. It's better than jail . . . though I bet some days he wonders.

He makes eye contact with me across the lobby outside the high school auditorium. And mouths *help me* over Miss McCarthy's bent head.

I give him the thumbs-up.

"Pay attention, god damn it!"

The little punk rolls his eyes . . . and then he straightens up and pays attention.

After Callie heads backstage, I jog out to the Jeep and grab a few things from the back. Then I find David heading towards his seat in the auditorium. I grab his arm and pull him to the side. And I smack a bouquet of roses against his chest.

"Rule number one—when your girl's in a play, you get her flowers. Every night. Got it?"

David looks down at the flowers. "Layla's . . . not my girl."

"Do you want her to be?"

Over the last few months, while David was in the Boy's Home, Layla told Callie he would sneak out of his room to the pay phones, to call her after lights out.

Frigging stupid? Epically so.

Romantic? To a teenage girl . . . absolutely.

He glances at the still-curtained stage, like he half-expects Layla to be there. "Yeah, I do want her to be."

I nod. "Flowers are a good start to making that happen. Keeping yourself the hell out of jail will go a long way too."

He grins, rolling his eyes again, and taking the flowers. "Got it. Thanks, Coach D."

"Anytime."

David lifts his chin towards the other bouquet of roses in my hand. "Those for Miss Carpenter?"

I nod. "Damn straight."

The show is fantastic—and I'm not just saying that because I'm doing the theater teacher. It's genuinely good. The sets, the songs, the kids—they're all so energetic . . . so awesome. By the time they take their curtain call, everyone in the auditorium is on their feet, clapping. When Callie appears center stage the applause get louder, I press my fingers to my lips and whistle.

She shines on that stage—looking so lovely—she was born to be there. And standing amongst the kids who gaze at her with adulation in their eyes, it's even more true.

Afterwards, backstage, it's all chatter and laughter as the kids change out of their costumes and take off their stage makeup. They talk about the cast party, make final plans on where they're meeting up and what they're going to do. Back in the day Callie and her theater friends used to drive down to the beach after a show, to watch the sun rise. She must've told them about it, because the kids' plans tonight are the same.

"Don't be idiots!" Callie calls after them, as the big, heavy school door closes behind the last one.

After he sweeps the stage, Callie sends Ray, the janitor, home, promising to lock up. And then it's just the two of us—here, together, where it all began.

The auditorium lights are dark, and the overhead stage lights are dim—a soft, golden glow. It's all quiet, peaceful, and still.

I hold out my hand to her. "Come on."

Callie grasps the roses I gave her in one hand and takes my hand with the other. I lead her onto the stage, our shoes clicking on the old oak floor. My fingers slide across my phone, and I find the song I'm looking for. "Perfect" by Ed Sheeran pours clear and distinct from the speaker, filling the silence with the strumming guitar and meaningful words. Words about finding love when you're just a kid, and not really realizing what you have until the second time around.

I set my phone on the stage and look up at Callie. "I heard this the other day, and it reminded me of us. I figured it could be our new song—officially."

Her pink lips stretch into a smile and her eyes shine on me. "I love it."

I stand up and hold out my hands. "Dance with me, Callie."

She comes quickly, eagerly, stepping into the circle of my arms, threading her hands behind my neck. We press close and rock together, turning slowly in the halo of the stage lights over our heads.

I gaze down into her eyes, breathing slow. "I've been thinking."

"Dangerous," she teases.

"Sexy," I tease back, making her smile grow.

And then I basically crack open my chest and let her see my heart. The one that beat for her when we were kids, the soul that breathed just for her—and now does again.

"I know you'll never ask me—so I'm just going to tell you. At the end of the year, when you go back to San Diego . . . I'm coming with you."

She breathes in quickly, gasping.

"I'll sell the house," I tell her. "I'll put my résumé together . . . find a teaching job in San Diego."

Her face is all soft and tender. Her fingers toy with the hair at the back of my neck, and she swallows. "Garrett . . . you don't have to do that."

I touch her cheek, stroking down her jaw, as we rock together to the music.

"I've thought about it, turned it around in my head, trying to figure out a way that this will work. This is how. I don't want to live across the country from you, Callie. And there's no fucking way I'm letting you go . . ."

Slowly, she shakes her head, tears rising in her voice and her beautiful green eyes.

"You love this town."

I nod softly. "Yeah, I do."

"You love coaching this football team."

"That's true."

One lone tear slips down her cheek.

"You love this school, these kids . . ."

"Also true." I catch her tear with my thumb, wiping it away. "But you know what else is true?"

A hiccup shudders in her chest.

"What?"

"I love you more than all those things. That's what I've realized this year, Callie—I can live in another town, teach at another school . . . I can live without coaching football if I have to." I dip my head, leaning in closer. "I can't live without you. Not anymore . . . not ever again."

Callie's face crumples, because my girl's a crier. But I know, this time, they're happy tears. She presses her forehead to mine.

"I didn't want you to have to give up anything for me."

"I'm not, baby. It doesn't feel like I'm giving up a damn thing. I'm getting you . . . I'm getting the chance to build a life with you . . . and that's all I really want."

I kiss her lips, tasting the warm salt of her tears. My arms squeeze tighter and her hands grasp my shoulders, clasping us together.

"The way I see it, I've been living my dream job for the last thirteen years. But you're just getting your shot at yours. And I want you to take it, Callie. I want to watch you and love you and be there, while all your dreams come true."

Big, diamond tears spill from her eyes, and she smiles so big at me. Like I'm the only thing she sees, the only thing that matters. And, Christ, that's a rush. I feel drunk . . . dizzy on her happiness.

"I want that, Garrett. I want you to come with me. I want to live with you, love you, every day until forever. I want that more than I have ever wanted anything in my whole life."

I brush her cheeks again, wiping away all her tears, and I kiss her lips.

"Then you got it, Callie."

CHAPTER
Twenty-Two

Garrett

"I can't believe you're not going to be teaching here next
year. My whole graduation aesthetic is totally de-
stroyed," Nancy whines, tapping on her phone.

In the weeks after opening night, word gets around town
pretty fast about my and Callie's moving plans. It doesn't go
over well with the kids.

"This blows. Who's gonna keep us in line?" Reefer asks.

I point at him from my desk chair. "You're going to keep
yourselves in line."

"Yeah, right," he scoffs, "like that'll happen."

"I don't have to worry about that." David Burke smirks.
"Miss McCarthy's so far up my ass it's a wonder I can stand
up straight."

And I can tell by the way he says it that he really doesn't
mind at all. Kids are complicated little bastards. They may re-
volt and push back against it, but deep down, even if they

don't realize it, they want to be watched over.

"Who's gonna give a shit about us?" Dugan asks.

"Every teacher in this building cares about you guys."

"Not like you."

"Yeah, you're right—I'm pretty awesome." I smile. "But just remember what I told you—don't be idiots. You remember that, and you'll be okay."

"You're gonna forget about us. Go off to California and coach some other kids." DJ frowns. "Dicks."

They all pout and give me the sad puppy dog eyes.

And I admit it—they get to me.

"I'm gonna come home to visit. DJ—I'm gonna still be checking out the games, and if you guys aren't kicking ass and taking names, you're gonna hear about it."

Still not good enough.

So I cave, and offer to do something I swore I never would.

"All right . . . I'll join Facebook. You guys can all friend me."

Nancy bites her lip and laughs.

"Coach Daniels . . . no one's on Facebook anymore, except our parents." She shakes her head. "Old people are so cute."

Callie

"**H**ey, Cal!"

I stand in the bedroom near the open window with the warm, June breeze wafting in from the lake—watching a flock of geese land on the sun-scattered jewels of the water. The last few weeks have been busy—there's been so much to do. I turn and look around Garrett's bedroom. It's almost completely packed up. The top of the dresser is empty and the walls are bare, a tree-high pile of boxes stacked neatly in the corner.

And it makes me . . . sad.

I don't understand it. There was so much joy the night Garrett told me he was moving to San Diego with me. But the next day, and every day since, it feels like I'm walking around with a heavy gray blanket covering me. Every movement feels weighted and hard.

"Callie!" Garrett calls me again from downstairs in the kitchen.

My footsteps are sluggish as I walk down to him, and I chalk it all up to the packing and busy days—they've tired me out.

Garrett stands in front of the open cabinet doors. Those gorgeous muscles in his arms flex tight beneath his short-sleeved Lakeside Lions T-shirt as he reaches up, taking plates down from the shelves. He wraps them in newspaper, with those strong, graceful hands.

And something trips . . . tugs in my chest . . . as I watch him put them in the box.

Garrett catches the look on my face.

"Hey—you okay?"

"Yeah." I smile—but I have to force it. "What's up?"

"We need more boxes. I was going to make a run to Brewster's Pharmacy and grab some."

Woody's big furry paws pad into the room, smelling my shoes.

"I'll go. I'll take Woody for a walk."

Garrett leans over and kisses me. "Okay."

I grab Woody's leash and load him into Garrett's Jeep, and drive over to Main Street, parking a few blocks from Brewster's.

I walk Woody up the street and down the blocks, passing The Bagel Shop and Zinke Jewelers, that old haunted house on Miller Street, Mr. Martinez's furniture store and Baygrove Park. They're rebuilding after the fire—with newly planted trees and landscaping, and a big, bright, colorful swing set. I pass Julie Shriver, pushing her daughter in a stroller—she gave Miss McCarthy notice that she's not coming back to teach at the high school and has gone the way of my sister into full-time, stay-at-home motherhood.

Simone Porchesky's little brother rides past me on his bike, calling, "Hi, Miss Carpenter!"

"Hi," I call back.

But still, that sadness, the melancholy fills my chest like heavy sand.

By the time I walk back up Main Street, two hours have passed. I look to the left and see Ollie Munson, sitting in his chair on the lawn, waving to cars as they go by. Woody sticks his black puppy nose against Ollie's sneaker and he pats his head.

I move closer. "Hey, Ollie."

He smiles, but doesn't make eye contact.

"Do you think . . . would it be okay if I sat here with you for a while?"

He nods. And I sit down next to his chair on the grass. The muscles in my legs loosen and relax now that I'm off my feet. For a few minutes I gaze around and see the world the way Ollie sees it.

And I get it—I get how this can be fulfilling for him. Because Lakeside is a pretty interesting place to watch—its own little universe of people, woven into each other's lives, all different but still the same. I hear Garrett's words in my head—something he said to me once—in that steady, confident voice.

Growth is painful; change is hard.

And life-changing decisions are scary. It's easier to cling to the path that's already there. To the plan we know and have already pictured for ourselves.

But sitting here on the grass next to Ollie, looking as this little town that I know so well hums and buzzes around us—I don't feel scared. I feel safe. Welcome. I feel known and cared about. I feel like I'm exactly where I'm supposed to be. I think about my students—Michael, who's so smart and kind, and Layla, who's like a butterfly—just starting to come out of her cocoon. I think about Simone, whose hard exterior protects so much sweetness inside, and . . . David. My stomach shifts and emotions swirl around in my chest like a hurricane.

But then the whirlwind stops. And everything inside me slides into place. And it feels peaceful. It feels *right*.

A smile comes to my face—a real smile—and energy suddenly bubbles in my veins. Because I know what's been wrong with me these last few weeks. And I know what to do now—exactly how to fix it.

I stand up, brush the grass off my butt, and grab Woody's leash.

"Thanks, Ollie," I tell him. "Thank you so much."

For the first time in my life, Ollie Munson meets my eyes. His are calm and knowing.

Then a passing car beeps its horn, and Ollie turns away and waves.

I march up the front walk and spot the For Sale sign marring the perfect house. And it looks fucking terrible—wrong. I yank the sucker out of the lawn and throw it in the bushes.

I go in the front door and unhook Woody from the leash.

"Hey, you were gone a long time," Garrett says, setting the box in his hands on the dining room floor with a dozen others. "I was just going to come looking for you."

"Stop. Stop packing." I shake my head. "I don't want you to come to San Diego with me."

The dark-brown eyes that I have loved since I was fourteen years old crinkle with confusion.

"Babe . . ."

"I want us to live here. I want to quit the Fountain Theater Company and be a teacher. I want to be . . . your wife." I step closer to him. "I want us to have babies and raise them in this house. I want to teach them to fish and ice skate on the lake, and push them on the new swings at Baygrove Park. I want to take them to The Bagel Shop every Sunday and wave to Ollie Munson every single day."

"Callie . . . slow down." He rests his hands on my shoulders, squeezing. "This is a big deal. Have you really thought about this?"

I move closer, swinging my arms around his neck, pressing my body against his.

"I don't need to think anymore. This is right, this is real, this is what I want."

"But your job . . ."

"Managing the Fountain Theater isn't my dream anymore. They don't need me, Garrett. Not really. But our school, these kids, they need me . . . and I need them."

I shake my head, because the words stutter in my throat, and I'm not explaining it right. How sure I am.

"The night I got the call from Colleen, when she told me about the accident, I looked at Bruce and Cheryl and do you know what I said?"

"What?"

"I said, I have to go *home*. This is home, Garrett. It's always been home to me; I just forgot. But I know now. I could live anywhere with you and be happy—but if I can choose where that is, I want it to be here. I want our life to be here— you and me—together, in our home."

I know him well enough to see the relief that lights up his face—the joy. And I know, deep down, this is what he wants too.

Garrett hugs me in those strong, solid arms and my feet leave the floor. Then he sets me down, holding my face in his beautiful hands and my future—*our* future—in his eyes.

EPILOGUE 1
Mrs. Coach (I)

Callie

G arrett and I met the first time in the fall, and we reunited in the fall . . . so it's fitting that we get married in the fall too. He proposed on a sunny, summer Sunday, while we were on his bass boat, in the very middle of the lake . . . with the same ring he bought me all those years ago. After I said yes and Garrett slid that beautiful ring on my finger, I rocked his world—both our worlds—literally.

I flung myself into his arms so fast, the boat capsized.

But even when we fell into the water . . . Garrett didn't stop kissing me.

When we eventually came up for air, he offered to replace the diamond with a bigger stone, but I shot that idea straight down. My ring is perfect, just the way it is.

Picking the location for the wedding wasn't as easy. Garrett wanted to get married on the fifty-yard line on the high school football field.

Yes—really.

Because he's a guy, through and through. A quarterback, so to him, the football field will always be a sacred place. I wanted to get married in a beautiful old theater about an hour away—because—guilty as charged—I guess I'll always be the theater girl who loves the lights and smell of the stage. We toy with the idea of getting married on the lake . . . but neither of us like the thought of my dress dragging through goose shit, so that idea gets kicked to the curb pretty quick.

We settle on a beach wedding. One of Garrett's old teammates from Rutgers, who did pretty well for himself, owns a big Victorian house with a private strip of beach in Brielle. It's close enough, open enough, that the whole town can come . . . and they do.

I peek out of the white tent at the clear, churning blue ocean. I spot the football team taking up the last three rows of pale wooden chairs on the groom's side. My theater kids are in the same rows across the aisle—David and Simone, Michael, Toby, and Bradley. Miss McCarthy is here, checking her watch and *tsk*ing that we need to get this show on the road. The whole faculty is here—Jerry Dorfman and Donna Merkle finally came out of the relationship closet and are actually holding hands.

The kids are going to lose their minds over that development this week.

My sister, Colleen, is my matron of honor. Cheryl and Alison and Sydney are my bridesmaids—all wearing matching silk pale-blue gowns.

Garrett stands beneath an arch of white roses—so tall and handsome in his black tux. He's confident—not nervous like most grooms—his mouth settled into that relaxed, gorgeous

GETTING Schooled | **273**

smile. Dean stands beside him—his best man—because he couldn't choose between his brothers. Woody sits at Garrett's feet, adorable and perfectly behaved—wearing Snoopy's blue collar around his fluffy neck—our something beautifully borrowed.

Layla agreed to sing at my wedding. And when the flute echoes and the string quartet joins in, and her beautiful voice starts to sing our wedding song—"After All"—I take my father's arm and step out onto the red, carpeted aisle that covers the sand.

Everyone we care about—everyone we love, from our childhood days until now—is here to celebrate with us. They all stand, watching me with wide eyes and delighted faces.

Garrett's gaze finds mine. His eyes drift slowly down over my long, white, strapless beaded gown. He pauses at my boobs—because they're still his favorite. And then he gives me a devastating grin that makes my stomach flip deliciously and tears spring into my eyes.

They say you can't go home again . . . but they're wrong.

I did.

I came home and found the love I never really lost.

The air is September warm, the breeze is light, and the sun is just starting to set. Halfway down the aisle, I stop and turn to my dad.

"I love you, Daddy."

He smiles back, warm and proud. "I love you too, my Callie-flower."

I glance at Garrett and turn back to my father . . . because it's unconventional, but it feels right.

"I think . . . I think I'm going to go the rest of the way on my own, Dad."

My father nods. Then he lifts my veil and kisses my cheek. "Go get him, sweetheart."

I turn back towards Garrett, kick off my shoes, lift the hem of my dress—and I run. I run to the boy who always had my heart . . . to the man who always will.

My bouquet bursts when I jump, showering us in white and indigo petals. And Garrett catches me, laughing. He'll always catch me.

He kisses me long and deep. Then he sets me on my feet, and the priest from Saint Bart's begins the ceremony. And I become Mrs. Coach Garrett Daniels.

At last.

EPILOGUE 2
Baby D

Garrett

It's our first game in October—Parker Thompson's a junior this year—still a great kid and now, post-growth spurt, he's a full-out monster on the field.

"Yes!" I clap my hands as he completes a thirty-yard pass for a first down. "Beautiful! That's the way to do it, boys!"

"Nice play, Parker! Woo!"

I hear my wife's voice loud and clear from the stands behind me. My wife. I look down at the thick platinum band on my left hand. How fucking cool is that?

Then I turn around, finding her pretty blond head, checking up on her. She's safe and sound, sitting between her parents and her sister. Callie's wearing a long-sleeve white shirt under an extra-large Lakeside Lions football jersey that I had custom made for her last month. It matches the one I'm wearing right now, but where mine says COACH D. across the back, Callie's reads, MRS. COACH D. across her shoulder blades. And in front—right above her round, adorably gigan-tic, pregnant belly—it says BABY D.

On the field, the ref makes a shit call and throws a flag on one of my guards. I open my mouth to bitch . . . but Callie beats me to it.

"What the hell was that? Get some glasses or get off the field!"

The pregnancy has made Callie fantastically insatiable in bed . . . and ferocious in the stands. It makes my heart . . . and my cock . . . a very happy camper.

Even though she's scheduled to pop any second now, she's been teaching the first few weeks of school—she loves it that much. After the baby comes, she'll take a maternity leave, but has sworn to McCarthy she's coming back. Between my parents and her parents, her sister and my sister-in-law, we have no shortage of child-care helpers who will adore the hell out of our kid. We've spent the weekends getting the nursery ready and more hours than I can say, just staring at her bump, watching our baby move and stretch inside her.

It's miraculous. More exciting than football—the most wondrous thing we've ever done.

I don't worry anymore about not being as good of a teacher because I have a kid of my own, or screwing them up when they get here. Because Callie and I make the best team—it's impossible for us not to be awesome at anything we do together.

Sammy Zheng kicks a beautiful field goal, adding another three points to our side of the board. I clap and tap the players' backs when they run in . . . and then I realize something's wrong. Because I don't hear Callie cheering.

At that same moment, the voice of Callie's theater student

and the announcer for the football games, Michael Salimander, comes through the speakers. His tone starts off semi-robotic, the way rote announcements always sound.

"Coach Daniels, please report to the announcer's box. Coach Daniels please report . . ."

And then rote goes right out the fucking window.

". . . what? Holy shit, Miss Carpenter's having the baby!"

My head whips around so fast it almost snaps off.

Then Miss McCarthy's voice echoes in a hail of loud-speaker feedback.

"Daniels! Get your ass up here now!"

In an instant Dean is at my side, eyes flaring wide behind his glasses. "Dude. Looks like there's somewhere you need to be."

I throw my clipboard and headset at him—swing my legs over the fence and practically leap up the stands in a single bound.

The way Superman would if he knocked up Lois Lane.

Callie stands in the announcer's box with her dad's arm around her back, her hands on her stomach, and a giant wet spot on her maternity jeans.

"Apparently that last call was so bad it broke my water," she tells me.

Holy shit, we're having a baby. I don't know why this thought is really just occurring to me now—but it is. Holy. Fucking. Shit.

Mrs. Cockaburrow whispers something to Miss McCarthy, who turns to us raising her arms in protest. "There is no giving birth on school grounds! Our insurance premiums will go through the frigging roof!"

I hold up my hand. "I got it."

My father-in-law tells me they'll meet us at the hospital. I swoop my wife into my arms and Miss McCarthy's voice follows me out the door.

"Remember—Michelle is a beautiful girl's name!"

The football game has temporarily stopped and as I carry Callie down the stands, everyone claps and cheers and wishes us good luck—even the refs and the opposing team's players. Callie smiles and waves like the homecoming queen she was.

I jog towards my black SUV—I got rid of the Jeep—my precious cargo needed a safer ride.

I look down at Callie. "You doing okay?"

She rests her head against my shoulder, smiling serenely. "I'm in your arms, Garrett—that means I'm great."

Twelve hours later? Not so much.

"Uhhh!!" Callie collapses back against the pillows after contraction number seventeen-thousand rips through her.

"You're doing so good, Cal." I dab her forehead with a cold cloth. "Remember, visualize the win. See it happen—"

"Oh, fuck your visualization!" Callie yells in my face.

At this particular point in our relationship—and her labor—I know not to argue with her.

"Okay, you're right—fuck the visualization—you don't need it. You got this, Callie."

Her face crumples and she sobs.

I think my heart may literally be breaking for her. I hate this—it kills me that she's hurting and there's dick all I can do to make it better. I wish I could do this for her, take the agony for her.

She shakes her head, pitifully. "I don't got this, Garrett."

I shift closer from my chair next to her bed, gathering her in my arms, pressing my head against hers. "Yes you do. Yes you do, baby. You're so strong, I'm in awe of you. And I'm right here with you. I've got you . . . we've got this together."

Callie closes her eyes, breathing me in. And my words seem to calm her. I brush her sweat-soaked hair back, off her face.

"We're gonna have a baby, Callie. *Our* baby. Focus on that, sweetheart. You're almost there; you're so close."

She nods against me. And when she opens her eyes, the determination and strength is back in their emerald depths. "Okay . . . okay . . ."

I nod and squeeze her hand. "Okay."

"Another contraction coming," Sue, the nurse, announces.

I help Callie sit up, one arm around her back, the other holding her leg, under her knee. And when the contraction hits, she tucks her chin, grabs her knees, and groans long and loud, pushing with everything she has.

And a few seconds later, an indignant, truly pissed-off cry fills the room.

"Here he is!" Dr. Damato announces. "He's a boy!"

And he lays the wet, squirming, amazing bundle on Callie's bare chest. My whole world shifts and goes blurry as more tears come—from Callie's eyes and mine.

"You did it, Cal. You did so good."

I hold her and we laugh and cry and gaze down at the pure perfection we made together.

Later on, after everyone is cleaned up and settled, I lie next to Callie on the hospital bed, with our swaddled little guy between us. Callie looks tired and so damn beautiful, my chest aches.

We've been kicking around a few names, but decided to hold off on a final call until he got here. "Okay—first round picks for his name on three," I tell Callie. "Three . . . two . . . one . . ."

We both say it at the same time.

"William."

Callie's smile grows and new tears spring up in her eyes.

"Will Daniels," she says softly. "It's a good name. A handsome, strong name . . . just like his daddy."

Will's fist wraps around my finger, holding on tight.

"He has your hands," my wife notices. "I wonder if he'll play football?"

It would be awesome if he plays—I love the game—and I hope he'll love it too. That it'll bring him the same joy it's always brought me.

On cue, Will lets out a healthy squawk.

"He has your voice. It projects." I laugh. "He might like theater."

Whatever he wants, as long as he's happy, I'll be good with it.

Callie gazes at me with her big, green, adoring eyes. "I love you, Garrett."

"I know." I lean over and kiss her forehead. My voice is a hushed, sacred whisper. "I love you too, Callie."

EPILOGUE 3

Us

Callie

I walk out of the auditorium where the Lakeside Players Group just finished meeting and planning the dramas and musicals we'll be performing this year. I head up to the practice field, where my hot coach of a husband is running his August football practice.

"Hey, Mrs. Coach D." Addison Belamine, a senior and captain of the cheerleading squad, waves as she passes me.

Yes, that's what Garrett's kids—his students and the cheerleaders and the football players—call me. I think it's cute—it makes me feel all warm and fuzzy inside. And Garrett loves it . . . he gets that sexy, tender, possessive-caveman look in his eyes whenever he hears it.

"Hi, Addison." I wave back as I make my way up the path.

And speaking of sexy . . .

There is nothing that turns me on more than seeing Garrett on a football field, holding our son. I suspect he knows this, which—besides the obvious benefit of hanging out with his boy—is another reason I think he brings Will to practices every chance he gets. My beautiful, dark-haired son chews on his hand and watches the players with rapt attention, from his outward facing spot in the carrier on Garrett's chest.

"What the fricking frack, Damato?" Jerry Dorfman yells. "Wrong play—get your head out of your butt!"

Garrett and the coaches have been pretty great about watching their language when Will's around. His first word was "Da"—but God only knows what it would've been otherwise. Probably dumbass.

"No, no, no!" Garrett waves his arms at a player on the sidelines. "Jesus Christ—you're fumbling because you're holding the ball too tight!"

"No, no, no, no, no, no . . ." Will chants. That was his second word.

"It's god damn genetic." Garrett shakes his head.

That would be Patrick O'Riley. He's a clencher—like his older brother Nick before him.

Garrett takes Will out of the carrier and holds him with one arm, his head in Garrett's large hand, tucked against his side. "This is how you hold the ball—this is the amount of pressure you use to keep the ball."

Then Garrett puts our ten-month-old in the sophomore's arm and points.

"Now run."

Will giggles as he's jostled around, having a blast. And I'm not concerned, because I know that Garrett would cut his arm off before he ever put our son at risk.

Still, as the football player jogs past me, I add my two cents.

"You drop my kid, O'Riley, I'll hurt you."

"Don't worry, Mrs. Coach D., I won't drop him."

Garrett smiles as I approach, his eyes sliding up and down over me and liking what he sees. "Hey, you. You all done with your meeting?"

"Yep. I'm going to head home with Will. We'll take Woody for a walk around the lake."

Garrett nods, his dark hair falling over his forehead in my favorite way. "We'll be done here soon too—another hour." He wraps his arm around my lower back, pulling me closer. "Let's go out tonight. *Twelfth Night* is playing at the Hammitsburg Theater. You can get dressed up, we'll enjoy the show . . . then I'll take you home and undress you."

I giggle. "Hmm . . . who's going to watch the baby?"

"My parents have Ryan and Angela's girls, and Connor's boys—he's got a date tonight . . ."

Connor's divorce from Stacey was finalized last year. He's got his own house in town now and he's been trying to get back into the dating scene. It's been . . . adventurous.

". . . so I figured we'll drop Will off with them too—give them a full deck of grandchildren. They live for that shit."

I rest my hands on my husband's broad shoulders.

"You have the best ideas."

He wiggles his brows, his pretty brown eyes full of love and filthy thoughts.

"Baby, I've got ideas for tonight that'll blow your mind."

Garrett does a quick scan of the field—making sure his players are all otherwise occupied. They are. So he slides his hands into the back pockets of my jeans, giving my ass a play-ful squeeze, then he bends his head and kisses me.

And this is us. This is our home, our life, our love . . . this is our always.

The End

ABOUT THE
Author

New York Times and *USA Today* bestselling author, Emma Chase, writes contemporary romance filled with heat, heart and laugh-out-loud humor. Her stories are known for their clever banter, sexy, swoon-worthy moments, and hilariously authentic male POV's.

Emma lives in New Jersey with her amazing husband, two awesome children, and two adorable but badly behaved dogs. She has a long-standing love/hate relationship with caffeine.

Follow me online:

Twitter: http://bit.ly/2reW1Dq
Facebook: http://bit.ly/2rgHAi3
Instagram: http://bit.ly/2jnzfpt
Website: http://bit.ly/2reCeUs

Follow me on Bookbub to get new release alerts
& find out when a title goes on sale!

BookBub: http://bit.ly/2IEDh8r

Also by Emma Chase

THE ROYALLY SERIES
Royally Screwed
Royally Matched
Royally Endowed
Royally Raised

Royally Series Collection

THE LEGAL BRIEFS SERIES
Overruled
Sustained
Appealed
Sidebarred

THE TANGLED SERIES
Tangled
Twisted
Tamed
Tied
Holy Frigging Matrimony
It's a Wonderful Tangled Christmas Carol

Getting Schooled

Coming next from Emma Chase,

ROYALLY YOURS

a sexy new standalone royal romance!

Releasing in ebook, print and audiobook August 14th

To receive updates and details on this new release,
sign up for Emma's newsletter:

http://authoremmachase.com/newsletter/

Turn the page for a free excerpt of

ROYALLY SCREWED

Now available in the newly released
ROYALLY SERIES COLLECTION

ROYALLY
SCREWED

New York Times Bestselling Author

EMMA CHASE

PROLOGUE

MY VERY FIRST MEMORY isn't all that different from anyone else's. I was three years old and it was my first day of preschool. For some reason, my mother ignored the fact that I was actually a boy and dressed me in God-awful overalls, a frilly cuffed shirt and patent-leather brogues. I planned to smear finger paint on the outfit the first chance I got.

But that's not what stands out most in my mind.

By then, spotting a camera lens pointed my way was as common as seeing a bird in the sky. I should've been used to it—and I think I was. But that day was different.

Because there were hundreds of cameras.

Lining every inch of the sidewalk and the streets, and clustered together at the entrance of my school like a sea of one-eyed monsters, waiting to pounce. I remember my mother's voice, soothing and constant as I clung to her hand, but I couldn't make out her words. They were drowned out by the roar of snapping shutters and the shouts of photographers calling my name.

"Nicholas! Nicholas, this way, smile now! Look up, lad! Nicholas, over here!"

It was the first inkling I'd had that I was—that *we* were—different. In the years after, I'd learn just how different my family is. Internationally renowned, instantly recognizable, our everyday activities headlines in the making.

Fame is a strange thing. A powerful thing. Usually it ebbs and flows like a tide. People get swept up in it, swamped by it, but eventually the notoriety recedes, and the former object of its affection is reduced to someone who *used to be* someone, but isn't anymore.

That will never happen to me. I was known before I was born and my name will be blazoned in history long after I'm dust in the ground. Infamy is temporary, celebrity is fleeting, but royalty . . . royalty is forever.

CHAPTER
1

Nicholas

ONE WOULD THINK, as accustomed as I am to being watched, that I wouldn't be effected by the sensation of someone staring at me while I sleep.

One would be wrong.

My eyes spring open, to see Fergus's scraggly, crinkled countenance just inches from my face. "Bloody hell!"

It's not a pleasant view.

His one good eye glares disapprovingly, while the other—the wandering one—that my brother and I always suspected wasn't lazy at all, but a freakish ability to see everything at once, gazes toward the opposite side of the room.

Every stereotype starts somewhere, with some vague but lingering grain of truth. I've long suspected the stereotype of the condescending, cantankerous servant began with Fergus.

God knows the wrinkled bastard is old enough.

He straightens up at my bedside, as much as his hunched, ancient spine will let him. "Took you long enough to wake up. You think I don't have better things to do? Was just about to kick you."

He's exaggerating. About having better things to do—not the plan to kick me.

I love my bed. It was an eighteenth birthday gift from the King of Genovia. It's a four-column, gleaming piece of art, hand-carved in the sixteenth century from one massive piece of Brazilian mahogany. My mattress is stuffed with the softest Hungarian goose feathers, my Egyptian cotton sheets have a thread count so high it's illegal in some parts of the world, and all I want to do is to roll over and bury myself under them like a child determined not to get up for school.

But Fergus's raspy warning grates like sandpaper on my eardrums.

"You're supposed to be in the green drawing room in twenty-five minutes."

And ducking under the covers is no longer an option. They won't save you from machete-wielding psychopaths . . . or a packed schedule.

Sometimes I think I'm schizophrenic. Dissociative. Possibly a split personality. It wouldn't be unheard of. All sorts of disorders show up in ancient family trees—hemophiliacs, insomniacs, lunatics . . . gingers. Guess I should feel lucky not to be any of those.

My problem is voices. Not *those* kinds of voices—more like reactions in my head. Answers to questions that don't match what actually ends up coming out of my mouth.

I almost never say what I really think. Sometimes I'm so full of shit my eyes could turn brown. And, it might be for the best.

Because I happen to think most people are fucking idiots.

"And we're back, chatting with His Royal Highness, Prince Nicholas."

Speaking of idiots . . .

The light-haired, thin-boned, bespeckled man sitting across from me conducting this captivating televised interview? His name is Teddy Littlecock. No, really, that's his actual name—and from what I hear, it's not an oxymoron. Can you appreciate what it must've been like for him in school with a name like that? It's almost enough to make me feel bad for him. But not quite.

Because Littlecock is a journalist—and I have a special kind of disgust for them. The media's mission has always been to bend the mighty over a barrel and ram their transgressions up their aristocratic arses. Which, in a way, is fine—most aristocrats are first-class pricks; everybody knows that. What bothers me is when it's not deserved. When it's not even true. If there's no dirty laundry around, the media will drag a freshly starched shirt through the shit and create their own. Here's an oxymoron for you: journalistic integrity.

Old Teddy isn't just any reporter—he's Palace Approved. Which means unlike his bribing, blackmailing, lying brethren, Littlecock gets direct access—like this interview—in exchange for asking the stupidest bloody questions ever. It's mind-numbing.

Choosing between dull and dishonest is like being asked whether you want to be shot or stabbed.

"What do you do in your spare time? What are your hobbies?"

See what I mean? It's like those *Playboy* centerfold interviews—*"I like bubble baths, pillow fights, and long, naked walks on the beach."* No she doesn't. But the point of the questions isn't to inform, it's to reinforce the fantasies of the blokes jerking off to her.

It's the same way for me.

I grin, flashing a hint of dimple—women fall all over themselves for dimples.

"Well, most nights I like to read."

I like to fuck.

Which is probably the answer my fans would rather hear. The Palace, however, would lose their ever-loving minds if I said that.

Anyway, where was I? That's right—the fucking. I like it long, hard, and frequent. With my hands on a firm, round arse—pulling some lovely little piece back against me, hearing her sweet moans bouncing off the walls as she comes around my cock. These century-old rooms have fantastic acoustics.

While some men choose women because of their talent at keeping their legs open, I prefer the ones who are good at keeping their mouths shut. Discretion and an ironclad NDA keep most of the real stories out of the papers.

"I enjoy horseback riding, polo, an afternoon of clay pigeon shooting with the Queen."

I enjoy rock climbing, driving as fast as I can without crashing, flying, good scotch, B-movies, and a scathingly passive-aggressive verbal exchange with the Queen.

It's that last one that keeps the Old Bird on her toes—my wit is her fountain of youth. Plus it's good practice for us both. Wessco is an active constitutional monarchy so unlike our ceremonial neighbors, the Queen is an equal ruling branch of government, along with Parliament. That essentially makes the royal family politicians. Top of the food chain, sure, but politicians all the same. And politics is a quick, dirty, brawling business. Every brawler knows that if you're going to bring a knife to a fistfight, that knife had better be sharp.

I cross my arms over my chest, displaying the tan, bare forearms beneath the sleeves of my rolled-up pale-blue oxford. I'm told they have a rabid Twitter following—along with a few other parts of my body. I then tell the story of my first shoot. It's a fandom favorite—I could recite it in my sleep—and it almost feels like I am. Teddy chuckles at the ending—when my brat of a little brother loaded the launcher with a cow patty instead of a pigeon.

Then he sobers, adjusting his glasses, signaling that the sad portion of our program will now begin.

"It will be thirteen years this May since the tragic plane crash that took the lives of the Prince and Princess of Pembrook."

Called it.

I nod silently.

"Do you think of them often?"

The carved teak bracelet weighs heavily on my wrist. "I have many happy memories of my parents. But what's most important to me is that they live on through the causes they championed, the charities they supported, the endowments that carry their name. That's their legacy. By building up the foundations they advocated for, I'll ensure they'll always be remembered."

Words, words, words, talk, talk, talk. I'm good at that. Saying a lot without really answering a thing.

I think of them every single day.

It's not our way to be overly emotional—stiff upper lip, onward and upward, the King is dead—long live the King. But while to the world they were a pair of HRHs, to me and Henry they were just plain old Mum and Dad. They were good and fun and real. They hugged us often, and smacked us about when we deserved it—which was pretty often too. They were wise and kind and loved us fiercely—and that's a rarity in my social circle.

I wonder what they'd have to say about everything and how different things would be if they'd lived.

Teddy's talking again. I'm not listening, but I don't have to—the last few words are all I need to hear. ". . . Lady Esmerelda last weekend?"

I've known Ezzy since our school days at Briar House. She's a good egg—loud and rowdy. "Lady Esmerelda and I are old friends."

"*Just* friends?"

She's also a committed lesbian. A fact her family wants to keep out of the press. I'm her favorite beard. Our mutually beneficial dates are organized through the Palace secretary.

I smile charmingly. "I make it a rule not to kiss and tell."

Teddy leans forward, catching a whiff of story. *The* story.

"So there is the possibility that something deeper could be developing between you? The country took so much joy in watching your parents' courtship. The people are on tenterhooks waiting for you, 'His Royal Hotness' as they call you on social media, to find your own ladylove and settle down."

I shrug. "Anything's possible."

Except for that. I won't be settling down anytime soon. He can bet his Littlecock on it.

As soon as the hot beam of front lighting is extinguished and the red recording signal on the camera blips off, I stand up from my chair, removing the microphone clipped to my collar.

Teddy stands as well. "Thank you for your time, Your Grace."

He bows slightly at the neck—the proper protocol.

I nod. "Always a pleasure, Littlecock."

That's not what she said. Ever.

Bridget, my personal secretary—a stout, middle-aged, well-ordered woman, appears at my side with a bottle of water.

"Thank you." I twist the cap. "Who's next?"

The Dark Suits thought it was a good time for a PR boost—which means days of interviews, tours, and photo shoots. My own personal fourth, fifth, and sixth circles of hell.

"He's the last for today."

"Hallelujah."

She falls in step beside me as I walk down the long, carpeted hallway that will eventually lead to Guthrie House—my private apartments at the Palace of Wessco.

"Lord Ellington is arriving shortly, and arrangements for dinner at Bon Repas are confirmed."

Being friends with me is harder than you'd think. I mean, I'm a great friend; my life, on the other hand, is a pain in the arse. I can't just drop by a pub last minute or hit up a new club on a random Friday night. These things have to preplanned, organized. Spontaneity is the only luxury I don't get to enjoy.

"Good."

With that, Bridget heads toward the palace offices and I enter my private quarters. Three floors, a full modernized kitchen, a morning room, a library, two guest rooms, servants' quarters, two master suites with balconies that open up to the most breathtaking views on the grounds. All fully restored and updated—the colors, tapestries, stonework, and moldings maintaining their historic integrity. Guthrie House is the official residence of the Prince or Princess of Pembrook—the heir apparent—whomever that may be. It was my father's before it was mine, my grandmother's before her coronation.

Royals are big on hand-me-downs.

I head up to the master bedroom, unbuttoning my shirt, looking forward to the hot, pounding feel of eight showerheads turned up to full blast. My shower is fucking fantastic.

But I don't make it that far.

Fergus meets me at the top of the stairs.

"She wants to see you," he croaks.

And s*he* needs no further introduction.

I rub a hand down my face, scratching the dark five o'clock shadow on my chin. "When?"

"When do you think?" Fergus scoffs. "Yesterday, o' course."

Of course.

Back in the old days, the throne was the symbol of a monarch's power. In illustrations it was depicted with the rising sun behind it, the clouds and stars beneath it—the seat for a descendent of God himself. If the throne was the emblem of power, the throne room was the place where that sovereignty was wielded. Where decrees were issued, punishments were pronounced, and the command of "bring me his head" echoed off the cold stone walls.

That was then.

Now, the royal office is where the work gets done—the throne room is used for public tours. And yesterday's throne is today's executive desk. I'm sitting across from it right now. It's shining, solid mahogany and ridiculously huge.

If my grandmother were a man, I'd suspect she was compensating for something.

Christopher, the Queen's personal secretary, offers me tea but I decline with a wave of my hand. He's young, about twenty-three, as tall as I am, and attractive, I guess—in an action-film star kind of way. He's not a terrible secretary, but he's not the sharpest tack in the box, either. I think the Queen keeps him around for kicks—because she likes looking at him, the dirty old girl. In my head, I call him Igor, because if my grandmother told him to eat nothing but flies for the rest of his life, he'd ask, "With the wings on or off?"

Finally, the adjoining door to the blue drawing room opens and Her Majesty Queen Lenora stands in the doorway.

There's a species of monkey indigenous to the Colombian rain forest that's one of the most adorable-looking animals you'll ever see—its cuteness puts fuzzy hamsters and small dogs on Pinterest to shame. Except for its hidden razor-sharp teeth and its appetite for human eyeballs. Those lured in by the beast's precious appearance are doomed to lose theirs.

My grandmother is a lot like those vicious little monkeys.

She looks like a granny—like anyone's granny. Short and petite, with soft poofy hair, small pretty hands, shiny pearls, thin lips that can laugh at a dirty joke, and a face lined with wisdom. But it's the eyes that give her away.

Gunmetal gray eyes.

The kind that back in the day would have sent opposing armies fleeing. Because they're the eyes of a conqueror . . . undefeatable.

"Nicholas."

I rise and bow. "Grandmother."

She breezes past Christopher without a look. "Leave us."

I sit after she does, resting my ankle on the opposite knee, my arm casually slung along the back of the chair.

"I saw your interview," she tells me. "You should smile more. You used to seem like such a happy boy."

"I'll try to remember to pretend to be happier."

She opens the center drawer of her desk, withdrawing a keyboard, then taps away on it with more skill than you'd expect from someone her age. "Have you seen the evening's headlines?"

"I haven't."

She turns the screen toward me. Then she clicks rapidly on one news website after another.

PRINCE PARTIES AT THE PLAYBOY MANSION

HENRY THE HEARTBREAKER

RANDY ROYAL

WILD, WEALTHY—AND WET

The last one is paired with the unmistakable picture of my brother diving into a swimming pool—naked as the day he was born.

I lean forward, squinting. "Henry will be horrified. The lighting is terrible in this one—you can barely make out his tattoo."

My grandmother's lips tighten. "You find this amusing?"

Mostly I find it annoying. Henry is immature, unmotivated—a slacker. He floats through life like a feather in the wind, coasting in whatever direction the breeze takes him.

I shrug. "He's twenty-four, he was just discharged from service . . ."

Mandatory military service. Every citizen of Wessco—male, female, or prince—is required to give two years.

"He was discharged *months ago*." She cuts me off. "And he's been around the world with eighty whores ever since."

"Have you tried calling his mobile?"

"Of course I have." She clucks. "He answers, makes that ridiculous static noise, and tells me he can't hear me. Then he says he loves me and hangs up."

My lips pull into a grin. The brat's entertaining—I'll give him that.

The Queen's eyes darken like an approaching storm. "He's in the States—Las Vegas—with plans to go to Manhattan soon. I want you to go there and bring him home, Nicholas. I don't care if you have to bash him over the head and shove him into a burlap sack, the boy needs to be brought to heel."

I've visited almost every major city in the world—and out of all of them, I hate New York the most.

"My schedule—"

"Has been rearranged. While there, you'll attend several functions in my stead. I'm needed here."

"I assume you'll be working on the House of Commons? Persuading the arseholes to finally do their job?"

"I'm glad you brought that up." My grandmother crosses her arms. "Do you know what happens to a monarchy without a stable line of heirs, my boy?"

My eyes narrow. "I studied history at university—of course I do."

"Enlighten me."

I lift my shoulders. "Without a clear succession of uncontested heirs, there could be a power grab. Discord. Possibly civil war between different houses that see an opportunity to take over."

The hairs on the back of my neck prickle. And my palms start to sweat. It's that feeling you get when you're almost to the top of that first hill on a roller coaster. *Tick, tick, tick . . .*

"Where are you going with this? We have heirs. If Henry and I are taken out by some catastrophe, there's always cousin Marcus."

"Cousin Marcus is an imbecile. He married an imbecile. His children are double-damned imbeciles. They will never rule this country." She straightens her pearls and lifts her nose. "There are murmurings in Parliament about changing us to a ceremonial sovereignty."

"There are always murmurings."

"Not like this," she says sharply. "This is different. They're holding up the trade legislation, unemployment is climbing, wages are down." She taps the screen. "These headlines aren't helping. People are worried about putting food on their tables, while their prince cavorts from one luxury hotel to another. We need to give the press something positive to report. We need to give the people something to celebrate. And we need to show Parliament we are firmly in control so they'd best play nicely or we'll run roughshod over them."

I'm nodding. Agreeing. Like a stupid moth flapping happily toward the flame.

"What about a day of pride? We could open the ballrooms to the public, have a parade?" I suggest. "People love that sort of thing."

She taps her chin. "I was thinking something . . . bigger. Something that will catch the world's attention. The event of the century." Her eyes glitter with anticipation—like an executioner right before he swings the ax.

And then the ax comes down.

"The *wedding* of the century."

Now available individually and in the newly released

ROYALLY SERIES COLLECTION

CPSIA information can be obtained
at www.ICGtesting.com
Printed in the USA
LVHW041538241019
635237LV00002B/145/P

9 781984 370617